S0-BEC-724

"You don't understand, do you?"

Mike caught Kelsey's hand before she could walk away, and continued, "To you, that ride was a game. A chance to court death and win. To me it was like watching the destruction of everything that's good." His eyes turned darker still as he talked. "Just as if it were actually happening, I saw you hit that truck and fly off your bike onto the road."

"Mike, life is risky," Kelsey said.

"After what you've been through, how could you put yourself in such jeopardy again?"

"Why do you think I'm taking this trip? To test my strength and endurance, certainly, but also to prove I can still take risks. I refuse to spend the rest of my life afraid."

Placing both hands on her arms, he looked down at her. "And I refuse to spend the rest of my life without you."

BOOK EXCHANGE
1317 NORTH MAIN STREET
SUMMERVILLE, SC 29483
803-875-2582

ABOUT THE AUTHOR

Kate Logan likes to accumulate experience points
in the game of life. Going to new places and
meeting new people provides a rich background
for her stories. She loves her husband, is in awe of
her children, treasures her friends and is happy to
live in Utah where she can ride her bicycle all year
'round due to mild winters.

Blue Skies and Promises is Kate's first published
romance novel.

KATE LOGAN

BLUE SKIES AND PROMISES

Harlequin Books

TORONTO • NEW YORK • LONDON
AMSTERDAM • PARIS • SYDNEY • HAMBURG
STOCKHOLM • ATHENS • TOKYO • MILAN

For Sandra,
who shares the miles and understands the dreams.

Published August 1991

ISBN 0-373-16402-5

BLUE SKIES AND PROMISES

Copyright © 1991 by Kathy Lloyd. All rights reserved.
Except for use in any review, the reproduction or utilization
of this work in whole or in part in any form by any electronic,
mechanical or other means, now known or hereafter invented,
including xerography, photocopying and recording,
or in any information storage or retrieval system, is forbidden without
the permission of the publisher, Harlequin Enterprises Limited,
225 Duncan Mill Road, Don Mills, Ontario, Canada M3B 3K9.

All the characters in this book have no existence outside the
imagination of the author and have no relation whatsoever to
anyone bearing the same name or names. They are not even
distantly inspired by any individual known or unknown to the
author, and all incidents are pure invention.

® are Trademarks registered in the United States Patent and
Trademark Office and in other countries.

Printed in U.S.A.

Chapter One

"Don't you think your obsession with that woman is a little weird?" Jerry asked from the doorway.

"First," Mike said, "I'm not obsessed with her. I'm interested in her. Second, since it's not an obsession, it can't be weird."

"You were staring at those pictures of her when I walked by ten minutes ago, and you still are." Without waiting for an invitation, Jerry came in and pulled one of two armchairs around so he could sit with his ankles propped on Mike's desk. Since his partner always treated furniture without respect, Mike chose not to notice.

Instead he stepped back to get a better perspective of his entire wall of photographs. They were samples of his best work, taken in the ten years he'd been selling free-lance.

Four were of Kelsey Sumner. In the first she was silhouetted against the sky, adjusting her harness. An arrow-patterned hang glider waited by her side. With his telephoto lens he'd caught the gleam of excitement in her eyes. The second had been taken almost straight up, from the edge of the cliff to the glider flying above the ocean. The next picture was after her return to earth. Everything about her, from her stance and her smile to her hold on the glider, proclaimed exhilaration. Finally he had a close-up of her.

She'd pulled off her helmet, and the wind caught at her chin-length dark auburn hair.

Her features were too sharp to be classically beautiful. Her cheekbones, nose, jawline and eyebrows were angular rather than curved. But her dark eyes sparkled with joy, and she seemed to be looking straight at him.

She was a woman who lived for adventure. It showed in her fit body, her laughing expression, her grace in the air. In his photographic pursuit of those who lived for risk, Mike had run across her in person or by reputation more than once.

But that had been before the accident. Now, four years later, she was active again, taking on another adventure. She made the questions that had always intrigued him take on new dimensions: Why do people risk their necks for adventure? What inner need does danger fulfill?

"So what is it, if not an obsession?" Jerry persisted.

"Interest, curiosity, respect."

"When are you going to ask her?"

Mike plunged his hands deep into the pockets of his wool-blend suit pants. "This afternoon."

"It'd serve you right if she turned you down flat."

Turning to face Jerry, Mike leaned his shoulder against the wall, his face just inches from the close-up of Kelsey. "I don't intend to take no for an answer."

THE STORE WAS crowded. Three boys in their early teens were checking prices on pads for their dirt bikes. An older man wanted to compare different models of mileage computers. A woman had brought her daughter's bicycle in for repairs. Answering questions and writing the repair report, Kelsey kept her eye on the boys. She liked kids and was glad when they shopped in her store, but she'd been ripped off more than once, and usually when she was trying to do too many things at a time.

"I can have this ready for you on Monday," she told the woman.

The daughter's face clouded. "I wish I could have it by Saturday. We're having a bike safety program at school."

Doing a quick mental calculation, Kelsey decided she could manage it if she worked late again tomorrow. "How about if I see what I can do?" With a smile she slid the form across the counter for the mother to sign. "Call me first thing Saturday morning to see if it's done. I'll do my best."

Relief lit the woman's eyes. "Thank you so much. Come on, Wendy."

Before the woman could leave, two guys Kelsey knew who raced came in with their bikes. Wearing cleats, they walked awkwardly on their heels. "Can we use your compressor to fill our tires?"

She waved them into the back, checked on the boys again and turned back to the man looking at computers.

"You might like the solar model. Then you never have to worry about batteries."

"Does it do everything? Trip miles, average speed, highest speed—"

"All of it. Here, let me show you."

Another woman with a baby and a child of about four came in. The store was never this busy on a Wednesday. Of course, the weather had suddenly turned sunny after a week of rain, and it had been a typically wet Oregon spring. That alone would make people think of ways to be outside. Kelsey wished Blaine were working; being on her feet for so long made her leg ache. But he and his wife were rock climbing in Yosemite, and he'd have entire responsibility for the store all summer.

When the bell over the door signaled yet another customer, she glanced up automatically.

Wearing a three-piece suit, the man seemed totally out of place. Her customers generally dressed casually, more like her own jeans and henley shirt. He hesitated at the door, looking straight at her. She caught a flash of recognition in his eyes, but she couldn't remember ever having seen him before. Too busy to give it much thought, she pulled another calculator from the glass display case and handed it to the older man, then she went back to see how the boys were doing.

They'd finally decided on the pads they wanted, so she took their money and watched them leave with a sigh of relief. The woman with the children was looking at little two-wheelers with training wheels.

"I think I will take this solar one," the older man said.

"I'm sure you'll be happy with it." Writing the bill up for him, Kelsey noticed that the man in the suit was following her with his eyes. Because she was working the shop alone, it made her a little nervous, but not much. Maybe she was too trusting, but she doubted someone who had trouble on his mind would be dressed for success, right down to the conservatively striped tie.

The guys with racing bikes came back from the rear of the shop. "*Muchas gracias,* Kel. You coming to watch the criterium this Saturday?"

"Not this week. But good luck, okay?"

"It's my turn to win," one of them said.

The other punched him lightly on the shoulder. "You won last time."

"It's still my turn."

They wheeled their bikes outside, and Kelsey watched through the window as they swung onto them. She loved the way athletes moved, so sure of the bodies that were as highly tuned as their bicycles.

While she was writing up the sales slip on the mileage computer, two more bikes came in, obviously for repairs. First, though, there was the man in the suit. He'd moved to the counter and now leaned with his hip against it. He still watched her intently.

Resisting a compulsive urge to tuck her hair behind her ear, she went to see what he wanted. She suspected he hadn't come to buy bicycle equipment. He looked more like an insurance salesman.

He was somewhere in his early thirties, and his skin was barely tan, unlike the deep bronze of someone who spent all his time outdoors. He was tall, with broad shoulders and trim hips. His black hair had been trimmed with precision.

Good-looking, well-built, the right age, no ring on his left hand, not the outdoor type. If he'd come this time last year—or in four months from now—she might have been tempted to flirt with him.

"Can I help you?"

"Go ahead and take care of them first."

His voice was deep and confident and his tone polite. Kelsey could only assume he wanted her complete attention, probably for a sales pitch. Well, she had no intention of changing policies, and she didn't have time today, anyway. It took only a few minutes to write up both repairs and wheel the bikes into the back of the shop, then she helped fit the four-year-old with an appropriate model.

As Kelsey worked, the shop began to clear. When no new customers came in, she realized she'd soon be alone with the man. Good. She could find out what he wanted and send him on his way.

When her last customer left, she wiped her damp palms on her jeans, then turned to face him.

"What can I do for you?"

Even with the counter between them, she was now close enough to notice his eyes. They were clear and piercing, of an unusual grayish blue shade. Under thick black brows they were especially striking.

"You *are* Kelsey Sumner?"

She nodded. It wasn't the opening remark she'd expected from a salesman.

"I'm Mike Kincaid." He held out his hand and she accepted it. His grip was firm and as commanding as his presence, his palm uncalloused. He looked like a salesman, and he talked like a salesman. So why wasn't he acting like a salesman? Unobtrusively she slipped her hand free of his clasp.

"I understand you're starting on a transcontinental bicycle trek soon," he said.

Ah, understanding began to dawn. "Yes, I am. And I have all the equipment I'll need, thank you."

"What?"

"Whatever you're selling, I don't need it."

For a split second he stared at her blankly, then he laughed. Spreading his hands out in a gesture of openness, he shook his head. "That's not why I'm here. I'm a part-time free-lance photographer. I specialize in adventure-type activities, and I'd like to come along for the first week or so of your trip, take some pictures and write a couple of articles."

"Why?"

He smiled in reassurance at the challenge in her tone. "I know about your accident, that four years ago you crashed while hang gliding. I think there's a lot of human interest in the fact that you're finally undertaking another major adventure."

She looked past him out the window, wishing he *had* been a salesman. They were so much easier to deal with. Four years ago her survival had attracted widespread attention. Someone had even contacted her about writing something to submit to *Reader's Digest*'s "Drama in Real Life." Since then, she'd learned that not dying was only the tip of the iceberg where survival was concerned. And survival was a very, very private matter.

"I'm afraid I can't help you, Mr. Kincaid." Picking up a loose repair-order form, she tucked it on the stack underneath the counter. A couple of pens were lying around, so she put them next to the cash register. "Now, if you'll excuse me, I have work waiting for me back in the shop."

He met her at the end of the counter and stopped her with his hand. "Will you at least think about it? In spite of how many people are doing it, a cross-country ride is still a major achievement. The fact that you're going against great odds would be of interest to a lot of people."

She jerked free of his hold. "Look, Mr. Kincaid. My accident was personal. Now my trip is personal. I don't need some voyeur along for the ride. Please, I have work to do."

She marched past him with as much dignity as she could muster, but he followed her into the workshop.

Turning on him impatiently, she didn't wait for him to speak again. "My answer's no."

For a brief second, silence reigned between them, then he smiled gently.

"I just want to come for the first few days, and then meet you again at the end."

"It's still no."

"I won't exploit your feelings or your experience."

"No."

"I can furnish references."

"No."

His smile took on an air of challenge. "You're not leaving for two weeks. That gives me plenty of time to convince you."

"Mr. Kincaid—"

But her protest met only his broad, tailored back as he left the store.

BY THE TIME KELSEY LOCKED up at seven and climbed on her bike to ride home, her leg ached from her waist to her knee. It only hurt this bad when she got too tired, but when she was tired it was easy to let the pain get her down. The trouble with a sudden improvement in the weather was that every bicyclist in Portland wanted his bike to be ready for the new season. She didn't mind the work; it meant increased profits, and profit meant money to play on. She hated the residual weakness left from her accident.

The five-mile ride from the store to home took twenty minutes. With a sense of relief she saw her brother's car in the driveway. She knew she depended on Rob too much. Even now that she was self-sufficient again, he offered her strength when she didn't have enough of her own.

She dropped her helmet and backpack just inside the door and rubbed her thigh. Thankfully, pedaling seemed to ease the soreness some. Peeling off her gloves and shedding her jacket, she let them fall on top of her backpack.

"That you, Kel?" Rob called from the back of the house. "Are you hungry?"

"Not very. Maybe later."

He met her on her way to the bathroom. One look at the way she limped down the hall and concern filled his eyes. "How bad does it hurt?"

"I'm okay. I just spent the entire afternoon on my feet."

"Let me fill the tub."

She nodded and slipped past him to her bedroom. She heard the water running while she undressed, and for about the millionth time, she thanked God and all the fates for Rob. She never, never could have made it if he hadn't willingly put his own life on hold to help her.

The water was still running when she went into the bathroom, and she could hear Rob whistling in the kitchen. He'd added her favorite oil to the bath, and it made the room smell like wildflowers. A clean towel lay folded neatly on the toilet seat. With relief at finally getting off her feet, she stepped into the water.

Lying back and letting the heat close around her, she knew that her fatigue went beyond the physical. Mike Kincaid's visit had distressed her.

She despised the idea of exploiting misfortune for commercial reasons. The only thing that set her apart from anyone else making a cross-country ride was her past.

Except Kincaid honestly didn't look like the exploitive type. He didn't seem either sincere enough or sleazy enough. He hadn't come with any religious zeal to write about a miracle, nor had he spread out an armful of inducements.

She wondered who he wrote for. Part-time free-lance, he'd said. Which meant the whole idea might be speculative.

So why had he chosen her?

Four years ago the question would have been easier to answer. The interest in her miraculous survival had lasted several weeks, but recovery processes are long and slow and boring, and soon other dramas overshadowed hers.

Running her hand from breast to thigh, Kelsey counted the scars. One where her ribs had punctured a lung, one to take out an ovary and repair her damaged uterus, two to piece the pelvis and hip back together, one to pin her thigh.

She could never resent them. The medical technology they represented had saved her life and allowed her to walk again. Because of them, she was going to make a three-thousand-mile bike ride.

Also because of them, she'd rearranged her thinking about her personal life. She'd been engaged at the time of the accident, but Alan hadn't been able to deal with the prognosis. She'd tried to give him the benefit of the doubt. Adventure was his life, just as it had been hers, and at the time it looked as if she would never be able to share that with him again. Then she'd realized that a relationship built only on good times wasn't worth crying over.

Now she knew she'd never again choose a man preoccupied with the next thrill. She'd want someone well balanced, with a variety of interests, preferably someone who had a desk job. Of course, he would also have to accept her as she was, but she'd want someone who wouldn't put his fun before her welfare.

Maybe someone like Mike Kincaid. He seemed the antithesis of the men she usually associated with, the men who biked, packed, flew, dived, sailed, climbed. She tried to envision him kayaking down a river and failed. She tried to imagine him riding a loaded bicycle up the Columbia River Gorge and smiled.

He would probably never know the favor she was doing him by telling him he couldn't come along.

A sudden knocking startled her from her thoughts.

"How are you doing, Kel?" Rob asked through the door.

"The bath's perfect. I'll be out in a few minutes."

"Will you want an ice pack?"

"I can get it, Rob. You don't need to bother."

"That's okay. Hey, Skip Newberry called this afternoon. He's coming over later and bringing a six-pack."

"Sounds terrific."

A beer with Skip would be nice. Of all Rob's friends, Kelsey liked him the best. He had more on his mind than how to pull the cords on his parachute so he hit the X perfectly every time. He was finishing up a political science degree at the university in June.

She listened to Rob go back down the hall, then slipped all the way under the water to get her hair wet. The ache in her leg had eased a lot. Washing off the sweat and grime from work lifted her spirits. By the time she climbed out of the tub, she felt almost rejuvenated.

After toweling herself dry, she frowned at her hair in the mirror. It was the wrong length for an extended bike trip. If it were longer, she could pull it back in a braid. Instead she'd have to get it cut. She'd need a style that stayed out of her eyes and took little care. The trouble was, very short hair made her chin look too pointed and her eyes too large. She shrugged. Since she'd be wearing a helmet six or eight hours a day, comfort and convenience were far more important than appearance.

A few minutes later she found Rob in the kitchen. A sandwich and a glass of milk were at her place, and an ice bag lay on her chair. Cheered even more by such little attentions, she gave him a hug before sitting down and fixing the ice against her hip.

"Thanks, pal."

"Are you sure you're okay?"

"You fuss too much."

He leaned back in his chair and folded his arms across his chest. "I don't want to take any chances on a setback when we're leaving in two weeks."

Seeing him sit like that, Kelsey was struck, not for the first time, at what a good-looking man he was. His hair was brown, without the red she'd inherited from their mother, his eyes blue like their dad's. Nineteen at the time of her accident, he'd been hardly more than a kid. Now his chest was broader and his features more narrow. But he hadn't lost his freewheeling, all-or-nothing attitude. She was counting on that to carry her on to full recovery, the way his attention to her physical needs had brought her this far.

"How's the bedroom set coming?"

"I'll be done. I finished the chest today."

"Can I see it?"

Rob laughed and shook his head. "Not tonight. Tonight you rest."

"Yes, boss. Can I stay up for a beer with you and Skip?"

"He'd be disappointed if you didn't. I don't know why all my friends are in love with you."

"Neither do I. I'm too old for any of them."

Rob snorted. "Three or four years. You make it sound like twenty."

"Sometimes I feel twenty years older."

"Sorry, sweetie, you don't look it."

An hour later Kelsey was lying on the couch reading the paper when the bell rang. Rob went to the door, and Kelsey heard a feminine voice mingle with those of the men. Skip came in first, then Rob and a woman.

When she started to get up, Skip waved her back. "Stay. We're not company. Have you met my sister? Angela, Kelsey." He pointed from one to the other, obviously considering that an adequate introduction.

Rob led Angela to one of the easy chairs, then sat on the floor beside her. Skip handed bottles of beer around before sprawling in the other chair.

While people got settled, Kelsey studied Angela. She wore tailored maroon pants and a gray blouse. Her blond hair was carefully styled, and her nails so beautifully manicured Kelsey wondered if they were real. She looked the antithesis of Skip, who wore faded jeans, cowboy boots and a denim jacket.

When Rob absently began to resume sanding a knob of oak to a beautiful sheen, Angela leaned over his shoulder to watch. "Is that for the bedroom set?" she asked. Her voice was as polished and precise as the rest of her.

He held the knob up and it caught the light. "There's one for each bedpost. What do you think?"

"It's perfect. Like everything you make."

The tiniest hint of color stole up Rob's neck, and Kelsey watched the exchange in fascination. She'd imagined she knew everything about Rob, his work, his play and his friends. She knew he dated, but at some point he'd spent enough time with Angela Newberry to invite her into the shop in their garage. Quickly she smothered a sting of jealousy.

Kelsey accepted that her brother deserved a life of his own, especially now that she was mostly on her feet again. And although she wouldn't have picked Angela Newberry out of the crowd for her brother, maybe he needed someone who was the opposite of himself—for the same reasons she wouldn't want a relationship with another adventurer. They made an unusual couple. Rob dark and rugged, Angela elegant and fair. Kelsey decided she was glad for Rob. She hoped whatever he had going with Angela could survive three months of separation.

"Kelsey's got the right idea," Skip said, slumping down in the chair with his legs stretched out and looking down his nose at Rob. "What's with this working nonsense? Jack's becoming a dull boy."

"If Jack doesn't work, Jack doesn't play," Kelsey said lightly. "Leave him alone, Skip. I can't go without him."

"Sure you could. I know a dozen people who would jump at the chance to take his place."

Except none of them would understand the reasons she had to make this trip, or accept her limitations the way Rob did. "Who?" she asked, more to make conversation than because she wanted to know.

Skip took a long drink from his bottle, then grinned. "Well, Johnny Witzel for one."

"He wants to ride the RAAM." Kelsey could just imagine trying to keep pace with someone who wanted to beat the record for the fastest time across the U.S.

"Mandy Adler."

Rob made an uncomplimentary sound. "She rides like a grandmother. Have you ever seen her bike? It's got a seat this wide." He held his hands about twelve inches apart. Kelsey laughed at his exaggeration, and Skip went on to name a few other people, most of whom she didn't know.

Scooting into more of a sitting position, Kelsey leaned on one elbow. "Have any of you ever met a man named Mike Kincaid?"

Rob shook his head, and since he had a knack for remembering names and faces, Kelsey turned to Skip.

"Photographer type?" Skip asked.

"He said he was a photojournalist."

"Yeah. I've met him. He shows up a lot when things are happening. Did you see that spread in *Mountain!* of Doug Carpenter and his group on Whitney? Kincaid did that."

Kelsey remembered the pure beauty of those pictures. They'd made her want to take her rock climbing gear out of mothballs. They'd made it difficult to imagine Blaine and Cindy spending a week in Yosemite without her. But her leg wasn't strong enough anymore. She'd already resigned herself to the fact that it might never again be dependable for that kind of activity.

"He wants to join us for the first few days," she told them.

Rob's hands stopped rubbing the knob. "When did this happen?"

"He came into the store today. He wants to do a little story on my recovery. I said no."

"I don't know, Kelsey," Skip said. "He takes good pictures. I bet he'd get some terrific ones of you."

"I'm not interested."

"Hey, think about it. You and Rob riding up the gorge, the river on one side, the mountain on the other, sweat dripping off your faces. Great moments in sports."

"Definitely sounds like a scene worth capturing," Kelsey said dryly.

"I'd buy one. Especially if Rob wasn't in it."

"I'd buy one if he was," Angela murmured.

"Did he say who he wanted to do it for?"

"No, and I didn't ask."

"I think you should invite him along." Skip waved his arm grandly. "Think of the publicity, the fame, the glory."

"I did think about the publicity. And now it's time to change the subject."

But Skip turned to Rob. "You ought to talk to her about this. She's turning down the chance of a lifetime here."

Kelsey glanced at Rob and saw that he'd totally stopped working. He sat with his legs crossed and his elbows resting on his knees, looking at her. She also noticed that Angela was watching Rob, an expression of resignation on her face. Whether Rob knew it or not, Angela wasn't excited about the trip.

"Kelsey makes her own decisions," Rob said.

Skip shrugged and started talking about something else, but Kelsey could tell Rob was still turning the conversation over in his mind. She knew that after his friends left, he'd bring it up again. And if he did, it would be because he thought she was wrong. She decided not to wait around for his private opinion.

When Skip went to get second rounds of beer from the refrigerator, Kelsey excused herself.

Rob watched her leave, and if the Newberrys hadn't been there, she knew he'd ask if she were all right.

By the time she'd climbed into bed, Kelsey's leg felt almost normal. Of course, since the weather promised to be sunny and warm, tomorrow would probably be just as hard at the store. Plumping her pillows up against the headboard, she took her big map out of the drawer of her nightstand and spread it open on her knees. With her finger she traced their proposed route from Portland, Oregon, to Portland, Maine.

Across the United States on a bicycle. As a teenager she'd dreamed about such a trip. After her accident she'd pushed it aside with every other dream, until she knew she'd be able to walk again, swim again, ride again.

And even now, if it weren't for Rob...

A short knock on the door startled her, and she checked the clock beside her bed. It was well after eleven. She wished she'd turned off the light and gone to sleep. Now it was too late to pretend.

"Come on in," she called.

"You okay?"

"I'm fine. Stop worrying."

Without an invitation Rob sat on the side of her bed. "I've been thinking about that Kincaid guy."

"I told him no, Rob."

"Yeah. But think about it, Kel. We both know you're still not sure how you'll do. If you let him write about you and it got published, then finishing would be more important. You couldn't quit."

Kelsey pulled her lip between her teeth and looked away. All her life, confidence had come as easily as breathing. She'd lived for the wind in her face. She'd taken any dare. She'd always wanted to go farther and faster and higher.

Now she missed that person she used to be.

"I'm not a heroine, Rob. I don't want somebody to make me out as something I'm not. What could he say about me? I crashed and spent a long time in the hospital and now I'm back on my feet. Nothing else is important, but he'll want more than that. I know he will."

"You *are* more than that, sweetie. You're a survivor, and people like to read about survivors."

She hesitated. In the process of getting well, she'd come to depend on Rob's judgment. "Do you really think it's a good idea?"

He took both her hands in his. "I really do. I think you need something besides me pushing you to finish. Besides, it will only be for the first few days. How bad could that be?"

"It's not having him with us that bothers me."

More important was the matter of having anyone else along. She knew Rob wanted this trip as badly as she did, and in a way, going was her gift to him for sticking by her. They'd become close during the past few years, much closer than most siblings. Since they both wanted this trip to be perfect, adding someone else might upset the balance.

"I'm afraid of what he'll say about me," she continued.

Laughing, Rob gave her hands a quick squeeze and stood up. "He'll say you're hell on wheels. But I meant what I told Skip. This is your decision. If you don't want him along, that's fine with me. Just think about it, okay?"

"Oh, I'll think about it. But I'm pretty sure I won't change my mind."

Chapter Two

"So there we were, Cindy was below me. I got my next piton in the rock . . ."

Only half listening, Kelsey cranked the pedal of the bike she was adjusting and ran the derailleur through its gears. Even though vicarious involvement wasn't as good as doing it herself, ordinarily she'd have enjoyed Blaine's account of his week in Yosemite. Today it didn't hold her interest.

Two weeks from today she and Rob would be out of the Columbia River Gorge and riding through the middle of Washington. After a year of planning and dreaming, it seemed impossible that they should be so close. Except there were still hundreds of details to take care of.

"You'll be sure and get our quarterly taxes mailed off in June," she said.

Blaine had a hub apart on the workbench and was washing the bearings. With a short laugh he threw a wadded-up paper towel at her. "Kelsey, we've already been over the list a hundred times. Nothing's going to go wrong with the store while you're away."

She shifted on her high stool and dropped her hands into her lap. "I know. I'm sorry. Three months is a long time to be gone, and I keep worrying I'll forget something."

Of course, she shouldn't worry about the store. As an equal partner, Blaine had as much reason to keep things running smoothly as she did, and he'd managed just fine whenever she'd had to go back into the hospital.

Blaine resumed greasing the hub and carefully adding the bearings one at a time. "I'll tell you what. If I need you for anything while you're gone, I'll just track you down and drag you home."

Cheered by the absurdity of his promise, she turned back to the derailleur. She had Rob to help cover the trip's details, and Blaine at the store. She needed to be reminded that nothing major could possibly go wrong. "Thanks. I knew I could depend on you."

"Damn right."

"Okay. Finish telling me about your climb."

By early afternoon the store was busy with customers again. It took both Kelsey and Blaine to handle the load, leaving repairs to accumulate in the back.

"When did it start like this?" Blaine asked after writing up yet another tune-up order.

"Wednesday."

"Bummer. Did you manage okay?"

"Just fine." She patted his cheek. "And it made me feel a lot less guilty about leaving for the summer."

Before he could reply, she hurried over to help a woman select a mountain bike.

The bell over the door rang constantly with people going in and out, but since she wasn't alone, she didn't pay close attention.

"Kelsey." Blaine called to her from the counter.

Interrupted from a discussion on seat height, she turned to him in surprise.

"Special delivery package for you."

She excused herself long enough to sign for the package, then stuck it under the counter until she had time to open it.

Despite how busy she was, the rest of the afternoon seemed to drag by. Every time she went behind the counter, she glanced at the package, and every time, her curiosity grew. It was big, probably eighteen by twenty inches, but only two or three inches deep. It bore no return address. She began to check her watch with increasing frequency, and had to force herself to be patient with her customers.

Finally at about six, the store emptied. Kelsey felt grimy from the dirt and oil of dozens of bicycles. Her leg ached and her shirt was damp with sweat. While Blaine finished up with a man who wasn't giving any buying signals, she took her package to the back, washed her hands, got a Coke from their ancient refrigerator and sat down at the workbench.

She cut the tape and folded back the heavy brown paper, then unwrapped a layer of bubble pack. When she came to a layer of tissue paper, a strange prickling sensation lifted the hair on the back of her neck. She set the package on the workbench, hesitant to look further.

"What is it, Kel?" Blaine came to stand behind her.

"I don't know." Slowly she lifted away the paper. First there was a copy of *Outdoor Adventure,* a magazine she'd stopped subscribing to after her accident. Setting it aside, she pulled off another sheet of protective paper.

In a narrow wooden frame was an enlarged, professionally matted photograph of herself. In it, she hung against a wall of rock in a rappeling descent, her head bent to one side to see her way, her eyes seeming to look straight into the camera.

In spite of herself, tears burned behind her eyelids. The definitions of the muscles in her arms and legs made her look strong and capable. Her expression was one of confidence. Sheer joy shone in her eyes.

When Blaine put his hand on her shoulder, she reached up and covered it with her own.

"You'll get there again, Kel. Just give yourself some time."

"I know. It's just that whoever took this picture caught the past too well."

"He sure caught the real Kelsey. The one we all know and love."

Kelsey ran her finger along the side of the frame. "I wonder who he is. Who sent this?"

"Maybe the answer's in the magazine." Blaine pulled up another stool and sat beside her.

Kelsey picked it up and thumbed through it. *Outdoor Adventure* specialized in any kind of activity that took people to the sea or the sky or the wilderness. Using pictures generously, the articles invited the reader into the out-of-doors. But of all the photographs, a series on a kayak run down the Salmon River caught her immediate attention. There was a certain quality about it that made her look again. The byline said Michael Kincaid.

She pointed to his name with her finger. "Have you ever heard of him?" she asked Blaine.

"Sure. Haven't you? He turns up all the time at motorcycle climbs or skydiving exhibitions. Things like that."

"What sports does he participate in himself? Do you know?"

Blaine didn't answer immediately, but his forehead furrowed in thought. "You know, now that you mention it, I don't think I've ever seen him do anything except take pictures."

"Have you ever met him?" she asked.

"Once. Nice guy. Quiet. He uses these long lenses—must be able to catch a fly on a rock at a thousand yards."

Kelsey laughed. She didn't believe that even spy satellites were that good. Then she looked again at the enlargement of herself and remembered the location, the long, sheer wall of the cliff as it dropped toward the ocean. In this instance the photographer must have been a very long way away.

"I think he took this one."

"Why? Kelsey, what's going on?"

Like a video replay, all the details of Mike's visit came flooding back again. "Probably nothing." She held the picture up at arm's length. "What do you think of it?"

"It's great. It's you. What are you going to do with it?"

"Should we hang it over the workbench?"

"Not here! The dust and oil in this place would ruin it. Take it home with you."

Knowing Blaine was right, Kelsey took both the picture and the magazine into the front part of the store. An intense yearning welled up inside her as she looked at it again. This picture was the essence of the person she used to be, the person she intended to become again, and Mike Kincaid had captured it, making it live.

And with this picture, he'd gotten her attention.

He might look like the office type, but his heart, she could tell, was that of an explorer, someone willing to push beyond the limits. Chances were, he was a man after her own heart.

Such a possibility tempted her.

Quickly she thrust the idea away. The *last* thing she wanted was another adventurer. Alan had been so self-centered that their relationship hadn't been as important as seeking the next thrill. If and when she decided she wanted another man in her life, she'd pick someone as different from herself as Angela Newberry was different from Rob.

The next day a bracelet arrived. It was a thin silver chain with six charms on it. A bicycle, a hot-air balloon, a kayak, a kite and a set of skis. In the lid of the box she found a hand-printed card bearing Michael Kincaid's name, an address and a telephone number.

She tucked them both in her backpack before Blaine saw them and began asking questions. She had too many of her own that needed answers. When Mike had indicated he intended to change her mind, she hadn't considered a siege by messenger service.

Now that the battle had begun, she needed to learn more about her opponent. Just before closing, she called Rob to tell him she'd be a little late, then rode to the public library.

In the magazine index she found a list of articles written by Michael Kincaid, all of them appearing in outdoor magazines. When she tried to look them up, she found five.

Like his work in *Mountain!* and *Outdoor Adventure,* the emphasis was always on the photographs. They were brilliant in both conception and execution. Some of them were of people she knew.

It was the copy that finally influenced her. More than an overview of the adventure, Kincaid knew how to probe beneath the surface. What was the appeal? How did it feel? When did the adrenaline high begin? Was it frightening? What about the sense of risk? Did the challenge make you grow?

Kelsey wasn't ready to agree to his proposal, but she wanted to know more before she made a final decision.

WITH HER PULSE BEATING a little too fast, Kelsey stepped into the wood-paneled elevator and punched the button that would take her to Michael Kincaid's office on the eighth floor. Built on a wedge of land between two busy streets, the building was an odd triangular shape, with an open solarium in the middle and skylights in the roof. For a part-time free-lance photographer, Mike worked in a pretty posh environment. She wondered what else he did.

The oak outer door of his office bore two names, one of them Mike's, lettered in black on gold-toned plates. Inside, the reception area was decorated in blues and grays with dark red accents. An original watercolor of the ocean hung behind a pair of elegant wing chairs, and there was a spread of magazines on a small table between them. Three doors with oak trim indicated more offices beyond. It occurred to Kelsey that she was as out of place here as Mike had been in her store.

A woman in her late thirties sat behind a large desk, which held a computer, a phone, and had an open file spread neatly across the surface. She looked up with a professional smile. "May I help you?"

"Is Michael Kincaid here?"

"Do you have an appointment?"

"No." She hadn't expected him to have a secretary, and she hadn't known what she'd say to him on the phone. If he wasn't in, she doubted she'd have the courage to try again. "Tell him it's Kelsey Sumner."

"Just a moment, please."

The woman picked up the phone and repeated Kelsey's message. This time when she smiled, it held a little more warmth. "He says he can see you." Leaving the desk, she opened the door on the left for Kelsey, then retreated discreetly.

Mike crossed the room and held out his hand. He'd taken off his suit coat and loosened his tie. His shirt was white with a woven stripe so subtle she noticed it only when he got close. Whether because he was now in his own element, or because his chest looked broader without his coat, he seemed more imposing than she remembered.

A slow smile pulled at the corners of his mouth as his hand closed over hers. "This is a surprise."

"Is it? I thought you wanted to hear from me."

"I did."

She pulled free of his touch. No matter what fantasies she might have indulged in the past couple of days, no matter how good it might feel to let her hand rest in his, she'd come for only one reason. To find out why she was leaning toward letting him join her. She rarely changed her mind once she'd decided on a course to take. This time, for some reason, was different.

"Won't you sit down?" He guided her to one of two armchairs, then took the other.

"Your work is very impressive," she began.

"I hoped you'd like it."

He'd known she would, she could tell from the confidence in his voice.

"Why did you take that picture of me?"

He seemed suddenly to see into the past, and his eyes became a deep and smoky gray. "You were like a poem, hanging there against the rock."

Embarrassed, she looked away. No one had ever compared her to a poem before; no one had even talked to her in poetic terms. If any of the people she associated with thought in analogies and figures of speech, they kept it to themselves. But somehow it didn't seem out of character for Mike to say something like that out loud. Maybe it was because he was also an artist.

"And the bracelet?"

"For all the different sides of you."

"That was a long time ago. When you can only take one step at a time, quantity and variety tend to lose their importance."

"No." His hand, firmly grasping hers, brought her back to face him. "Nothing could change what you are inside."

She pulled away and stood up. "What do you know about who I am?" How could he think he knew what she had or hadn't lost? Even Rob wasn't that presumptuous. "A part of me died in that fall."

On his feet beside her, Mike looked down into her eyes. "No," he said again. "And that's why I want to come with you. It's the human spirit that drives a person, Kelsey, and a physical injury doesn't change that. Not by itself. The very fact that you've chosen to make such a trip proves that your spirit came out intact. Agree to let me come, just for the first week.''

Pivoting away, she paced the length of his room. Caught between the persuasiveness of his argument and the force of his personality, she wavered in indecision. The inclination to say yes kept growing stronger, but she didn't feel any closer to an answer.

What was it that nudged at her to agree? She turned to look at him. He projected the image of the conservative professional. Cool. Rational. Successful in true yuppie tradition. ''What do you really do? Besides take pictures.''

''I sell insurance.''

In spite of herself, she laughed. ''Insurance. You know, that's what I thought when you first walked into my store.''

He sat on the edge of his desk with his hands resting casually in his pockets. His smile became broader, and for the first time, she saw a recklessness in his expression. It challenged her to push away her fears and accept him. She decided a smile like that should be illegal.

''What else did you think?'' he asked.

''Oh, I don't know. That you were as out of place as a prince in a flea market.''

''A rather extreme analogy.''

''Maybe a knight or a count.''

''Still a little high for my blood.''

She swept her eyes over his office. ''What kind of insurance?''

''Corporate. We specialize in designing manuscript policies to fit a company's specific needs, from fire and liability to developing an investment portfolio for top management.''

''You obviously do well.''

''I work hard at it.''

Yes, she imagined he did. Michael Kincaid would never do anything halfway. She'd seen it in his art, in his ability to capture the essence of both the people he photographed and their sports. Now she could see it in his office. Every inch had been designed to make a specific impression. From the oil painting on one wall to the display of pictures on the other.

Suddenly her heart skipped a beat. Some of them were of her. Hang gliding. Four eleven-by-fourteens. Framed and matted like the one he'd sent. A chill raced down her spine and settled in the small of her back. Mesmerized, she moved closer.

Memories washed over her in waves, buffeting her like a piece of flotsam until she felt battered and weak. Closing her eyes, she felt Mike behind her, steadying her. With a fierce determination not to be weak, not to succumb to the inner hurt that never quite went away, she stiffened and stepped away.

"Why?" she asked.

"For the art."

She didn't believe him. "Why me? Hang gliding, rappeling, how many times have you been there, spying with your camera?"

With a wave of his hand toward the rest of the pictures, he dismissed her protestations. "You, a hundred others. People who do the kinds of things you do interest me. Your trip interests me."

She didn't believe that, either. But meeting his eyes, messages she didn't understand invaded her mind.

"I think I was right the first time. It would be better if you didn't join us."

When she started toward the door, he stopped her with his hands on her arms.

"You know I won't exploit you. That's why you came here today, because you've seen my work and know it's honest. You need for me to go, to share your story. How many other people are out there, hurt by some force they couldn't control and waiting for the right catalyst to over come a past trauma? Be their inspiration. Share you strength with the world.''

Kelsey didn't feel all that strong. The whole reason for thi trip was to take another step toward her old level of confi dence. Rob said she needed an extra commitment to insur she wouldn't quit. Well, maybe she did.

''What's in this for you?'' she asked.

''A three-part series in the newspaper, then a color sprea on Sunday. It will mostly be a write-up of the trip. How yo pack, how far you ride, what it's like, how you camp an eat. But I also want to let people know what it took to ge you to this point. I'll want you to talk about the acciden and your recovery.''

If that were all, perhaps she could give him what h wanted. ''One week?''

''I'd like to ride with you the first week out, with the op tion of a day or two more if I think I need it. Then I want t join you again at the end, to see how you've done and wha changes you had to make in your routine along the way.''

It was crazy. Kelsey knew it right to her fingertips. Bu coupled with Rob's opinion, Mike's arguments made sense.

''All right,'' she said. ''We leave on the twelfth.'' Sh turned quickly before she could change her mind. ''It woul be a good idea if you met my brother before we left.''

''When?''

''Sunday?''

''Sure.''

At the door she paused. ''I forgot to ask if you can ride bike?''

His smile sent a shaft of warmth straight to her heart ''Yes.''

''Fifty miles a day?''

''I don't think you need to worry.'' He reached past he for the doorknob.

With a nod she accepted his assurance. "Good. If you don't have all your equipment, I'll expect you to buy the rest in my store."

"I wouldn't dream of going anywhere else."

"Fine. Then I guess I'll see you on Sunday."

Opening the door, he stepped back and held out his hand. Accepting it, Kelsey hoped she hadn't just made the biggest mistake of her life.

"I'm looking forward to it," he said.

Chapter Three

The first twenty miles were fairly easy. It took them that long to get out of Portland and across the river into Washington. After another ten, Mike suspected an hour a day on an exercise bike at the health club was inadequate preparation for a steady uphill grade. Although the temperature hovered around seventy, his jersey was wet with sweat. In his pursuit of risk takers over the years, he'd found himself in a lot of interesting situations, but he'd never had to work this hard.

Ahead of him Kelsey and Rob talked and laughed together side by side, so in tune with their bikes and the road that they seemed to anticipate traffic coming from behind them. Automatically one or the other of them would fall back to single file whenever necessary.

A seed of jealousy began to germinate as he observed them. Logically Mike knew that he couldn't expect to keep up—at least at first. Philosophically he respected all highly athletic people. Emotionally he felt excluded by their relationship.

He quickly quenched the feeling. Successful relationships weren't based on emotion, and those that were tended to self-destruct.

But he wasn't after a relationship. True, Kelsey Sumner fascinated him in ways no other woman ever had. From the first time he'd seen her, that day he'd photographed her hang gliding, he'd been drawn to her. Something even then made her stand out from the rest. The few other times their paths had crossed, his first impression had simply been reinforced, but there had never been an opportunity to actually meet her.

Then came her accident. Crashing, surviving, recovering, taking on something this major. He assumed there had been changes, although he was sure that the inner fire that had drawn him to her in the first place still existed. Now, finally, he was going to discover what made her different, what made her so intriguing.

They passed another mile marker, and whenever Mike lifted his eyes from the road, all he could see were Kelsey's legs. They were long, strong and gorgeous, but not quite enough to take his mind off the laboring of his lungs. The road seemed to be getting steeper. A little farther and he'd have to stop for a rest, whether the Sumners did or not. Luckily they weren't pushing. In fact, he began to notice that Kelsey set a moderate pace and Rob held back for her.

Eventually they pulled off at a rest area at the edge of the river. The water roared fast and white down the gorge, its thunder rumbling up the cliffs. Mike leaned his bike on its kickstand with his helmet on the seat and flopped onto the ground. His heart beat too fast and his thighs burned. Linking his hands behind his neck, he closed his eyes and tried not to think about how tired he was.

Almost automatically his thoughts turned to the woman he'd come here to write about. Always fascinated by those who endangered their lives in the name of sport, this was the next question: what does the risk taker do after the crash-and-burn? Before her hang glider fell out of the sky, Kelsey's life had been one of constant adventure; now she was struggling to regain her identity. Where once he'd seen laughter and a swashbuckling romanticism, he now saw vulnerability, although she did her best to hide it. For four years he'd heard people talk about her. Since deciding to make this trip, she'd become a legend.

He wanted to know her mind, what motivated her, and what trade-offs she'd had to make.

He sensed her sit beside him. She didn't touch him, and he couldn't have heard anything over the sound of the river, but he knew she was there.

"Are you all right?" she asked.

"Sure." Without changing position, he opened his eyes. She sat only inches away, parallel to him, with her hip near his side. Matted against her head, her hair was damp with sweat and so dark none of the red showed. Because of the angularity of her features, rather than in spite of them, she was a beautiful woman. He liked the slant of her eyebrows and the prominence of her cheekbones. He appreciated the slender slope of her shoulders and the smooth, firm proportions of her body.

Undoubtedly Jerry was right to question his motives in joining Kelsey and her brother. But Mike had always been drawn to risk takers the way a moth is drawn to a light. He'd never met one who wasn't half-crazy. They did stupid, foolhardy things and didn't give a damn about anyone else. They rarely considered that if they got hurt, other people might suffer. But they still fascinated him.

And maybe because Kelsey didn't seem to fit the mold, she fascinated him more than any of the rest.

Good sense might tell him he should be home pursuing a hot new lead that could net him thousands of dollars annually. Instead he was engaged in that elusive quest of trying to understand what drove people beyond their limits—what drove Kelsey Sumner.

"Have you ever ridden mountains before?" she asked.

No use denying the obvious. He shook his head. "But I'm doing okay."

"We can go slower this afternoon." She pulled her knees against her chest and wound her arms around them. At the hem of her shorts he saw the tip of a narrow, fading scar on her thigh. For all his listening to the grapevine, he'd never been able to discover the specifics of her injuries—only that she'd spent six or seven months in the hospital. It was time to start learning the answers. From the cargo pocket of his shorts he took out his minicassette recorder.

Kelsey nodded her assent before he could ask permission. Rolling to his side, he propped himself up on his elbow and clicked it on. "When did you first start bicycling?"

She laughed lightly. "When I was a kid. When did you?"

The question made him smile. "When I was a kid. I guess I want to know when you fell in love with it. You've toured before—you own a bike store."

"I raced some when I was in high school, but I didn't like the time commitment it took to win. There were too many other interesting things to do besides ride. I put myself through college by working in a bike shop, and then Blaine and I decided we could do better on our own."

"Why didn't you go into business with Rob?" Watching how smoothly she and her brother worked together, he thought it would have been the natural choice.

Kelsey glanced at Rob, who was walking along the bank of the river. Mike continued to watch her. He noticed that her eyes softened and an affectionate smile touched her lips.

"Rob's love is wood. He has a shop of his own where he makes beautiful handmade furniture." She laughed again and turned back to Mike. Her eyes invited him to share a secret. "For which he charges absolutely obscene prices. We should have had him show you."

"Maybe when you get back."

"Sure." She passed it off the way casual acquaintances agree to stay in touch. "Have you decided what you're going to say in your first article?"

He dropped on his back. "That riding uphill is damn hard."

Her laughter rippled in counterpoint to the roar of the river. "You phony. You're tired, but you stayed with us all morning. You knew before we started it would be tough."

"I'll let you read my first draft when I finish it."

"I'd like that."

"Still worried about having me along?"

"A little."

Reaching out, he took her hand in his. It was small. Too small to do all the things she'd done. "I won't say anything that will hurt you, Kelsey."

"Won't you?"

When she started to pull away, he let her go. "You know I won't, or you wouldn't have let me come."

"Sometimes things we do have consequences we don't expect."

It was a surprising thing for a risk taker to say. But maybe he shouldn't be surprised to hear it from Kelsey. He already knew she was different.

The sun filtered through the trees and turned her drying hair to fire wherever it touched in the shifting shadows. "How much farther will we go today?"

At first she didn't answer. Her eyes searched his, and he saw they were a rich hazel color, partly green, partly brown, not too dark and not too light. Faint, fine laugh lines radiated from the corners. "About ten miles."

She stood up abruptly. "We'd better get something to eat."

As she hurried toward her brother, Mike noticed that she limped slightly. He thought back over the other times they'd been together—in his office, at her house on Sunday, even this morning. Not once before now had he seen a sign of a limp. Already, it seemed, the ride was exacting a toll.

He wondered how much residual disability was left from her accident. It was a question he hadn't considered before, simply because he knew so little about her recovery. People talked about her, but usually more in speculative terms than in hard facts, and usually just because she'd survived a killer crash. Since she was embarking on a three-thousand-mile bicycle ride, he'd assumed she was totally well. Obviously an erroneous assumption.

The woman had guts. A sense of humor, eyes a man could drown in, a perfectly proportioned body, and guts. Suddenly he had the uncomfortable feeling that if he ever got close to Kelsey Sumner, he'd have a hell of a time backing away. Clicking on his recorder, he dictated a few more notes as he watched her walk away.

BECAUSE KELSEY HAD RIDDEN the gorge before, albeit when she was still in college, she'd known what to expect. While training for this trip, she'd tackled a few of the canyons closer to home. Some of them were steeper than this, but none of them was as long.

By midafternoon she knew she was in trouble. Her thigh had begun to hurt half an hour earlier, but since they weren't far from their goal for the day, she hadn't wanted to stop. Now the pain radiated from her hip to her knee. Rob had slowly outdistanced her until he'd disappeared around the curve of the road. She could see in her rearview mirror that Mike was just a few yards behind.

She bit her lip and forced her feet to push the pedals. This was only the first day. Her leg couldn't give out now, before they hardly got started.

Except the pain cut like a knife thrust. She braked to a stop and balanced her weight on her good leg. Closing her eyes, she concentrated on breathing deeply.

"Terrific view." Mike's voice came from behind her.

Without turning, she nodded.

"Kelsey, what's the matter?"

Suddenly his hands were on her shoulders, and she felt him take the weight of the bike. Not trusting herself to speak, she used her hands to lift her leg over the crossbar, gritting her teeth against the agony of movement. He lowered her bike to the ground, then swung her into his arms and carried her away from the road.

"Put me down, dammit. I'm okay."

"Like hell."

He set her in the shade of a tree, and she stretched her leg straight. Soon, she knew, the pain would ease. Too bad she didn't have any ice. Leaning back against the tree, she closed her eyes.

She felt him unfastening the strap of her helmet. His hand was hot and dry and gentle. He smoothed her damp hair off her forehead. When his fingers drifted to her throat, she looked at him.

He crouched on his heels, his eyes studying her, his expression unreadable. "Do you have medication to take for your leg?"

"Really, I'm okay. I just need to rest."

"There must be something I can do." He looked tense, and worried.

She smiled to reassure him. "Move our bikes?"

With a light laugh he dropped his hand. "Good idea."

Watching him wheel the bikes away from the edge of the road, Kelsey wished she knew what he was thinking. Maybe he felt sorry for her. Maybe he thought she wouldn't be able to go on. *That* would be an interesting ending for his article. Well, he'd soon discover she had more grit than that.

When he came back, he brought her water bottle and sat beside her while she drank. The pain had dulled to a steady throb. She'd been a little worried about leg failure, but she certainly hadn't expected a problem the first day.

"Does this happen often?"

Meeting his eyes, she shook her head ruefully. "Not any-more."

"Can I do anything for you?" His hand touched her arm, and to her surprise she found it more comforting than alarming.

"I'll be fine in a few minutes."

"Should I go find Rob?"

"He'll be back soon to see what's wrong."

Mike leaned back on one arm and draped the other over his raised knee. "It's easing up."

"You're very perceptive."

"Where you're concerned."

A simple statement. Bald and unsettling. Kelsey concentrated on relaxing her leg and felt the muscles ease. Looking at Mike through her lashes, she decided enough time had been spent discussing her physical condition.

"Are you going to make enough selling four articles to the newspaper to justify a week of your time?"

The concern didn't leave his eyes, but to her relief he accepted her change of subject. "I'm supposed to be asking the questions."

She grinned. "Except right now you think anything you ask might be wrong."

This time he laughed clearly, without hesitation. "You have your own share of perception."

"So why are you here?"

"Life-story time?"

At her nod, he sat beside her on the ground and rested one elbow on his bent knee. Idly he plucked a strand of tall, wild grass and chewed the end.

"When I was a kid, I hated to climb trees. I hated the high-diving board and the soapbox derby. I couldn't stand riding in the back of a truck, and thunder scared me. I refused to play football."

Mike Kincaid? Six feet of pure hunk? "What a wimp."

"That's right," he agreed, unabashed. "And I ate my share of crow because of it. But I couldn't stay away from the kids who walked along the tops of high fences and climbed on roofs. I guess I took some kind of vicarious pleasure from watching them. When I got my first camera, I started taking pictures of people doing the things I avoided."

"And then you outgrew your fears?"

"No." He shook his head decisively. "I didn't."

Of course, she didn't believe that, not after what she'd read into his work. "Then how do you get within photographic distance?"

His smile made her as light-headed as any pain medication, but it helped her relax, too. "I use *very* long lenses."

"I saw those pictures in *Mountain!* of Doug Carpenter. You were at the same altitude."

"Helicopter."

"Liar."

"Mountain goat?"

"Ropes and pitons?"

Holding his palm up in protest, he shook his head. "Not me. I keep both feet firmly on the ground at all times."

At his light, bantering tone, Kelsey shrugged. Perhaps the way he achieved his photographs was a professional secret.

"I found thirteen titles listed in the magazine index of stories you've done," she said. "Does that pay enough to make it worth your while?"

"Is this trip making *you* any money?"

"This is a vacation," she protested.

"Photography is my hobby. The rewards have nothing to do with money."

Since she'd always tried to integrate her hobbies with other aspects of her life, she could understand that.

"I'd like to take your picture," he said suddenly, getting to his feet. "Now. While you're sitting like that."

"I probably look a mess."

Brushing off the seat of his shorts, he shook his head. "You only look as if you've been riding a bike all day."

Watching Mike go for his camera, Kelsey realized that in biking shorts and a jersey, he looked as much at home on the road as he had dressed for business in his office. He still wasn't as tan as most of the outdoor types she knew, but he also ran an obviously successful insurance agency, which probably took a lot of his time.

She settled back against the tree and closed her eyes. Talking to him just now had been as easy as being with a lifelong friend. Almost as easy as talking to her brother.

"Nice," Mike said.

She looked up with a grin. "Do you want me to pose or anything?"

He was folding the case back over his camera. "I already got what I wanted."

"That was fast."

"I wanted to catch you when you weren't looking."

"How many did you take?"

With a shrug he crouched next to her again. "Enough. How's your leg?"

Actually she'd stopped thinking about it. "It doesn't hurt anymore." But his simple question forced her back to reality. "I wonder where Rob is."

As if she'd conjured him up by saying his name, she heard Rob call out, then he appeared around the curve in the road.

"Kelsey! Are you okay?" Before she could object, he was kneeling beside her, literally elbowing Mike away.

"I am now. My leg gave out."

"How bad?"

Mike stood up and stepped back, but he didn't leave. "I thought she was going to pass out."

"I never faint," she said firmly.

"I shouldn't have gotten ahead."

"That's absurd. I'm fine. Besides, Mike was here."

Without so much as glancing at Mike, Rob continued to hover over her. "I could wet a shirt in the river—it might be cold enough to give you some relief."

Embarrassed by Rob's suddenly curt attitude toward Mike, Kelsey decided it was just because he was worried. "It doesn't even hurt anymore. Really. It's no big deal."

"There's a place we could camp just around the next bend. It's not a campground, but there's water and privacy."

"Sounds great."

Offering her hand to Rob, she let him pull her up. Shifting a little weight to her left leg, she felt it refuse to hold her. Focusing on her muscles and breathing deeply, she concentrated on one step at a time. Using all the techniques learned in years of physical therapy, she walked slowly to her bike.

Each step took less effort. Okay. Easy now. Leg over.

With her bike pointed east and her foot in the toe clip, she felt as if someone had just hung an Olympic gold medal around her neck. Grinning, she turned to Rob.

Her success was mirrored in his eyes. He knew what that ten feet had cost her. "All *right*, Kel!"

Then she sensed Mike beside her, watching. He didn't say anything, and the humor they'd shared no longer filled his eyes.

She hoped he'd interpret Rob's attitude as one of concern for her rather than insult to him. Otherwise, the week would become very uncomfortable.

THE SPOT ROB LED them to was lushly green. Coniferous and deciduous trees, berry bushes, ferns and wild grasses combined to turn it into a tiny paradise. A stream babbled along on its way into the Columbia River.

Kelsey insisted on helping Rob set up camp with the same routine they always used. It took only a few minutes to put up their two-person dome tent, and then they changed out of their shorts and jerseys and hand washed them, hanging them on their bikes to dry. By washing every night, they got along with only one change of riding clothes. In camp they wore regular shorts or sweat suits that doubled as pajamas on cold nights.

She noticed with satisfaction that Mike was easily as proficient in setting up as she and Rob.

They cooked one of their packages of freeze-dried stew for dinner. The trick to successful bike packing was being prepared for any contingency.

After dinner Mike retreated to his tent to write. With her leg stretched out straight, Kelsey sat by the fire to play rummy with Rob. The sun hovered just above the western mountains, slanting golden rays through the trees. A crisp wind blew up from the river, and Kelsey zipped her jacket on over her sweatshirt.

From where she sat, she could see Mike, spread out on his sleeping bag, his tent flaps rolled up to allow more light inside. A narrow shaft of dying sunlight lit the side of his face and fell on his hand.

A day spent in his company had made her curious about him. How did his denial of pursuing adventure fit in with the truth she'd seen in his photographs? And then, there was the way he'd reacted to her weakness. Not for one minute had he made her feel inferior or inadequate.

With a thoughtful expression on his face, he lifted his eyes from the notebook. He started tapping his pen against his thigh, and then he looked straight at her.

For a brief, heart-stopping moment their eyes locked before he grinned and went back to work.

It was the grin that convinced her there had been nothing unusual in the exchange of glances. She refocused her attention on the cards in her hand.

"You're worried," Rob said.

"Of course not." She rearranged her cards, then drew from the stack.

"At least he won't be with us long." Rob laid down a run of high diamonds. There was a tension just beneath the surface. She could hear it in his voice and see it in the thrust of his jaw.

"What's wrong?" she demanded.

"I don't like the way he hangs around you."

"That's what he's here for," Kelsey protested. "As I recall, you thought it would be a good idea."

With his arm balanced on his leg, Rob leaned toward her and lowered his voice. "He gets a greedy expression in his eyes when he looks at you."

"Oh, come on, Rob. He does nothing of the kind." If he did, she would no longer feel so comfortable around him. "Look, we know he doesn't assassinate people with his pen."

"We're not discussing his writing."

"You worry too much."

"It's a habit."

"Try to break it."

"Kelsey—"

Refusing to get drawn in deeper, she changed the subject. "I'm sorry about today."

For several interminable seconds, Rob continued to study her in the dying light. When he shrugged and turned his attention back to his cards, she felt some of the tension drain away. Perhaps the less they talked about Mike, the better.

"If the pain's gone," Rob said, "we could run through some exercises tonight."

"That'd be a good idea." She closed the fan of cards in her hand and leaned back on one arm. "I'm going to make it, Rob. What happened this afternoon doesn't change anything. I refuse to let it get me down."

"We'll just take our time."

And really, Mike Kincaid's presence and his articles should have nothing to do with how well the trip went overall.

But a longing she wasn't willing to identify stirred deep within her. She glanced at Mike again. The sun was gone, leaving the interior of his tent in shadow.

"Kelsey, there's more here than you're letting on. He bothers you, too. What is it? That picture of you on the mountain?"

She shifted her eyes back to her brother. Rob read her too easily. "The only thing worrying me is that if we don't relax about him, we won't enjoy the next few days. I don't want anything to ruin this trip."

"As long as he doesn't step out of line."

"Pretend you like him, okay?"

"I like him all right."

Touching Rob's hand, she smiled. "Then act like it. We're not exactly discussing my virtue, you know."

He grinned back. "Okay, sweetie, no shotguns."

As dusk settled in, it became too dark to see the cards. Beyond Rob's shoulder, Kelsey saw Mike get out a flashlight to finish by. Rob threw another piece of broken branch on the fire. Overhead, stars began to fill the sky.

At that moment the world seemed perfect. A squirrel chattered somewhere in the rustling trees, and the wind carried the scents of pine and cold water and made her skin tingle with the evening chill. How many times since her accident had she remembered nights like this and feared she'd never experience one again?

"I want to take every possible side trip and see every scenic attraction along the way. I wish we had a year."

Rob chuckled dryly. "Call Blaine, offer to sell him your interest in the store. Then when we eventually get home, you can start all over again."

Almost incidentally Kelsey realized Rob hadn't mentioned Angela Newberry's name all day. She didn't know whether to be glad or sorry. A girlfriend at home could become a major complication, but for the entire four years of her recuperation, Rob had hardly dated at all. This trip would prove she didn't need that kind of doting attention anymore.

"When we get back, I want to buy a sailboat and go around the world," she said.

"You inviting me to go along?"

Tossing a twig in the fire, she laughed. "Do you need to be invited?"

"I'd want to build the boat. Could you wait that long?"

She heaved an exaggerated sigh. "I guess I'll just have to keep working a little while longer."

Suddenly Mike's light clicked off. In the darkness he moved like a shadow, coming out of the tent toward them.

"Finished?" Rob asked with no hint of rejection in his voice. "Pull up a chair."

"Thanks. Got a beer?"

"In the fridge. Help yourself."

Mike sat on the ground near Kelsey. The fire lit the planes of his face and left his eyes in shadow. So subtly she could hardly identify how it happened, the mood changed. She decided it had to be Rob. Whatever was bothering him, she hoped he'd get over it quickly.

"What a place," Mike said. "Nothing but stars and space debris between us and God."

"Where all have you camped?" Rob asked, his voice too neutral.

Mike didn't seem to notice. "Oh here and there. The Cascades, of course. A little bit in the Sierras. I used to backpack in the lake country of Minnesota."

"Different from the mountains."

"Flatter."

To Kelsey's surprise, Rob chuckled. "And wetter, probably. You from the Midwest?"

"Duluth."

"I heard there's good fishing there."

"Some of the best."

"You go with your dad?"

"Never with him." Mike said it without emphasis of any kind, but beneath the surface Kelsey sensed a cold shutting off of the past. "I mostly went with friends."

When Rob kept the conversation going easily, Kelsey sat back. Perhaps she'd been reading things into Rob's attitude. There certainly were no undercurrents of tension in this discussion of canoeing and the merits of fly rods. Good.

Mike, it turned out, had a lot more of that kind of experience than Rob, but Rob made up for it in enthusiasm. Then the conversation turned to other activities, the kind Rob participated in and Mike claimed only to record, and Rob warmed to the topic.

It seemed to Kelsey that Rob's range of experiences exceeded Mike's. Or was that Mike's way of giving her brother his head? If so, it was no wonder his interviews with adventurers were so good. He won their confidence and delved beneath the surface, and the subject of the interview didn't even realize he was being handled by a master.

She considered their brief conversation earlier in the day. Yes, she'd been that at ease with him, too. She wondered if she'd said more than she'd realized. Rob was certainly opening up like a flower to the sun. As Mike asked all the right questions to keep Rob rolling from anecdote to anecdote, Kelsey decided to be more alert with him in the future.

For tonight, however, it was nice that Mike and Rob had found an interest in common. With any luck it would keep Rob's temper from erupting.

When Rob began telling Mike about his furniture, Kelsey levered herself to her feet. "I think I'll turn in."

Both Rob and Mike stood up immediately. "I can come now, too," Rob said.

With a quick glance at Mike, she shook her head. "Take your time. I'll be awake for a while."

Mike touched Kelsey's arm. "It's been a long day. You can read what I wrote in the morning when there's light."

"I want to." She couldn't discern his features, but the feel of his hand on her arm conveyed unspoken messages.

Backing away, her foot slipped slightly, and his clasp tightened.

But surely it was only the dark night and the cool breeze that made her believe there was anything significant in his touch.

"Good night," she said.

Another quick squeeze, and he released her. "Sleep well."

Pivoting away, she hurried to her tent.

Chapter Four

Mike felt as if he'd been run over by a truck. Even with a high-density pad under his sleeping bag, the ground was hard and uneven. Oh, he'd done his share of camping, but as an adult it had only been when the pursuit of risk takers took him to remote locations. He couldn't imagine wanting to sleep in a tent for three whole months. And yesterday's climb through the gorge had taken a toll. His leg muscles screamed every time he moved, his feet were stiff and his shoulders protested.

Hearing movements around the camp, he stretched and unzipped his tent flap. The sun slanted gold, making prisms of the dew that hung motionless on the morning grass. He had a side view of Rob, crouched at the fire circle. Kelsey didn't appear to be up and about yet.

Rolling onto his back, he linked his fingers behind his head. His interest in Kelsey Sumner was the same interest he had in all risk takers, wasn't it? Whether he liked it or not, the answer was no. It wasn't, and it never had been. Perhaps Jerry was right. Perhaps he was obsessed with her.

She was exciting, alive, challenging, brave. And yesterday he'd seen an inner strength in her that awed him. He marveled at the determination it must take to go on, to face three thousand more miles when thirty had almost been too much.

That didn't mean he wanted a relationship with her. He only wanted to discover whatever it was that gave her the power to overcome.

Of course, with her brother acting as guardian, exploring the surface was probably the best he could hope for. Yesterday he'd gotten the message to keep his distance. He wondered if Rob thought he was protecting her health or her virtue.

After a few minutes, when Kelsey still hadn't put in an appearance, Mike threw aside his sleeping bag. Obviously he was going to have to confront Sir Galahad, defender of maidens, by himself.

Stripping off his sweats, he climbed into a fresh pair of riding shorts and joined Rob. In the fire circle a hatch-work of dried grass and twigs waited for a match.

"How about if I make coffee," he offered.

"Good idea," Rob agreed simply, "before Kelsey gets to it. She's getting some water."

"Stream water?" Mike asked in surprise. Contracting giardiasis had never been high on his list of things to try.

"It's okay if we boil it long enough. We don't have much water left in our bottles."

Not one to reject a peace offering, Mike hunkered down near Rob and began handing him twigs and sticks. Yesterday's abrupt change in plans didn't seem to bother either of the Sumners, and Mike admired that.

"What's wrong with Kelsey's coffee?"

"It always tastes like river water when she makes it over the fire. Outdoors, nobody ruins coffee like Kelsey."

Under Rob's careful tutelage, the flame came to life.

"I think I understand Kelsey's reasons for making this trip," Mike said. "What are yours?"

"You going to include me in your article?"

"A passing reference, maybe. I don't want it to seem as if she's out here alone."

Rob nodded and blew lightly on the growing fire. "When we were kids, writing dream lists was one of our favorite pastimes. You know, things like walk on the moon, explore the Nile to its source, climb the world's ten highest mountains. This was one that kept rising to the top. Last summer, when Kelsey was in the hospital recovering from her last operation, we promised ourselves we'd make it happen."

"After just one day I can see the appeal," Mike said, stretching the truth only slightly. "Bicycling opens your senses to the world, doesn't it? Three months with nothing to do but experience."

Resting his weight on his heels, with his elbow on his knee, Rob looked at Mike. "Ever wanted to do it?"

"Not anything this long. You're unusually close to your sister," Mike replied, turning the conversation away from himself. "Is that because of the accident?" He hoped Rob would talk about it. Almost as much as risk takers, the idea of family loyalty fascinated and amazed him.

"Maybe some. But our folks moved around a lot when we were growing up. Most of the time we didn't have any other friends." A quick grin flashed, lighting his eyes. "Kelsey was adventurous from the beginning, and when she started hauling me around with her, I'd have done anything not to be left behind. I guess I sort of hero-worshipped her. Our mother probably spent half her time praying for our safety."

Then Rob sobered. "After Kel's accident I spent a lot of time with her, and when our folks went to Greece, I was all she had."

Rob's answers only created more questions. "Your parents are in Greece now?"

"They travel all over the world writing books and articles, the kind of stuff you see in *National Geographic*."

A serious fire now blazed in the circle. The heat dispelled the damp of morning within a short radius.

Kelsey was humming when she broke through the brush into the clearing. She was dressed in shorts for riding, her body fit and beautiful. In the early light the red in her short hair glistened like dark gold, and around her neck hung a pair of high-powered binoculars. In her hand she carried a miniature aluminum coffeepot full of water.

"Took you long enough," Rob said, but Mike heard no censure in the other man's voice.

Kelsey stuck her tongue out at him. "There are your choices," she said. "Instant oatmeal or granola bars."

"Which way do I get coffee?" Rob asked.

"Either way. You have to wait longer for it if we have oatmeal."

"Then I vote for granola bars and coffee. What about you, Mike?"

"Granola bars are fine." He hated instant oatmeal. Catching Rob's eye, he grinned. "I'll make the coffee."

"Okay." Kelsey handed him the pot and dropped down next to the fire. He noticed that this morning she didn't favor her weak leg.

"See anything interesting?" Rob asked.

"Nothing rare or unusual, but they're all interesting. I actually saw a robin pulling a worm from the ground."

"Just like in the cartoons?"

Kelsey picked up a pebble and lobbed it at her brother. "Don't knock it until you try it."

"Boring."

Mike busied himself with the coffee. He was an outsider, since he'd invited himself along, so there was no reason to feel left out. He should just concentrate on getting the job done well.

With that in mind, he got his notebook from the tent while waiting for the water to boil clean of parasites. Kelsey took it without comment and began to read. In spite of his best intentions, he found himself watching her expression for any indication that she approved. Because they had yet to discuss her accident, he'd focused on their preparations and the first day of riding. He hadn't skimmed over the difficulty.

Kelsey's face gave nothing away. A couple of times he saw her eyes dart back to an earlier place in the text, and once she returned to a previous page. He estimated he'd only written about a thousand words, but it seemed to take forever for her to finish.

Finally she closed the notebook and handed it to him. Then, without a word, she stood and walked toward the stream.

He watched her go, and a chill crawled up his back.

"Leave it, Mike." The tone in Rob's voice brought him around.

"I want to find out what's the matter."

"If there's a problem," Rob said firmly, "I'll deal with it."

Closeness was one thing, ownership quite another. Rob assumed a proprietary attitude about Kelsey that Mike didn't like. "We're talking about something *I* wrote. I'm going to her."

Rob blocked his way. "If you hurt her—"

"The point is, I'm trying *not* to hurt her." Pushing past, Mike strode after Kelsey without looking back.

He found her sitting on a boulder that protruded far enough into the stream that the water rushed around it in a white torrent. Never actually looking his way, she acknowledged him with the posture of her shoulders. He climbed on the rock to sit behind her.

"I don't have to send it in," he said. "I can write something else."

"No, it's okay."

"It upsets you."

She turned then, and it brought her so close her breasts almost brushed against his shirt. In the early sunlight her eyes looked more green than brown, as if reflecting the foliage around them. Her breath caressed his chin. He wanted to touch her.

"Not really. Everything you wrote is straightforward, all your facts are right. Yet you make me seem bigger than life, and I'm not."

He thought of things he'd wanted to say but hadn't. "You have courage and determination."

"Not more than anyone else."

Unable not to, he cupped her cheek with his palm. Tentatively he brushed his thumb across her lower lip. The past few years had left their mark on her face, adding character, defining her inner strength. "Much more than most people."

"Mike—"

He silenced her protest with his mouth. Her lips were soft and smooth. She smelled of wind and wildflowers. She tasted like the morning sun. Almost imperceptibly she responded to him, and then she drew away.

"No, please."

She'd given him the merest taste of what it would be like to really kiss her, and now she was pulling away. Good. Firmly he reminded himself he didn't want to get involved with her. He should be glad of her brother's watchdog attitude.

In the meantime he had several more articles to write, and he'd need Kelsey's full cooperation. With a grin he dropped a brotherly kiss on the tip of her nose. "If the water hasn't boiled away by now, it's probably pure enough to make coffee with."

Relief flashed in her eyes as she quickly picked up on his change of tone. "Which you're going to make. We'll see if it's any better than Rob's."

Sliding off the boulder, he took her arm to help her down. "What's wrong with Rob's?"

She pulled a face and shuddered. "It would dissolve nails. A couple of swallows, and you want to give up coffee forever."

They hated each other's coffee. Mike wondered if they both endured it without comment. In his family it would have been grounds for a perpetual fight.

ALL THAT DAY ROB RODE either right at Kelsey's side or immediately behind her, and Mike decided that was for the best. Kelsey set a slow enough pace that he had no difficulty staying with them. Except that his crotch still wasn't conditioned to hours on the saddle, the riding seemed to be getting easier. Still, he looked forward to the rest stops.

That afternoon they rode into a tiny town that boasted a population of less than four hundred. It did have a post office, though, so Mike took his carefully handwritten pages and his first rolls of film, put them in an express envelope and sent them to his editor with a note about which type of picture he thought would go best with this first copy.

They bought bread and cheese, fruit, orange juice and gingersnaps in the town's one grocery store, then went down to the river to eat a late lunch. Picking a nearby rock to sit on, Rob found a gnarled piece of driftwood and attacked it with his pocketknife.

Mike guided Kelsey to a spot several yards away and put his tape recorder unobtrusively on his thigh. "You and Rob seem a lot closer than the average brother and sister," he began.

"I think he saved my life." A smile softened her mouth as she watched Rob whittle. "I was in a coma for three days. No one knew for sure if I would come out of it, or when, but Rob almost camped at the hospital."

To Mike's surprise, she talked easily. He hadn't expected her to tell her story without a lot of gentle encouragement.

"Rob would talk, or read to me. Sometimes he brought his ghetto blaster and played music. Of course, I don't remember any of it, but somehow I knew he was there.

"He sloughed off his classes at the university and ignored his friends, and spent his time sitting by my bedside."

Even having heard Rob's side, Mike found such devotion incomprehensible. While he was growing up, his two sisters were annoyances rather than friends. His likes and dislikes confused them. They resented the fact that he wasn't a star athlete, or, barring that, best friends with the guys who were. Even now, they wrote to each other infrequently, if at all.

"Where were your parents?"

"In Brazil at the time of my accident, and they came right home. But I don't remember sensing them the way Rob's presence remained with me."

"He said they're in Greece now."

She nodded. "I think we got our flair for adventure from them. They had the house in Portland, the one Rob and I live in now, but every couple of years we'd go off somewhere—Iceland, the Riviera, Kenya."

"Do you miss them?"

"Of course!"

Just as if all parents and all children loved each other unconditionally, Mike thought ruefully.

"I miss the traveling, too," she continued. "They asked me to go to Greece with them, but by then I only wanted to get back on my feet and start living a real life again."

"What about your friends? How did they react to your fall?"

"My friends." In her eyes and the angle of her head, he could see that her memories had changed abruptly. "I stayed in the hospital for seven months. That's a long time. People have their own commitments.''

There was a wistfulness in her voice that made him wonder if she referred to someone specific. If so, the memory wasn't pleasant. When she didn't go on, he continued with his own questions.

''Rob said your parents write for *National Geographic*.''

''Sometimes. Mom is an artist with a camera, just like you are. She has a master's in sociology. Dad got a doctorate in anthropology. They do social and historical research, and romantic travelogues, and whatever else catches their interest.''

Mike encouraged her to talk on about her family, what it was like growing up so footloose, why she'd decided to open her own store and how her partnership with Blaine gave her freedom to live the kind of life she wanted. Then he turned the subject back to the trip.

''I guess bicycling is addictive. The smells alone are incredible.''

She grinned suddenly. ''The best is yet to come.''

''What could be better than wind and pine?''

''Skunk. Manure. Fertilizer.''

Mike gave a shout of laughter. ''I expected you to say flowers or something.''

''Flowers are good. So is freshly turned earth, or catching a whiff of baking bread. But it's all part of the whole.''

Again, she was wearing the binoculars around her neck. Mike flicked the strap with his finger. ''Tell me about this.''

''Bird-watching.''

He laughed again, this time in disbelief. *''Bird-watching?''* He'd been studying risk takers informally for years, and without exception they were single-minded in their quest for thrills. ''Isn't that kind of tame for someone like you?''

With her heel she hollowed out a hole in the dirt. "What is someone like me like?"

Suddenly he wasn't sure. Every adjective he'd been using had a synonym with a negative connotation. And although he was fascinated by risk takers, he generally didn't have much use for them personally.

Kelsey Sumner had always been an exception, which was why he was following her on this trip. Because she was different, he knew he shouldn't be so surprised when the differences became apparent.

"You know, you may be creating someone with these articles of yours who doesn't really exist."

"I'm trying to be honest."

"You're only seeing what you want to see."

"So, tell me about the bird-watching."

She leaned forward and turned to face him. "There's nothing to tell. It's a hobby. My father introduced me to it when I was about nine, I think. When my mother discovered it was something that would keep me on the ground, she not only encouraged me, she bought me posters and spotter's guides and tapes of birds' songs."

"Rob doesn't share your interest."

With a low chuckle she glanced at Rob and shook her head. "I told you, Rob's love is wood."

By the time they started riding again, Mike wondered if he'd ever understand Kelsey Sumner.

THEY TOOK SIX DAYS to ride across Washington, and to Kelsey's relief her leg didn't give out again. By the time they crossed the border into Idaho, she thought that success alone would carry her the rest of the way.

Of course, they still had several mountain ranges to climb, including the Rockies, but she felt stronger with each day—with each mile.

She'd also adjusted to Mike's omnipresent camera and tape recorder. He took pictures so often she soon didn't notice. And she accommodated herself to the things he wrote. She didn't recognize the woman he portrayed; that person seemed too dynamic on the one hand, and too ethereal on the other.

She decided it didn't matter. Maybe, as he'd said, his articles would inspire people who didn't know her. They would certainly provide entertainment for her acquaintances.

They entered Lewiston just before noon and picked a campground with showers and laundry facilities. Situated at the confluence of the Snake and Clearwater rivers, the town was a gateway to wilderness activities. Billboards and advertisements by various concessionaires prompted Kelsey to suggest that they spend an extra day and take a float trip on the Snake River.

"Sure thing," Rob agreed quickly.

After doing some laundry and picking up a few groceries, they stopped at the little cabin that served as a visitor's bureau.

Rob headed straight for a giant map displayed on one wall. Kelsey started picking through the brochures with Mike at her elbow. "Which sounds best to you? A raft or canoes?" After a week of riding with him, she was more sure than ever that his protestations about preferring to observe were a sham. Every time it had come up, he'd deflected her probing with a joke.

Now he held up a hand in protest, although a smile hovered around the corners of his mouth. "You and Rob can do whatever you want. I'll watch."

"You can't watch a river trip," she objected. "It's a participation sport."

"I told you. I use very long lenses."

"But you wouldn't feel the spray on your face."

Mike pointed to a folder with the picture on the front of a ten-person raft diving nose first into white water. "You know where I'd be? Huddled in the middle with my arms over my head."

She passed off the idea with a laugh. "Once when I was on the Green River in Utah, a couple of us rode the minor rapids standing on the cargo box in the middle."

"That's the kind of thing I try to get on film."

She looked at him in disbelief. "You actually sound serious."

Calmly, not one bit embarrassed or annoyed, he grinned. "I am."

Kelsey tried to equate the different images Mike Kincaid projected. In a business suit he could probably sell ice to the Eskimos. In biking shorts he looked as if he'd worn them every day of his life. He had the build and coordination of an athlete and the presence of a lion tamer. And here he was saying he didn't want to challenge a little white water.

"Is it because you sell insurance? You spend all your time assessing other people's risk so you don't want to take any yourself?"

"Maybe it's the other way around," he suggested. "Maybe I sell insurance because I'm fascinated with risk."

"That doesn't tell me why you'd rather not go with us."

Having missed the exchange, Rob came between them, holding an open tri-fold. "This canoe place looks the best, Kel. I can taste the rapids already."

Kelsey lifted the brochure out of her brother's hands. "It wouldn't be the same as kayaking." She handed him one for a rafting company. "Mike votes for the more comfortable ride, and since it'll be our last day together, I feel generous."

Mike took the raft brochure out of Rob's hands and replaced it with the canoe one. "Do whatever you want. I have other plans."

"Like what?" Kelsey demanded.

"Like washing my hair."

She couldn't help it. She burst out laughing.

"Sounds like a good idea," Rob said with a touch of asperity. "Take a little time off from all the excitement."

Kelsey swung toward her brother in dismay. His inflection indicated he'd be glad if Mike didn't come with them, but although she'd felt hostility rise a couple of times during the week when he thought Mike was getting too close, he'd kept it to himself. "Rob—"

Rob held up his hand in a gesture of acquiescence. "Hey, I'm easy. Mike knows I didn't mean anything, don't you, Mike?"

Mike met Rob's eyes steadily. "Sure. And I wouldn't miss the excitement for anything."

"Then canoeing it is," Rob said.

Mike's lips compressed briefly before he smiled. "Sounds like a terrific day." And if his tone didn't match his words, who was Kelsey to point it out?

MIKE DIDN'T KNOW why he'd risen to Rob's challenge. He'd stopped taking dares when he was a kid. It hadn't been easy, back then, to ignore the taunting of the macho types his neighborhood produced, the guys who constantly had to prove they were tough by pounding on others. He knew photographing them in their exploits had been a form of self-defense. It appealed to their vanity even while they scoffed at him. By the time he left home, he'd vowed never, never to let a bully push him around again. He learned the best way out was to ignore them. He learned that art and intelligence beat brute strength any day.

So why had he felt compelled to prove something to Rob? Now he was committed to spending the day rocketing down the river in a canoe. Already his palms were clammy enough to slip on the paddle.

It wasn't that he was a coward. It wasn't that he thought he'd get hurt. He wasn't even afraid he'd make a fool of himself by throwing up over the side.

He just didn't get a kick out of defying nature. Which was why he usually melted quietly into the background with his camera.

Now, not for the first time in his life, Mike tried to identify if there were some logical progression from excitement to discomfort to fear.

People had phobias, and they weren't all caused by bad experiences. He'd read recently that fear of spiders might be caused by a chemical imbalance. At the other end of the spectrum were the people who courted danger. Some researchers speculated there were physiological reasons why. From a strictly personal point of view, Mike didn't care about the mechanics. For as long as he could remember, he'd belonged to one group, and people like Kelsey Sumner belonged to the other.

In spite of his father's prodding, he'd never envied the thrill seekers or dreamed of being like them. He watched them, though, with the fascination of a scientist studying a bug under a microscope.

After forty minutes on the river, he stopped thinking about motivations. Ahead he saw another patch of white water. The runs so far had been easy, but that didn't lull him into a false sense of security. He dug his paddle into the water. Behind him he heard Kelsey's shout when they hit the first dip.

Through a piece of adroit maneuvering, he'd managed to get the front seat of her canoe, leaving Rob to go with an extra man from another party. Rob hadn't liked the arrangement, but Mike could live with that. Instinctively he knew that if he'd drawn Rob as a partner, Kelsey's brother would have picked the wildest route through any rapid with relish, and not just for the thrill of the ride.

So Kelsey sat behind him. He tried to translate his own perceptions into the excitement he heard in her voice.

Dip, lurch, tilt, roll. For a brief second he closed his eyes and tuned into the sensations. He felt the shifts in temperature when they passed from sun to shade and back again. He smelled the water and the darker scent of leaves decaying on wet earth. Barely, above the rush of water, he heard the cry of a bird.

A surge of current sped the canoe, and a quick thrust of exhilaration burst within him. More than all the photographs he'd taken, this was a fleeting glimpse inside. He could almost imagine its becoming addictive. But running mild rapids was hardly like scaling walls of ice or jumping out of airplanes.

The worst white water was toward the end of the run. Mike noticed that Rob and his partner took any route promising the most action. With a quick glance over his shoulder at Kelsey, he tipped his head in the direction he preferred to go and she nodded back. As easily as if she controlled a real rudder, the canoe responded to her paddle, edging toward the right.

Seconds later, without warning, an enormous boulder seemed to rise out of the water directly in their path.

Mike switched his paddle to the right side of the boat. If he couldn't help turn, he might be able to push them away by brute force. He fought the current for all he was worth, and finally the canoe seemed to slide sideways. The bow lifted, listing slightly, and missed the rock by inches. With a jolt it slammed back against the water.

The momentum carried it too far. Like a log rolling on the tide, the little craft turned over.

"Kelsey!" He could hardly hear his own voice over the roar of the river.

The water was icy cold. Sputtering to the surface, Mike remembered the instructions of the guide and twisted so that he floated on his back with the current, feet first.

Where was she? He twisted in the water to see. The green canoe, still bottom up, shot past him, and he ducked out of its way.

Then he spotted her. She floated about a yard behind and an arm's length away. Relief surged through him. "Kelsey!"

Shaking her hair out of her eyes, she turned, grinning. "Hey, Mike!" The roar of the water mixed with her words.

"You okay?"

"Sure." She reached out her hand. It was solid and real.

His heart raced painfully, his breathing rasped his lungs and her eyes glinted with pleasure. He tightened his hold. *If he'd lost her. . .*

Together they rode the rest of the rapid on the buoyancy of their life jackets, then they headed for the bank.

Keeping a firm grip on Kelsey's hand, Mike pulled her into the shallows. Nothing had happened, thank God. No one was hurt.

Still knee-deep in water, with the fringe of the current pulling at their legs, she turned to him.

"What a ride! I'll bet you didn't expect that, did you?"

Her hair was plastered to her head. Even after she wiped at her face with her arm, droplets of water clung to her eyelashes. He recognized the light in her eyes. The glittering, joyful animation. He'd been drawn to it frequently since adding those pictures of her to the gallery on his office wall. Experiencing it was erotic.

"Hardly," he said dryly. "As a matter of fact, I thought I'd be safer with you than with Rob."

She laughed. "We'll never live it down. Rob loves it when I make a fool of myself."

"You can blame it on me."

Lifting an eyebrow, she acquired a pixie look. "You wouldn't mind if I called you a clumsy, incompetent idiot?"

"I think I had something milder in mind."

With a shiver she unstrapped her life vest. Her one-piece maillot clung to her curves, defining nipples taut with cold. She wore shorts over her suit. Weighted with water, they hugged her hips and thighs. He'd never seen so much of her body. Long and lean, firm and gentle.

The river still swirled around their legs, though he no longer felt the chill. Drawn like iron to a magnet, his fingers touched her cheek, and her lively eyes met his.

Whether he liked it or not, ten seconds of fear had done something a week on the road had not. His feelings toward this woman had coalesced. His interest was no longer academic; it wasn't professional. It was totally, deeply personal. He wasn't ready to explore what that meant in the long term. But for now, for right this minute, he wanted to touch, then taste.

"Do you have any idea how beautiful you are?"

If the experience had had the same effect on her, she didn't show it. For a moment their eyes locked, then she turned toward the bank, pulling him along behind her.

"I think we'd better make our way downstream. The current might be too strong for anyone to paddle back to get us."

Tall pines grew almost to the bank; the bushes and willows growing beneath the trees and along the river made the prospect of blazing their way unappealing. They sloshed onto dry ground, and water squished through the fabric of their canvas shoes. Mike turned Kelsey toward him and slid his hands slowly up her arms. For the first time since leaving Portland, he had her all to himself.

"Let's wait to get rescued," he said.

She laughed, refusing his unspoken invitation. "I hope someone caught the canoe."

Chapter Five

They sat on the bank, their wet clothes turning the dirt beneath them to mud, their life vests tossed casually aside. For fifteen minutes they'd battled the growth along the riverbank, sometimes wading to skirt brush they couldn't push through. Then they'd reached a bend so sharp the current swirled against the bank, cutting deeply into the earth. Left with two choices, swimming or waiting, they waited.

"Our guide's probably beside himself struggling to recover us," Kelsey told Mike. In the space of a simple trip down the river, something had changed. Suddenly Mike's presence enveloped her. She knew his thoughts, felt his magnetic pull. She decided her only defense was to pretend it didn't exist. "It's not good business to lose clients in the river." Her shoes were filthy from trudging through the soft mountain dirt, and she kicked her feet in the water to wash off the mud.

"Rob, too."

She turned. Mike leaned back on his elbows, twisting a strand of tall grass through his fingers, watching her. Though not quite smiling, his expression made her breath catch. There was something in his eyes, something pulling at the corners of his mouth that deprived her of rational thought.

In one smooth, unbroken movement, he levered himself upright, then bent forward. She knew he was going to touch her, possibly kiss her. Her tongue brushed across her lower lip as she waited. It would be good. It would be right. Reason and rationalization had no place at a time like this.

Then he pointed to a spot past her shoulder. "What kind of birds are those?"

Relieved, disappointed, she swiveled around to see. Her heart was beating too fast, she could hardly breathe around the lump in her throat, and she had to blink several times to make her eyes focus. With the discipline of years of pain therapy, she forced her body to relax. Okay, so maybe she was reading things into this situation that didn't exist.

Across the river a flock of perhaps a dozen birds rose into the air in a tight formation, then settled together in a tree about ten feet from where she sat. They were small and brown, and even from this distance she could see the black throat and eyebrow streak and the reddish orange tips on the inner wing.

"Cedar waxwings," she said.

"Tell me about them."

Why? Why did Mike Kincaid send her heart into a tailspin just by looking at her with some subtle light of enjoyment in his eyes, and then want to talk about birds?

Hoping her voice wouldn't hint at that temporary moment of insanity, she pointed at the flock and told him what she knew of their eating and nesting habits. She was just warming up to their migration patterns when she realized Mike was only partly listening to her.

She shrugged. She'd always accepted that generally birdwatching didn't appeal to adventurers. Of course, she didn't know Mike well enough to make many assumptions about him.

With a self-conscious little laugh, she stopped midsentence. "Well, you asked."

"I did," Mike agreed. "And I apologize. Mostly I wanted to understand you better."

"There's not much to understand."

"Can I ask you a different kind of question?"

"Sure."

"Tipping over just added spice to the day for you, didn't it?"

Like an instant replay, she remembered the sudden rush of excitement at encountering the unexpected. Not only had it been fun, but it had given her back some of her lost confidence. "Actually, yes."

"You weren't scared?"

"There wasn't any danger."

"Of course there was," he said flatly with no argumentative undertones. "You could have hit that rock, or the boat could have hit you. The current could have dragged you into debris below the surface."

"None of those things happened."

"But they *could* have."

Kelsey swung her feet onto the bank, turning to face him, and wrapped her arms around her knees. "I've never let remote possibilities interfere with my life. Why should I start now?"

He didn't answer right away. Thoughtfully, as though considering one of the great questions of the universe, his eyes searched hers. In the space of seconds, half a dozen subtle changes worked through his expression.

"Did tipping frighten you?" she asked.

"It happened too fast."

"But you didn't like it. Did you enjoy any of the run?"

"It had its moments. It wasn't something I'd go out of my way to do for fun."

The more time she spent with Mike, the more complicated he became. She'd never doubt again that he *did* prefer keeping both feet safely on the ground. It was an attitude she still couldn't identify with, even after her own experiences. "I suppose fun for you is spending hours in a darkroom inhaling unpleasant fumes."

A smile, slow and sensual, pulled at the corners of his mouth. "Fun is *taking* the pictures. It's what I do best."

"Aren't you glad that in this case you didn't bring your camera?" They'd left their valuables in the outfitter's office.

Mike chuckled softly. "A fortunate decision." Then he sobered, and the questioning look returned. "Didn't you come out of your accident with any residual fears?"

How had they gotten from bird-watching to here? It was much easier to explain how cedar waxwings built their nests by interlocking twigs rather than weaving them.

Propping her chin on her knees, Kelsey tried to pick her way through the different angles his question presented. Every psychologist who had counseled her during her recovery had cautioned that she would. Except how could she know unless she faced them? "Probably. I often wonder if I'll ever fly again."

"But you didn't hesitate today."

"Well, yes, I did, but not for long. Of course, it's not exactly the same."

"Speed is speed," he persisted. "It seems to me that it's the unmanageable aspects of a situation that might frighten you. The unexpected. The chance of losing control again."

"Like tipping a canoe. Is that what makes you nervous?"

He grinned. "I'm the one asking questions."

With a light shrug she smiled. "Growing up, I was never afraid. Not in any physical sense. And in a physical sense, I can't let my accident traumatize me."

"Nobody is that cool." He spoke without censure, but she heard both amazement and disbelief in his voice.

"If by that you mean self-confident, then no, I have quite a few leftover hang-ups. But I can't afford to worry about crashing again. I refuse to let fear rob me of the good things life still has to offer. If anything, I feel that now I want to make sure an adventure is worth my time and energy, because I know how quickly it could be my last. But I admit that the bike trip, and maybe even coming on the river, are ways of testing the limits, to see what I *am* afraid of now."

"Then there *are* things."

"Sure," she said lightly. "Like how angry Rob will be, just because he'll have been worrying all this time."

Mike sat up, and his chest was within inches of her knees. Suddenly electricity filled the air between them. To Kelsey, it seemed he saw beneath the surface, yet she wasn't giving anything away. He didn't touch her; he didn't need to. Just with the sweep of his eyes, he sent weakness plunging through her body.

"Like you and me," Mike said.

"I'm not afraid of you."

"That's not what I mean, and you know it."

"I know you're leaving tomorrow, and we're going on."

"You'll be back."

"Three months is a long time."

"I'm a patient man."

Drawing a deep breath, she looked away. In the ribbon of sky open between the aisle of trees, a formation of cumulus clouds drifted on the wind. On a day like this, nature was peace. She wanted to tap into it, draw from it, use its ancient wisdom to guide her.

"I learned a lesson once. It was a good lesson, and I learned it the hard way. Shared experiences foster a kind of attraction. You do things with someone, you share good times with him, you think it will last forever. Then the good times end, real life intervenes, and the attraction isn't so strong anymore. Pretty soon it will probably disappear altogether, and if you're not prepared for that, you get hurt.''

Mike took her hand, and she dropped her eyes to see him twine his fingers between hers. ''You think I wouldn't want to make love to you if we weren't here, making this trip together.''

She swallowed, hard. ''That's what I think.''

Reaching out, he framed her face. Pulling her closer, he kissed her.

Not at all like their first kiss, that morning in the gorge—this one seared deep. It severed her defenses like a hot knife cutting through butter. Wrapping her arms around his neck, she shifted her knees out of the way to press against his chest. Passion flamed through her, igniting every nerve ending. Need robbed her mind of caution.

His hands slid down her sides, then up her back. She felt them on her bare flesh and hungered for more.

When his hands moved to her shoulders, she sensed the tension change. Slowly, raggedly, he broke away. The heat continued to pump through her veins.

''Company's coming,'' he said.

She dropped her forehead against his chest. This time his arms circled her gently as they each waited for their breathing to quiet.

About the time she could think again, she heard voices from the river. Rob's voice, calling her.

When she met Mike's eyes, his were dark, smoky. Still rich with emotion.

''I didn't expect that to happen,'' she said, half in amazement, half by way of apology.

''Didn't you? How could it have been any different?''

''*Kelsey!*''

Mike's arms slipped away, and she turned back toward the river. There were two canoes hugging the far shore, the side with the least current. Standing, she waved both arms over her head.

"You okay?"

"Fine." If he didn't hear, he'd at least be able to see for himself. And on the outside, she was as fine as ever. Inside, she didn't think she'd ever be the same again.

Gesturing, Rob indicated they'd have to go up farther, then cross back to get her and Mike.

"We should backtrack to a place where they can pull ashore," Mike suggested, offering his hand.

She hesitated, but only for a second. Scooping up both life vests by their straps, she put her hand in his.

AFTER DINNER that night they went to a movie. Briefly Kelsey considered making sure Rob sat between her and Mike. Instead she made sure he didn't.

For a whole week she'd been living in a state of ambivalence where Mike was concerned. Today had ended that.

But returning to town, registering in a campground, eating—the day-to-day stuff—put things in a different perspective. She doubted that passion would hold steady in the end, and she wasn't sure the friendship of a week was enough on which to hang any hopes.

Mike was leaving tomorrow, and it would be three months before she saw him again. One fourth of a year. In that much time anything could happen. So tonight she'd sit shoulder-to-shoulder with him for a couple of hours and absorb the sensations. When he reached for her hand, she reveled in the caress of his thumb across her knuckles.

After the show Kelsey felt both edgy and pleasantly tired. Walking back to their tents, Mike kept her hand firmly in his.

The wind blew briskly down from the mountains, chilling the air. Mid-May at this latitude meant spring was still going strong. Behind their tents a hedge of lilacs bloomed profusely, filling the whole area with their fragrance. It would be like sleeping in a floral shop, except this was the concentrated scent of only one flower.

Suddenly Rob stopped her with a hand on her shoulder. "Hold it, Kel. There's somebody in that car."

It was parked as close to their tents as a car could get. Inside, she made out the silhouette of a man sitting in the driver's seat.

Mike moved in close to her other side.

When the door opened abruptly, she jumped.

The man climbed out and came hesitantly toward them. "Are you Kelsey Sumner?" he asked, squinting toward them in the dark.

Mike's arm circled her waist protectively.

"Yes." There was no point in denying it.

Closing the remaining distance between them, the man held out his hand aggressively. "I'm Vince Lassiter, deejay on KYAK radio here in Lewiston. Pleased to meet you."

With Rob's body half in front of hers and Mike holding her close, she couldn't easily shake hands with him. She wasn't sure she wanted to. It was well after eleven o'clock, and the rest of the campground was asleep.

"What can I do for you?"

From the inside pocket of his flight jacket, he pulled out a handful of papers that rustled loudly in the night. "I knew you were coming here. I've been reading about you in the paper and figured you'd get to town about now."

She turned questioningly to Mike. It was too dark to see his face, but he lifted his shoulder in answer. Without him and Rob she would have been very nervous.

"So?"

"You're a mighty brave little lady. I'd like you to come on my show and tell folks about this trip you're making."

Kelsey laughed. So the romantic, exaggerated picture Mike had painted of her had caught someone's attention.

"What a kick," Rob said. "Radio. Maybe next week it'll be television, and after that the movies. You're going to be a star, Kel."

"Well, I just thought it would be interesting," Lassiter hedged.

"It'd be terrific," Rob agreed. "You can tell everyone how thrilling it is to ride through fifty endless miles of farm country. What it feels like to run out of water before you get to a place where you can fill up again. The great variety of our diet."

That drew a chuckle from Mike. "Side winds."

"Flat tires."

Kelsey laughed. "Is that what you had in mind, Mr. Lassiter?"

"I want to," Rob volunteered.

Lassiter picked up on it quickly. "Who are you? Her brother or the writer?"

"Her brother."

"How about the both of you? I promise my audience will love it. We have a lot of outdoors people in this area, and they really get off on great adventure stories like yours."

Great adventure stories. Kelsey groaned. If the truth were known, bicycling in and of itself was sixty percent boring. "I'm sure there are people in this town who have ridden bikes across the United States," she said. "Why don't you get one of them?"

"Wouldn't be the same," he persisted. "I'm not saying it wouldn't be good. Most of my guests are local. But you're en route, and that makes a difference."

"Come on, Kel," Rob begged. "This is my big chance. He wouldn't want me by myself."

"You're crazy."

"You'd love it, too."

Perhaps she would. New experiences were a part of what this trip was all about. "Okay, when?"

"I have a morning show. How about ten-thirty tomorrow?"

In the dark she exchanged glances with Rob. Grinning, she nodded. "Sure."

"Fine, fine. We'll really pump it up during the morning." This time she shook his hand when he stuck it out. "You'll be great. I'm excited. Come at least fifteen minutes early, okay?"

"Sure, Mr. Lassiter. See you then."

"Call me Vince. We're real informal. Thanks a lot."

"Good night, Vince."

As soon as he shut himself in his car, Kelsey burst out laughing. "I can't believe him. I can't believe I'm going to do this. Rob, I swear, you're out of your mind."

As naturally as if they'd always done it that way, Mike walked with Kelsey to her tent. In the dark Rob didn't seem to notice. He just made one joke about being on radio after another. Kelsey didn't hear them. She was aware only of Mike's arm around her waist, the feel of his chest against her shoulder, the smell of sunshine in his shirt. With Rob still rambling on, Mike turned her within his arms and kissed her.

His lips touched hers lightly, then he lifted his head. "I'll stay while you do this radio thing."

"Of course." To Kelsey, it went without saying. His articles were the reason they'd asked her at all.

Giving her a light hug, he released her and went on to his own tent.

Turning, she found Rob watching her. It was too dark to tell what he was thinking.

"I'm going to the john," he said.

She felt suddenly insecure and lonely. Today, for the first time since they'd begun, she suspected Rob had something to be concerned about. He'd picked up the pieces, after all, when Alan deserted her.

When Rob came back, Kelsey had her sleeping bag zipped up around her shoulders. Hunched over in the low tent, he stripped off his shirt and shorts. Waiting, she listened to him go through the movements of settling in.

"Are you falling in love with him?" Rob asked at last.

"No."

"He turns you on?"

How like Rob. "Sometimes. But he's leaving tomorrow. How he makes me feel doesn't make any difference."

"He's hot for you. I could tell it the first day."

"His tough luck." The words came easily in the dark, since soon she wouldn't have to pretend.

Rob laughed. Through both sleeping bags he nudged her with his elbow. "You sore about the radio deal?"

"Of course not. I'll probably be scared speechless when we finally get there, but what's the worst that could possibly happen? My mind will go blank, and you'll be left to carry on without me."

"This trip's been good for you already. You laugh again."

"I'm beginning to believe in myself again. For so long it was just wistful thinking, then it was hoping I actually could do something like this. Then it was praying I wasn't biting off more than I could chew. Maybe the mountains will still beat me, but it won't be without a fight."

"You'll be ready for them, Kel. No doubt about it."

"As long as you're on my side. Good night, Rob."

"WELL, ANYWAY, IT'S all those crazies out there that would worry me," the voice in her earphones was saying. "If you were my daughter, I wouldn't let you go, and that's all there is to it."

Kelsey rolled her eyes and looked at Rob. Just barely, he was managing not to laugh out loud. "That's why I'm not making this trip by myself." Kelsey spoke pleasantly into the microphone in front of her. "But there's a little risk inherent in everything we do. You know your bathtub is slippery when wet, but you still take showers. For me, making this trip was so important the risks didn't seem worth worrying about.''

Vince Lassiter winked at Kelsey and took over. "Okay, we have to break here. But you all just keep your dials tuned to KYAK 570, and we'll be back in two minutes with Kelsey and Rob Sumner."

In Kelsey's opinion two minutes was hardly long enough to catch her breath, but it was better than nothing. When Vince again opened the air to callers, she smiled to convince herself it was going well. So far she hadn't had one blank moment.

"Hi. I'm Travis," the next voice said. "I'm fourteen, and I'd like to try hang gliding but my mother won't let me. She says it's too dangerous. What do you think?"

Kelsey searched for the right words. "She's right, Travis. It's very dangerous. That's one of the reasons people like it so much. It's fun to flirt with death and win. Except it's a little like playing Russian roulette, and sometimes you lose."

"Like you."

"Actually I won. I'm still alive."

"Do you want to hang glide ever again?"

"Maybe someday. For a while I think I'll stick to ground-based adventures like bicycling."

"What did it feel like when you knew you were going to crash?"

Rob's hand covered hers, and she returned the pressure. Perhaps her answers to Travis's questions could help him and his mother work out their disagreement.

"It happened too fast for me to really know it was happening. Some friends and I had been flying off the cliffs over the ocean, and I was coming back to land. I was only about ten or twelve feet off the ground when the wind suddenly changed. It was a lot like crashing into a wall, then I fell. I don't remember anything after that. They told me I hit some rocks.''

"Did you take a lot of lessons to learn how to fly?''

"Yes, I did. And I had a good teacher. But sometimes accidents happen that we can't avoid. Travis, I can tell you really want to try it, but I can tell your mother loves you very much, too. Maybe it would be a good idea for you both to talk to a certified instructor before you make any decisions.''

"Thanks, Kelsey. Good luck on your trip.''

"Thank you, Travis. And good luck to you, too.''

Vince Lassiter nodded his approval and punched another button on his phone. "Hello, caller, you're on the air.''

This time it was a man whose voice placed him in the thirty-to-forty age range. "I'd like to ask Kelsey what kind of training it took to get ready for this trip. I was in a car wreck a couple of years ago, and broke my leg pretty bad. I used to backpack a lot before that, and now I get too tired.''

"That's a good question. Kelsey—'' Vince nodded her way again.

Kelsey drew a deep breath. This was the fifth caller who had referred directly to her accident. "I started on a physical therapy program right after my first surgery, with sessions several times a day. After I got out of the hospital, I still went for therapy every day, then three times a week, and finally only once a month. The last surgery didn't require so much follow-up, but my brother learned how to help me with the exercises, and we still do them often. Tell them what your goals are and see if they can set up a program for you.''

"Does it still hurt?'' the man asked.

Rob held up his thumb in a sign of encouragement. "My leg?'' Kelsey asked. "Sometimes.''

"Thank you, caller.'' Vince touched a button on the console, and in her earphones Kelsey heard a man's voice talking twice normal speed about new cars. She pushed the earphones back to hang around her neck.

"It's going great, Kelsey," Vince said. "You've got them hanging on every word. You too, Rob. Keep it up."

He stuck a cassette tape in a carrier and pushed another button. Outside the window of the sound booth, a woman taped a note to the glass. This one said, "Wall Street Report." To Kelsey the best part of being on the radio had been watching the inner workings. She'd only counted four people at the station, and they seemed to do it all.

Vince changed tapes in the carriers with quick efficiency. "We just have to make sure we don't use the same voice back-to-back," he said. "Okay, five seconds to air."

Kelsey put her headphones back on.

"Good morning, caller, do you have a question for our guests?"

"My name's Gloria, and I have a comment and a question for Kelsey. I've been reading the articles in the paper about you. I'd just like to say that I'm so in awe of you. The way you've conquered your difficulties and set new goals. So many of us just accept our lives like we can't do anything to change them. You have, and I think that's just so inspiring."

"Yes, Gloria," Vince cut in. "And you have a question?"

"Well, yes, I do. I wondered if you had insurance. Seven months is a long time to be in the hospital, to say nothing of all those operations. So many people these days can't afford adequate health care, and our legislators aren't doing anything about it, and it causes such a hardship. I mean, did you have to have help with your medical bills?"

Kelsey didn't consider this to be anyone's business but her family's. "Insurance covered most of it."

"Thank you, Gloria. Hello, caller, you're on the air."

Kelsey appreciated Vince's quick handling of a difficult moment.

The next few calls were easy: How many miles did they average in a day? Wasn't it going to be cold in the mountains? How did they carry enough stuff for all weather conditions? Rob answered a lot of them, and one girl wanted to know if it had been hard for him to give up his social life for a whole summer.

Toward the end of the program, the station secretary taped another note to the window. Vince cut to a commercial, smiled an apology to Kelsey and stepped to the door. After a quick whispered exchange, he returned to his chair, an expression of smug achievement on his face.

When he went back on the air, he smiled broadly at Kelsey. "Well, all you listeners, I have an exciting presentation to make. An anonymous cashier's check was just delivered to us here at KYAK made out to Kelsey Sumner. Kelsey, I'm sure I can say this for all the fine folks of Lewiston—we wish you the very best on this trip of yours, and someone in our listening audience wants to make sure you succeed. Here it is, a check for *five hundred dollars!*"

Chapter Six

Shocked into speechlessness, Kelsey took the check Vince thrust into her hands. Five hundred dollars. Just because she'd been on the radio? She didn't need the money. She didn't want it. And she certainly didn't know how she could accept it.

Except there was no way to return it. Glancing at Rob, she saw he was taken aback just as much as she was.

Vince was watching her expectantly. Silence hung over the tiny sound studio and throbbed through the air. Clearing her throat, Kelsey took a deep breath and spoke clearly into the microphone.

"I'd like to thank the generous person who made this donation."

Already the lights on Vince's console were beginning to light up. When he punched one to take the next call, she heaved a sigh of relief.

Five hundred dollars. What on earth was she going to do with it? Awash with embarrassment, she hardly heard the woman on the other end of the line until Rob stiffened beside her.

"...people like you who play on the sympathies of others just to swindle them out of their hard-earned money. If it's publicity you want, why don't you stand naked—"

Vince pressed a button, cutting the vitriol off in mid-sentence. "It takes all kinds to make a world, I guess."

Kelsey's stomach tightened into a knot, and her throat closed, making breathing difficult. What had she said to convey the impression she was a con artist? The check felt like poison rotting in her hand. Lights continued to flash on Vince's console. She knew she had to do something. She had to think.

Leaning forward to the microphone, she cleared her throat. "Vince, I'd like to say something about this donation. Although I don't need the money, I appreciate the concern that must have prompted it.

"The one important aspect of my story that I'd like to stress again is that I recovered, even though at first we didn't know if I would ever walk again. Well, there are thousands of people who are in similar situations. Many of them are children, and many of them will be able to walk only if caring people like you share your love with them. At the risk of misunderstanding the intent of this gift, I'd like to pass it on to the nearest children's hospital and designate that it be used specifically for those who are physically disabled. Let's give them some hope. I'm sure KYAK will be happy to help me do that."

By the time she finished, Kelsey's heart thudded so loudly she thought everyone listening in could hear it. Rob pulled her into his arms and hugged her enthusiastically, and outside the soundproof window, Mike stood with the people of the station clapping his hands.

"Ladies and gentlemen, that was Kelsey Sumner. Can you believe that compassion? We have to take a break and then we'll be right back."

Stunned by the turn of events, Kelsey could only stare at Mike. Strangely she understood the caller who'd attacked her more than the listener who'd sent the money. The last thing she wanted was to come across as needy or manipulative, but a donation that large made her seem as if she were both.

And it was all because of Mike. If he hadn't convinced her to let him come, no one would even know she existed, let alone be giving her money she didn't need. A cold ache closed around her heart. Was this what he'd wanted all along? To create something newsworthy out of nothing, with his byline on it? This morning she'd seen the copyrighted articles bearing Mike's name that had been picked up by the news service so that Vince Lassiter could find her.

What did she really know about Mike Kincaid? Both his art and his work indicated success. Was he driven to it? Did accomplishment come before human values?

She took off her headset and laid it on the table. "I think I'm finished, Vince."

"You can't go yet. The phones are ringing off the hook."

"I can't possibly talk to them all."

"Then just make a general comment over the air. We're almost out of time anyway."

Walking out would be too precipitate, even though she wanted nothing more than to wash her hands of this entire episode. She looked at Rob, who shook his head uncertainly.

"I wish you could see my phone right now," Vince was saying over the air. "Every light is blinking. Unfortunately we don't have time to talk to all of you personally, but Kelsey Sumner will make one final statement before we have to go."

At his nod, Kelsey cleared her throat. "I can only say that I'll remember Lewiston for the friendly, generous people we met here, because I know most of you are. Thank you."

Vince finished the program, but it was all a blur to Kelsey.

As they left the sound booth, Rob put his arm around her shoulder. "You handled it just right, Kel. Sending that money on was the perfect thing to do. You just can't let that woman get to you."

She turned and searched his eyes. "What did I say that would make someone want to give me money in the first place? Why are people interested in me at all? I don't understand any of this."

Rob hugged her close. "I know you don't. Maybe that's why they care."

"Some care. Some attack. Let's finish up here, then go pack."

"Sure thing, sweetie. The open road is calling again."

She chuckled dryly. "More invitingly than ever."

When she turned toward the outer door, she found Mike blocking her way. "You're one hell of a woman, Kelsey," he said.

At that moment she hated him. From the very beginning he'd manipulated her, pulling on her emotions, steering her the way he wanted her to go. "It looks like you got the publicity you were after." She pushed past him and marched out into the brilliant May sun.

Mike caught her arm and pulled her around to face him. "Publicity has nothing to do with it."

"Doesn't it?"

Mike stood his ground. "Nobody could have foreseen a call from a lunatic."

She faced him squarely. "You don't understand, do you? For all we know, that woman may be living on the edge of poverty and five hundred dollars to her might sound like a fortune. What she thinks doesn't bother me."

"Then what does? The donation?"

"Of *course* the donation."

The puzzlement in his expression lasted only a moment before it was replaced by one of warm comprehension.

"You are one hell of a woman," he said again. Softer this time.

"Heaven help me. Not you, too." Pivoting away, she turned toward her bike. Why couldn't people just accept who she *was?*

Again, Mike blocked her way.

"Kelsey, what did this hurt? Someone who doesn't know or understand you sent you money. It made them feel good. You gave it to a good cause. That made more people feel good. Five hundred dollars might help some kid walk, and then he'll feel good."

"It doesn't make me feel good. It makes me feel like a fraud. I don't need anyone's money. I don't want sympathy or pity or concern, especially from strangers. And I don't want to be someone's good cause."

"Then I apologize. I never expected those articles to get picked up by a service. I expected them only to be of local interest."

"Well, you were wrong."

"Are you going to hold it against me forever?"

As her own pain faded, she caught a glimpse of vulnerability in Mike's eyes. She'd considered him too strong to have doubts.

"What difference does it make? You're going back and we're going on."

His hand slid up her arm to her throat. His fingers began to lightly caress her chin and cheek. "You know what difference it makes." Almost perceptibly the color of his eyes darkened to a smoky gray, and the way he looked at her made her lungs tighten painfully in her chest. "I may be leaving you, but I won't be gone."

Right there, practically in the doorway of the radio station, Mike pulled her into his arms and captured her mouth. Still angry and confused, she tried to push him away. Instead he deepened the kiss with such possession she thought she would drown in the sensations.

When he released her, she stood weakly, looking up at him.

"Mike, I—"

He silenced her with a finger to her mouth and grinned. A heart-stopping grin that seemed more potent than his kiss. "I'm not leaving quite yet, Kelsey. I think you have one or two more hurdles to cross, and I don't intend to desert you."

She turned to see a car pulling to a stop only a few feet from where they stood.

A woman about Kelsey's age, dressed in jeans and a corduroy blazer, hurried over to them.

"Are you Kelsey Sumner? Thank goodness I caught you. I'm afraid I wasn't listening to KYAK while you were on, but a couple of guys at the paper were. And the phones have been ringing, let me tell you."

Mike's hand settled on her shoulder, and Rob closed in by her other side. When they'd assumed those same positions at the campground the night before, she'd hardly noticed. Now she realized how protective it must look, and how fragile it must make her seem.

Pretending a confidence she didn't feel, she stepped forward and extended her hand. "I'm Kelsey, and you're..."

"Brenda Croxton, with the *Lewiston Sentinel*. We're only a weekly paper, but we try to pick up on all the local news." She pulled a tape recorder like Mike's out of an oversize shoulder bag. "I understand you just turned a five-hundred-dollar donation over to handicapped children?"

"That's the plan." How had everything snowballed so quickly out of proportion? Kelsey's emotions were in such a tangled mess she couldn't think.

"Do you have any idea who donated the money in the first place?"

Maybe she needed the support after all. Kelsey shot a quick glance at Rob. "No. It was an unsigned cashier's check."

"Why did you donate it to physically disabled children?"

Kelsey repeated what she'd said on the radio, then answered a couple of questions about the trip so far.

When Brenda finally left, Kelsey wondered if that would be the end of it. Her personal challenge had taken on new dimensions.

"This whole thing seems ridiculous," she said. "I'm anxious to get back to just riding along and minding my own business."

"Let's do it," Rob agreed quickly, looking over her shoulder at Mike.

He'd seen the kiss; heaven knew what he suspected. Kelsey could feel tension radiating from him, but she was too immersed in her own problems to care. After Mike left, it would be academic anyway.

But at the campground Kelsey knew that things would never get back to normal. As she rolled her sleeping bag, her eyes kept straying to Mike. She wasn't sure how she felt about him, but she knew it would seem strange going on without him, his ever-present camera and his questions that seemed more like conversation. She wondered how often she would catch herself remembering the intimacy in his smile, the gentleness of his touch and the urgency of his kisses.

Determinedly she forced herself to concentrate on her own packing. In a day or two she would have forgotten all about him.

Surely that was true. Surely she wasn't standing there missing him while he was still only a few feet away.

It took just a few minutes to finish loading up, and when they walked their bikes to the pavement, Kelsey suggested she and Rob ride to the local airport with Mike. She told herself it was the polite thing to do and had nothing to do with the emotional withdrawal she felt barreling down on her. He'd be catching a commuter flight first to Spokane, then home.

Meeting her eyes, he smiled and shook his head. "The plane isn't leaving until six tonight. You don't want to hang around until then, so we may as well say goodbye now."

Goodbye.

The word hung in the air between them. Kelsey wondered if Rob could feel it, and what he would read into it.

"Write to me?" Mike asked.

"Sure. I have your address." Of course, vacation friendships rarely survived a week after parting. In spite of the feelings he stirred in her, she couldn't believe this one would be any different.

"I have your itinerary for the next couple of weeks." Then, although his bike was between them, he leaned across the bar and kissed her. "Until we meet again."

Like prophecy etched in stone, his words embedded themselves in her brain. Would they meet again? And if they did, would she be able to count on anything remaining the same?

It took Mike one solid twelve-hour day to catch up on all the work that had accumulated while he was gone. Phone calls, letters, adjustments and sales appointments. He rarely let his hobby interfere with his business to such an extent.

But, putting the last file on his secretary's desk, he knew the week with Kelsey had changed him. For long periods of time he'd forgotten his original purpose. Now it was time to get back to normal. Over the weekend he would reread his five-year plan and review his goals.

A part of him wished he could have gone on with her. Of course he wouldn't miss sleeping on the ground or spending so much time in the sun. Or Rob.

Walking back into his office, he moved automatically to the gallery on his wall. After getting to know Kelsey, the photos of her seemed two-dimensional, flat, uninteresting.

All his adult life he'd believed in out of sight, out of mind. One day away from Kelsey, and he knew that wouldn't work with her.

No woman had ever made him feel the things he felt now. Suddenly she was making him think of families and of permanence—things he'd decided long ago not to clutter his life with. Seventeen years of family life had been quite enough, thank you, and a couple of live-in relationships had only reinforced his determination. Trying to live with other personalities only pulled you in wrong directions.

He knew what he wanted to achieve with his life, and a wife wasn't part of it. Hell. Even if he wanted a wife, Kelsey would be the wrong sort of person. She'd keep his life in continual chaos. He should remember the fire and laughter in her eyes after they'd tipped into the river. She was probably half-crazy, surviving a fall like hers and learning nothing from it. Who needed a woman that delighted in such impossible situations?

But he couldn't forget the fear he'd felt before he'd seen her surface in the river. Already the separation from her seemed too much like losing her permanently.

That night his condominium seemed too sterile and quiet for comfort, so he went to the health club. Following his normal routine, he started with the stationary bike. To his surprise, he rode at a much higher level than he'd ever managed before, which was satisfying, and boring. No wind, no squinting against the sun, no straining at hills, no smells except sweat, no sounds except the clatter of machines and the blare of the radio.

He wondered what Kelsey was doing.

Did she miss him as much as he missed her?

BECAUSE OF KELSEY'S LEG, she and Rob had plotted their route down through Idaho and across the Snake River Plains rather than across the Bitterroot Mountains into Montana. If their circumstances had been normal, Kelsey would have voted to spend as much time in the mountains as possible. They would, after all, be in the Great Plains and Midwest for over a month after they crossed the Rockies. But she wanted to build up her strength before facing another major challenge.

Two days out of Lewiston they set up camp along the Little Salmon River. Kelsey started the fire while Rob put up the tent. When the sun was just beginning to dip behind the mountains, she went to the riverbank to watch the changing colors of the sky and the deepening shadows on the water. Making herself as comfortable as possible on the rough ground, she sifted her hand through the dirt, rolling the few remaining larger stones between her fingers. One at a time she began to pitch them into the water.

When Rob came to sit beside her, she welcomed him with a smile.

"You miss him, don't you?" he asked.

Kelsey heard the challenge in his voice and tossed another stone into the river. Between the current and the fading light, she could barely see where it hit. "Sure." But she said it lightly and indifferently. "Don't you?"

He made a derogatory sound. "No."

On the distant eastern peaks the last hint of sun disappeared. The clouds cooled from gold to gray. She wished her heated longings would fade the same way.

"It's better that he's gone," she said.

"Yes."

Throwing the rest of the rocks into the water together, she drew her knees to her chest and faced her brother. "This is what I wanted, to just come with you, without company, without publicity, and learn to know myself again."

With his forearms resting on his thighs, Rob looked deep into the shadows and shook his head. "I don't know, Kel. I think the publicity was probably good."

"You do?" The calm logic in his voice surprised her. He'd made no effort to conceal his animosity toward Mike. Why did he think the efforts of Mike's hand could be good?

"But it's so artificial. I'm not a celebrity."

Rob took her hand and held it loosely between his knees. "For four four years you've had to concentrate all your energy on yourself. Getting well, getting strong. Going back to work and planning this trip. It's all taken a lot of hard work. That donation made you think about someone else. Something else. I think the timing was right."

"But you didn't like Mike. Isn't that a contradiction?"

"I didn't like the way he moved in on you. You've been hurt enough without asking for more. That doesn't mean I object to the net effect."

The words were different, but in a way he was echoing the argument Mike had used to convince her to let him join her. To help others. To get out of herself. Until now she hadn't really looked closely at what it might actually mean. She recognized the wisdom in Rob's words, however, and some of her embarrassment and frustration about the money drained away. Except it was hard to see a new, less attractive side of herself. She hadn't realized before how wound up she'd been in the business of getting well.

"I've been awfully self-centered for a long time, haven't I?"

"Hey, Kel." He tightened his hold on her hand. "You had to be. And it's probably not over yet."

She leaned forward and kissed him on his cheek. This was yet another hill in the long climb toward recovery, and she appreciated his willingness to be blunt. "I owe you another one. At this rate I'll never be out of your debt."

With a self-conscious laugh, he stood and pulled her to her feet. "This trip makes us even, I promise. It's something we both wanted, and I can't think of anyone I'd rather do it with."

Kelsey knew as brothers went, he was one in a million. She wondered, walking back to their tent, how she could possibly miss Mike with Rob around.

But Rob wasn't Mike. Rob didn't make her heart leap when he smiled at her or heat her blood with his touch. On the other hand, Rob would never hurt her. She doubted any other result could come of falling in love with Mike.

TWENTY MILES OUT of Boise, with more than an hour of riding still ahead of them, a van with a television logo painted on the side waved them off the road.

The driver was a man in his mid-forties with tanned skin, carefully groomed hair and a health-club physique. Looking triumphant, he climbed out of the truck. A younger man chewing gum followed him.

"You're Kelsey Sumner, aren't you? And her brother Rob? I'm Gerald Ogilvie, KGEM news, and this is Dan-my-camera-man." He laughed briefly at the obviously old joke. One corner of Dan's mouth lifted in a wry smile. "We've been cruising this road for two days looking for you," Gerald continued. "How you doing?"

Kelsey exchanged glances with Rob, who shrugged his shoulders. First newspaper articles, then radio shows, now TV news. All because of Michael Kincaid.

"What can we do for you, Mr. Ogilvie?" Rob asked.

"Call me Gerald. We heard about that deal in Lewiston." He turned to Kelsey. "That was a mighty generous thing you did, giving the money to crippled children. Nine out of ten people would have kept it. Everybody at the station is still talking about it. Anyway, we called KYAK, and Vince Lassiter said you were heading this way, so we thought it would be great to talk to you on the air. If you wouldn't mind, we could get some footage of you riding along, then ask you a few questions about how your trip's been so far."

"If you've talked to Vince, you know the response wasn't all positive." No matter how philosophically Kelsey accepted the verbal attack, no matter how much she wanted to be the kind of person who automatically thought of others first, she didn't want a repeat performance. "Besides, you must have bicycle tourists through here all the time. We're no different than anyone else."

Like Vince, Gerald brushed off the argument. "Of course you are. Anyone who takes on a trip like this after what you've been through is special. Someone who gives away five hundred dollars is a saint."

"Look, Gerald, I'd really rather not."

"Hey, we know all about that bad call, but this is TV, not radio. It'll be taped instead of live. There's no chance something like that could happen here. This would only take a few minutes, fifteen at the most."

Rob lifted his shoulder and nodded slightly. Gerald's argument made sense. Kelsey decided this would probably be as good a place as any to start her new approach to life. And the sooner she gave him what he wanted, the sooner they could be on their way.

"Okay, a few minutes."

The minute he sensed her agreement, Dan hustled to the van. He came back loaded with a video recorder and all the accompanying equipment.

At first the questions Gerald asked were the same ones she'd gotten in Lewiston, the same ones Mike had asked. She repeated her answers, refusing the dwell on either her accident or her recovery. Then he asked about her motives in passing her donation on to a hospital.

"I know firsthand what it's like not to be able to move under your own steam. If that little bit of money gives hope to even one child, then I'm richer than I was before."

"So you'd do it again?" Next to Gerald, the camera on Dan's shoulder continued to hum along.

"Absolutely. In spite of all our available technology, progress is restricted by financial limitations. I'm sure every dollar helps."

From there, Gerald moved on to their plans for the rest of the trip, this time including Rob in the interview. Kelsey was glad to let her brother share some of the limelight.

When Gerald finished, Dan positioned himself in the back of the van and they shot some footage of Kelsey and Rob riding down the road. Kelsey thought the whole thing was totally ridiculous, and when Rob waved to the camera and mouthed greetings to his friends, she applauded silently. After five or six minutes of driving ahead of them and alongside of them, Gerald stopped the van again.

"I appreciate this. Now, my wife insisted that I invite you to dinner. She said you were probably tired of eating out after so long on the road."

Rob didn't even hesitate. "Where and when?"

Kelsey smiled her agreement. She could probably like Gerald, now that the interview was over.

He gave them the address and told them how to get there. "About seven? After we get through with the evening news?"

Agreeing that would be fine, Kelsey waved goodbye to Gerald and Dan. She thought Dan should be called Dan-the-silent-camera man.

WHEN KELSEY AND ROB turned into Gerald's driveway that evening, he came out of the house to meet them. His smile seemed to stretch across his entire face, and a knot of apprehension formed suddenly in Kelsey's stomach.

"You're not going to believe this," Gerald said. "During our newscast we got pledges and donations totaling over six thousand dollars, just because of you. Those kids you care so much about are certainly coming out on top this time. We're running the clip again tonight, with a follow-up. You've got to stay long enough to watch it."

Chapter Seven

Toward the end of the week, Mike had settled back into his normal routine. He no longer woke up cold in the morning and wanting a cup of coffee that had been boiled over a fire. He'd stopped thinking how long the ten weeks would be before he rejoined Kelsey and Rob.

Late Friday afternoon he stopped by the office to pick up his messages and a couple of files he wanted to work on over the weekend. Thumbing through the pink slips left by the secretary, he saw one from the lab that processed his photographs and one from a client who changed his policy an average of once a month. Then one from an editor at Seastone Books caught his attention.

Seastone. A San Francisco publishing house that specialized in high-gloss books on nature, travel and history. He not only admired the exceptional quality of their line, but he owned several volumes himself. Doing a book for them was part of his five-year plan.

He tried to return the call, but it was too late in the evening. Hanging up the receiver, he knew he'd spend the whole weekend wondering what they wanted.

On Monday morning he called right at eight. The receptionist put him straight through to the editor.

"This is Darlene Yim."

"Hi, Michael Kincaid, returning your call."

"Yes, Mr. Kincaid. I read your series on Kelsey Sumner and her brother with interest. Her story is really quite beautiful. How did you enjoy the ride?" Underlying the professionalism of her tone, a note of enthusiasm came through clearly.

"It was good."

"Well, I'll get right to the point. If you would consider rejoining the Sumners and making a photographic record of their entire trip, we'd like to publish it as a book."

Seastone coming to him! Well ahead of his private schedule. He'd planned to submit a proposal on a year of climbing Mt. Rainier, contrasting summer and winter assaults.

He could still do Rainier later.

"Is this a firm offer?" he asked.

"Yes, it is. We realize that a transcontinental bicycle trip isn't noteworthy in and of itself. There are several things, however, that separate this one. First, of course, is Ms. Sumner's past history, but we wouldn't want to emphasize that. We're not interested in a trauma story. The second is the publicity regarding her trip, which began with your articles. These donations she's getting are receiving wide attention, and we think more will follow. We envision this as the profile of a cause."

"Hold on," Mike interrupted. "There was only one donation."

"Oh, no. It's much bigger than that. Didn't you see Thursday night's news? A station in Boise interviewed her, and pledges poured in. At last count the total was nearly ten thousand dollars. It's been like a spontaneous telethon. The money is being sent to the Children's Medical Center."

Mike sank back into the chair. Ten grand. Well, good for Kelsey. After she got used to the idea, she'd probably run with it. In spite of her initial reaction in Lewiston, he didn't think for a second she'd back away from this kind of challenge. It would make one hell of a book.

He wanted to do it. Like being worth a million by the time he was thirty-five or owning a Mercedes, he wanted to do this particular book for Seastone.

The problem was in leaving his agency for ten or twelve more weeks.

"I don't think—" he began.

"We're prepared to give you a reasonable advance." Darlene Yim named a figure that surprised him. It wasn't a fortune, but it was more than he would have expected. "And royalties, of course."

"The idea has a lot of appeal, but I have a business to run. I'd lose nearly a whole quarter."

For a moment she didn't answer. The trouble with phone conversations was the invisibility of the other person. When she finally did speak, her tone seemed cooler, more distant. "I can understand that. I'm sorry we can't adequately compensate you financially for your time, but—"

"The money's only a part of it. I'd also be leaving my clients for that long."

"I see. Well, of course, you were our first choice. We've noticed your work before and knew you could provide the quality we look for. Also, you've had the advantage of already spending time with Kelsey and her brother. There are, however, one or two other people we can approach."

Mike imagined someone else riding with Kelsey. Some other man. "Are you saying that if I don't, you'll find someone who will?"

"It's a tremendous idea, Mike, one we would definitely like to pursue."

Under the smooth professionalism of her voice, he recognized an effort to manipulate him. And damn her, it was working.

"Can you give me a day or two to think about it?"

"Of course. I'll be looking forward to hearing from you."

"THE WHOLE IDEA'S CRAZY," Jerry said the next morning when Mike attempted to explain.

"Probably." But Mike couldn't keep his voice free of anticipation. Pacing around Jerry's office, he tried to forget all the details he had to take care of in the next few hours and concentrate on the one immediately at hand. "I'll arrange for you to keep the commissions on all the work you do for me while I'm gone." He knew Jerry would probably do it as a favor, but he couldn't ask him to take on that much extra responsibility for nothing.

Grinning, Jerry locked his hands behind his head and put his feet up on his desk. "Plus a kickback."

"Season tickets to the university football games in the fall?"

"Deal."

"Unless you lose one of my clients, then no tickets."

Jerry tried to look insulted. "You either trust me or you don't."

"Now that's a hell of a spot to put me in."

Jerry shook his head. "Don't lay that on me. This is a situation of your own making. I hope you know what you're doing."

Considering that he'd spent the past twenty-four hours wondering the same thing, Mike could only agree.

The whole idea was a risk, but like all risks, if he succeeded the reward would be worth it. So would the costs. Financially the advance and royalties off the book would probably barely cover the commissions he'd be turning over to Jerry. They wouldn't approach what he'd lose by not writing any new business for three months. By the time he recovered, he'd be half a year behind schedule. But Mike had never been one to let a goal become his master.

"Do you have a couple of hours you can spend this afternoon going over my accounts? I want to leave tomorrow."

Jerry whistled. "That soon? You're not wasting any time."

Mike didn't figure he had any to waste. Not if he wanted to connect with Kelsey and Rob. He'd gotten a postcard from her in Saturday's mail from some little town in Idaho.

The picture on the front was of a weird-looking brown rabbit with antelope horns. The message on the back said, "We're taking our time, enjoying the scenery. I love the song of the meadowlark. Because of you I have something to think about besides myself. Thanks, Kelsey."

Mike doubted he'd recognize a meadowlark if he heard one. He wondered what he'd given her to think about.

In the week spent riding with her, he'd learned that there were depths to her only someone who looked closely would see. Of course, rejoining Kelsey made about as much sense as owning an apartment building without liability coverage. Still, the potential rewards outweighed the possible risks.

Mike wondered how she'd react to the idea of the book. She'd probably hate it. He folded his arms across his chest and watched the clouds float past Jerry's window. She'd absolutely hate it. When she found out what he wanted, she'd turn him away without giving him a chance to explain. He'd never before met anyone as adverse to celebrity status as Kelsey.

On the other hand, after it was over and she could look back to see the final result, he suspected she'd be happy about what she'd accomplished.

Abruptly he realized that was the answer. He'd wait until the end to tell her. By then, she'd be able to see that her trip was bigger than her own personal quest. And she'd know him well enough to understand his motives.

''My guess is you left yesterday.''

Mike tried to pull his thoughts back to the matters a
hand. ''What?''

''I've been talking and you've been dreaming. No woma
is worth spending three months on a bike for.''

Kelsey is. ''I'm going to write a book.''

''Oh, right.'' Jerry stood up and shrugged into his sui
coat. ''I'll be back in the office about three-thirty. You ca
fill me in then.''

''Thanks.''

''I still think you're crazy.''

KELSEY AND ROB RODE into Ashton, Idaho, in the middl
of the afternoon. Depending on what the grades were lik
climbing toward the Targhee Pass, they'd reach Yellow
stone tomorrow, or maybe the day after. In spite of her bes
efforts to be optimistic, Kelsey felt nervous about hitting th
mountains. Logically she knew she could now handle
climb; she'd gotten progressively stronger with each con
quered mile. Emotionally she doubted her staying power.

''Mail stop, then food,'' Rob said.

Grinning, Kelsey nodded. To avoid possible mix-ups, they
planned mail stops for small towns with only one zip code
She'd noticed that twice Rob had gotten letters in pale green
envelopes. He didn't confide in her, but she suspected they
were from Angela Newberry, and she suspected he though
another one would be waiting for him today.

Aside from that, they hadn't heard from their parent
since Portland. Of course, international mails were unpre
dictable, and their timetable had been tentative at best. Bu
they had sent a list of towns along the route, and any day
letter would catch up with them.

And, although she would never have admitted it to Rob
she kept hoping for something from Mike.

At the post office, Kelsey let Rob go in. She sat on the bottom step in the shade and stretched slowly over her left leg, concentrating on relaxing the muscles from hip to toe. Her flexibility had improved along with her strength. Rob had been right. This was what she needed, and if she made it over the mountains, she'd never hesitate again.

Leaning lower over her knee, she took a long, deep breath. The breeze was full of sage and freshly turned earth. Only an occasional car broke the silence of the little farming community.

From a distance she heard the whir of a freewheel. Instead of looking up, she dipped deeper into her stretch. Far too often during the past five days she'd turned, expecting to see Mike. Every bicyclist they passed made her think of him. It had been like trying to exorcise a ghost.

The sound got closer, and she tried to shut the images out of her mind. Then a wheel stopped just inches from her toes.

Slowly she raised her head.

Mike.

He took off his sunglasses, and her heart caught in her throat.

"Hello, Kelsey."

Her pulse pounding, she scrambled to her feet. He looked just the same, tall and lean, his eyes shadowed by his helmet, his arms and legs darkened by the sun. Too wonderful to comprehend.

Stepping automatically toward him, she reached out her hand and he immediately took it in his. A kaleidoscope of sensations washed over her, feelings of warmth, acceptance, coming home.

Quickly she pulled away. She'd just spent an entire week adjusting to his absence. "What are you doing here?"

His eyes were more blue than gray, almost a reflection of the sky, and searching hers. When he smiled, it seemed as if a shaft of golden light shot straight to her heart, connecting her to him. Excitement danced across her skin like a breeze.

"Going with you." Reaching out, he slid his hand behind her neck and urged her toward him with the barest hint of pressure. "All the rest of the way." Then his mouth was on hers.

Not thinking, only feeling, she leaned toward him. He smelled of sun and a musky after-shave. Her shoulder brushed against his chest. Dammit, she'd missed him.

His tongue skimmed along her lower lip in invitation, at once questioning and demanding. Unresisting, she parted her lips in welcome.

His fingers lifted into her hair. When her thighs pressed against his leg and the crossbar of his bike, she didn't even mind the bite of the metal. For a few breathless moments, nothing mattered except the fact that he was here.

But it was all fantasy, of course. Digging deep for the last dregs of willpower, she pushed free and met his eyes again. "I gave you what you wanted, Mike. Going on with us wasn't part of the bargain."

"Not everything I wanted. There's more, and we both know it."

Kelsey knew excitement, and apprehension. "Why? This doesn't strike me as your kind of thing."

As lightly as the caress of the breeze, he stroked his finger across her cheek. "Because of you, of course."

Reason eluded her. She grasped at the flimsy strands of argument remaining. "You hardly know me."

"We spent one full week together, twenty-four hours every day, in circumstances where we had to trust one another. I think I know you fairly well."

"It's the unusual circumstances that bothers me."

He chuckled softly. "That's what convinced me. Understanding exists on many levels." His thumb traced her lip.

"So does promise, and there's enough of that between us to go on.''

"You don't know that. There are too many things you don't know. Maybe we should leave it at that.''

His hand drifted down her throat and followed the rounded neckline of her jersey. She knew he could feel every beat of her rushing pulse. "I can't, love. We've passed the point where I can walk away.''

Longing surged through her veins, a thousand times stronger than she'd ever wanted anything before. Even needing to walk again hadn't felt like this.

Just then, Rob came out of the post office, letting the door swing shut behind him. In his hand was a single pale green envelope.

Seeing Mike, he hesitated, eyes narrowing, then came slowly down the steps. "What are you doing here?''

"Mike's going with us,'' Kelsey said.

"The hell he is.''

Stung by the harsh vehemence in Rob's voice, Kelsey stared at her brother. His previous antagonism had been nothing like this. "I want him to.''

Rob gestured impatiently. "Suit yourself.''

"No!'' She grabbed his arm, making him face her squarely. "We'll talk about it!''

Mike touched her shoulder. "There's a café down the street. I can wait for you there.''

"Fine!'' Rob growled.

Without watching him, Kelsey listened to Mike's retreat. Partly she appreciated his strategic exit. Partly she felt his leaving was an omen. And not a good one.

"I don't think this is a good idea, Kelsey,'' Rob said immediately. "You haven't even looked at another man since Alan. You're vulnerable.''

Facts she already knew. "I'm trying to get well, Rob, in every way.''

"He could hurt you."

"I could get hit by a car tomorrow."

Concern replaced anger in Rob's expression. "One step at a time," he suggested, his tone softer. "That's all I'm asking. Make the trip first. There'll be plenty of time to put your emotions on the line when we get home."

"Is that what you're doing?"

"What?"

She couldn't expect him to follow her train of thought. She pointed to the envelope in his hand, crushed now from the strength of his feelings. "Is that from Angela?"

Using both hands, he straightened the paper. "Yeah."

"Does she make you confused?"

Rob slung his arm around Kelsey's shoulders and pulled her into a hug. "She doesn't understand why I'm here."

"At least Mike has that down."

Releasing her slightly, Rob looked down at her. "If he hurts you, I'll tear him apart."

"I don't know what lies ahead. But he's here, and I can't send him away."

"You're sure?"

"As sure as I can be under the circumstances. And the least you can do is go along. He wouldn't be here at all if you hadn't encouraged me to accept him in the first place."

SITTING IN A CORNER BOOTH with a Coke in front of him, Mike tried to make sense of the whole situation. He was here to do a book, wasn't he?

Like hell. The minute he'd seen Kelsey sitting there in the shade, bending over her leg, he'd known exactly why he'd come. Everything he'd said to her had been the truth. There *was* more between them than their original agreement. It *was* too late to turn back.

And leaving her to talk about it with Rob had been stupid. In business he never gave control of the decision to the client. That was why he was so successful, because he knew how to close a sale.

Of course, he couldn't have forced Kelsey to choose between him and her brother. Still, every second ticked in his mind like a time bomb.

He felt helpless. It could go either way, and he'd given up the opportunity for further argument. He suspected this was the way a defendant felt while the jury was out.

What would he do if her answer were no? He could tell her of Seastone's plan, tell her if he didn't come, someone else would probably show up later. He could smile pleasantly and walk away. He could fall on his knees and beg.

Never had he been so drawn to a woman. No one had ever wrapped herself around his imagination, or rooted herself in his mind. Thinking about Kelsey, he could almost feel the wind-dried softness of her skin, smell the sun in her hair, see the future in her eyes.

And he'd thought he knew himself so well. He knew he wasn't about to let events run whatever course they would.

Through the window he saw Kelsey and Rob park their bikes in front of the café. As though synchronized, they took off their helmets and hung them over their seats. They both tucked their gloves into the bungie cords holding the sleeping bags on their back racks. Rob was four or five inches taller than Kelsey, his hair was darker and lacked the red highlights, but their faces had the same angular planes and they moved with the same athletic grace. Their familial resemblance was obvious at a glance.

So was their close emotional relationship. It suddenly occurred to Mike that Kelsey might not have room in her life for anyone besides her brother.

They came into the café laughing together. Gritting his teeth against the picture of total harmony they presented, Mike stood up to greet them.

"We're going to stay here tonight," Rob said, "so we can check the mail again in the morning. Then it's straight on to Yellowstone."

Kelsey slid into the booth across from Mike, leaving room for Rob beside her. Sitting back down, Mike silently vowed that soon, very soon, she'd choose to sit with him.

"I expect the ride to be steep," Kelsey said.

"We'll be crossing the Continental Divide," Rob added, his voice full of challenge.

Obviously the kid didn't think he'd make it. Well, the kid had a lot to learn about Mike Kincaid. But they were saying "we," just as if his going were an accepted fact. So did they want him along, or were they giving him an out? He decided to play it for keeps.

"I can handle it."

"I'm sure you can," Rob said dryly.

Mike ignored the jibe. "Tell me about Boise."

To his surprise, Kelsey laughed. "I should be very angry with you."

He lifted an eyebrow in question.

"It was all your fault, after all."

"Should I apologize?"

She laughed again. "No. Rob says I've been too self-centered. I think it's terrific that something good finally came out of all that suffering."

Without knowing her story, Mike would never have guessed the suffering she referred to was her own. Impulsively he reached for her hand. "I understand you brought in over ten thousand dollars."

"Incredible, isn't it?" Rob asked, his voice neutral and his eyes dropping pointedly to where Mike's hand covered Kelsey's. "She's a one-woman crusade. While we were in Boise, calls came from all over the West—Wyoming, Nevada, Utah. Of course, the money went to a hospital in Utah, so that one's understandable.

After a moment's hesitation Kelsey drew away from Mike's touch. "It still seems too bizarre to be real."

"Where do you think it will go from here?" he asked.

Some of the laughter left her eyes. "Do you think it *will* go on from here? I'd much prefer becoming anonymous again."

If Darlene Yim's interest were any indication, Mike knew there was little possibility of that. "I think there's a good chance your trip will become a cause. You could become a symbol, or a rallying cry. If that hasn't happened already."

Enthusiasm faded from Kelsey's expression. Mike wanted to reach out to her, to tell her everything would be fine, but it was Rob she turned to. Rob shifted his body in an obvious effort to block Mike out with his back.

"Maybe we could change our route, or just stop calling attention to ourselves," Kelsey suggested.

With an emphatic shake of his head, Rob put his arm around her shoulders. "What happened to making the most of this? Keep remembering that if the publicity continues to build, and you raise more money, then you'll be helping a bunch of kids who could use it."

Mike recognized the twist in his gut as jealousy. He wanted to be the one who held her. Instead he pressed his hands firmly against his thighs in restraint.

The man was her brother, for God's sake. He'd earned her trust and affection. But knowing that didn't make it any easier. And it wasn't just the touching. Rob knew exactly what to say to quench the uncertainty in her eyes.

"People respond to you because you give them something to believe in. If you quit, you rob them of that." Rob flicked her chin with his finger. "And you'd be robbing us of a dream. So what if we have to share it once in a while along the way?"

Mike decided that one day she would smile at him the way she smiled at Rob. One day soon.

In the meantime he refused to be intimidated. "Rob's right," he said. "You'll run into it again, and as I see it, you have two choices. You can either balk and worry every time, or you can take it up yourself. Besides, I don't believe you're the type to run away."

Without even a glance in Mike's direction, Rob took up the argument. "You've already come a long way toward accepting it. Promoting it would be more fun than passively accepting whatever falls our way."

"You're both right. And I'd hate to slay anyone's dream, especially my own." Kelsey sat up straight and linked her hands together in front of her. "So, if we're going to promote this 'cause,' then we better do it right. We'll start by letting people know we're coming and when we'll be in their town. We'll decide in advance where donations are to be sent."

"Good for you, Kel," Rob agreed. "We can try to keep a running total so that radio stations can use it in their promotions."

"Maybe we could think up a theme or a slogan or something," she said.

Surprised at how quickly his suggestion had grown into a firm plan of attack, Mike sat back and listened. Darlene Yim was going to love it. The notion crossed his mind that by convincing Kelsey, even inadvertently, to take this cause business to its ultimate conclusion, he was meeting Seastone's needs more than her own. He quickly discarded it. The publicity would follow her, whether she liked it or not. By taking charge, she could control the situation rather than be controlled by it.

And success, such as raising money for a good cause, never hurt anyone.

Chapter Eight

"What did your parents have to say?" Mike asked.

They were riding a gentle incline, and when Rob pulled ahead, Mike had immediately moved up beside Kelsey. A quick glance told her he was already feeling the climb. There was a fine sheen of perspiration on his face, and his breathing came too hard for so early in the day. He could still talk normally while he rode, though, which was a good sign.

"They're just wrapping up the last details of their project in Greece, then they'll be in Barbados for a month or two before coming home." She couldn't keep the expectation out of her voice. They'd been gone nearly two years.

"They'll be back about the same time you will," Mike said.

"I think they planned it that way."

"What do they think of this trip?"

"They think it's great. My mother wants tons of photographs, but that's her thing, not mine. It kills her that I haven't got scrapbooks full of memories."

"I'll give you copies of everything I take."

Embarrassed, she laughed. "You don't have to. I wasn't hinting."

"It seems like the least I can do since you're allowing me to tag along."

"You would, of course, have gone meekly back to Portland if I'd said no."

He chuckled. "Actually, no. I wouldn't have."

"That's what I thought."

"How close did Rob come to sending me away?"

"*Trying* to send you away?" She cast another brief look in his direction, and this time his laugh was fuller. She loved the sound of it, the solidity of it. Mike Kincaid caused dozens of emotions to cascade through her, like winter melt overflowing a stream bed, and although some of them were uncomfortable, many more were pure pleasure.

This was one of the best. She liked him. Pure and simple.

"How close?" he repeated.

"Close."

"How close?" he insisted.

"I think it's better if you don't know. Especially since it doesn't make any difference."

"It makes a difference to me. I want to know where I stand."

"I'd say you stand about six-one, but if you tried to stand while riding, you'd be in a hell of a lot of trouble."

Before he could reply, she bent lower over her drops and put her shoulders into the climb. She quickly pulled ahead, and with no more effort than that, she could probably stay ahead the rest of the day if she wanted to.

They only made thirty miles before calling a halt. The grades were steep, Mike hadn't ridden in a week, and to Kelsey's dismay, she felt the strain in her leg. It didn't give out, but each time they stopped, she saw the concern in Rob's eyes. She managed to pass it off with smiles and reassurances.

By the time they got to Island Park Reservoir, only a few miles west of the Wyoming border, she knew she'd had enough. Since they stopped in the middle of the afternoon, there was no urgency to set up camp quickly. The dull ache in her leg was one of fatigue rather than stress, so she ignored the men and stretched out on her back on the picnic table to relax. Applying techniques that had become automatic, she closed her eyes and focused on releasing the tension.

Breathing deeply and using mental triggers, she slipped into a light trancelike state. She'd learned a lot about biofeedback and self-hypnosis in the hospital, techniques that continued to work for her. After about fifteen minutes she dozed off, and when she awoke she felt restored.

She drifted awake slowly without opening her eyes. A mild breeze whispered through the trees, bringing the scent of snow down from the high mountains and the murmur of water washing against the shore. An occasional bird called from a distance. There were no sounds of people. The sun, finding its way through a break in the trees, warmed her skin.

Sitting up, she stretched. And there, at the end of the table, Mike sat watching her.

"Feeling better?" he asked.

"Where's Rob?"

"He walked up along the shore of the lake. I think he still resents my being here."

"Probably."

When she didn't expand, Mike nodded toward the lake. "This is a beautiful place."

"It must be a lot different from the places you went as a kid."

He chuckled. "Just the trees, the underbrush, the terrain and the climate. I bet it'll be cold here tonight."

"You'll be glad you have a down bag."

"Why did you choose to start so early in the year? There's still snow on the north-facing slopes."

"I've heard that in July the mosquitoes in the Midwest will carry you away."

With a wry grin he nodded. "They will in Minnesota."

"And the humidity is terrible."

"So you chose the cold." He sat facing the lake with his back to the table, his elbows resting behind him and his legs stretched out toward the water. The way the sun slanted on his face made the shadow of his hair fall over his eyes. He had a fine white scar that ran from his lower lip to the crease in his chin. She'd never noticed it before and wondered how he'd gotten it. For all his protestations about walking the safe road, he'd stepped into harm's way at least once.

"I'd prefer not to get snowed on." She pulled her knees up to her chest and wrapped her arms around her legs.

"Then what would we do?"

"Build a snowman."

Laughing, he looked up at her. His eyes seemed almost blue, as if reflecting the sky and lake. "You're incredible."

She steeled herself against the flutter in her stomach. "Next week's the first of June. I doubt there's much probability."

With a single, fluid movement Mike moved to sit on the table next to her. Anticipation flared quickly, like a flame, but he only leaned forward and rested his elbows on his knees. She forced herself to relax. All day she'd been expecting something from him and she didn't know what. A sign perhaps, that his words were honest and her feelings were true. Instead he'd ridden, taken lots of pictures and stayed just close enough to keep her off balance.

"Why do you keep photographing me? You've finished that series for the paper."

For a moment he continued to stare off toward the lake, and when he turned toward her, she thought she saw hesitation flicker in his eyes. Then he smiled, a smile full of both warmth and confidence. She wasn't sure which made her the most nervous.

"Because you're beautiful."

Caught off guard, she laughed lightly, self-consciously. She was sweaty and tired, and her hair probably stuck out at strange angles because of her helmet. She was too angular and had freckles on her shoulders.

As if sensing that he'd made her feel embarrassed, he let it drop there. "I've never been to Yellowstone before."

"Neither have I. Strange, isn't it, when you could drive here in a day from Portland."

"And it's taken two weeks by bicycle. I'm beginning to see why you allowed three months to get to Maine."

"We didn't want to push." It was easier when they talked like this, without undercurrents pulling her in other directions. "Our longest day so far was after we left Boise. We did ninety miles because there was a good tail wind. I think by the time we finish, the average will be about fifty."

"The most I ever did at a time before was twenty."

Glancing sideways at him, she shook her head. "You have a lot of confidence, taking on something like this with so little training."

"I work out every day at a club, and I figured I could get used to road riding as I went."

With his thighs so close to hers, she could already see the increased muscle definition. "I'd say it's working."

"Tell me about your leg. It was hurting, wasn't it? When we stopped?"

She heard no special concern in his voice, no pity or morbidity. Just normal curiosity. This was a question he hadn't asked when writing about her, and she appreciated that. "When I fell, both my pelvis and thigh shattered. I broke both bones in my calf and three ribs, one of which punctured a lung. I have so much metal pinning me back together I can't walk through a security gate at an airport without setting off the alarm. I get tired and become stiff easily. Sometimes, as you've already witnessed, that leg gives out on me completely.''

She recited the list without emotion, and while she talked, she watched him closely. Although his jaw tightened slightly, he listened impassively.

''Because of my hobby,'' he said, ''I happened to be where you were a couple of times, while you were hang gliding and rappeling, and once when you were racing in Baja. Maybe one of the things that caught my attention was how invulnerable you seemed. It was as if you were a part of the mountain, or the air. When I heard about your accident, I couldn't believe it.''

What he said answered some questions, but brought others to mind. ''How did you hear about my trip? Why did you care?''

''You really don't have any idea what a heroine you are, do you?'' He turned to look deep into her eyes, and his knee touched hers. ''Ever since your accident, wherever I went, I heard your name. At first it was, 'Kelsey's in a coma,' then it was, 'Kelsey's gonna make it.' Pretty soon the talk wasn't whether you'd walk again, but whether you'd fly. When you went back to work, people cheered. When word got out that you were making this ride, they cried.''

Kelsey sucked her lower lip between her teeth and bit down hard. She didn't want to believe him. No one, not Rob, not Blaine, not any of her friends, had even hinted that she'd attained some kind of notability.

''Why?''

He shook his head. ''Maybe because they want to believe they could make it back, too, if the unthinkable ever happened to them. Maybe because you're a neat person.''

No matter what other people thought, Kelsey knew how ordinary she was, but maybe this was what Rob had talked about. About giving people hope.

Mike took her hand in his. "You know, what others think doesn't matter."

"But that's why you contacted me in the first place, isn't it? Because I'm famous in a way?"

"Only because you didn't let the accident stop you." His fingers wove between hers, and his thumb caressed her knuckles. "But every time I saw you, I was tempted to introduce myself."

"Why didn't you?"

"You were with someone else. Whenever we were in the same place at the same time, so was he."

Alan. The man who'd walked out on her because she was damaged and couldn't play the same games anymore.

She pulled free of Mike's touch and hopped to the ground. "I wonder where Rob is. He's been gone a long time."

Without looking, she sensed Mike stand behind her. "If he stays close to the lake, he can't get lost."

"Rob never gets lost. He has an unerring sense of direction."

Placing his hands on her shoulders, Mike turned her toward him. "Then you want him back so you won't be alone with me."

"That's not it."

"Liar."

He stood so close she could smell sun and exertion on his clothes. Her heart thudded against her chest until she thought he would hear it.

"Yesterday you said you wanted me with you," he continued.

"I do." But thinking about Alan made her doubt. What if Rob were right? What if she let herself become emotionally involved with Mike, and then he walked away?

"I'd never have guessed you for a coward," he said.

"I'm not."

"You wouldn't hesitate to jump out of an airplane, or climb the face of a glacier, but right now you want to run. From me and from yourself."

"Don't judge me, Mike."

His hands massaged her shoulders, and he laughed softly. "I'll never judge you, Kelsey. But one day I will understand."

For a moment she thought he would kiss her. The way he looked at her made her bones soften to unsteadiness and tempted her to lean against him. Instead he brought her against his chest, holding her gently while her breathing steadied, and then he stepped away. "I think I'll go set up my tent."

THAT NIGHT IT WAS COLD. Dressed in both thermals and sweats, Kelsey still huddled in her sleeping bag. The wind had picked up with the setting of the sun. Now it pulled at the fabric of the tent and whistled through the trees above them.

But even the moaning of the branches wasn't as unsettled as her thoughts.

Maybe letting Mike rejoin them had been a mistake. Knowing he wasn't an adventurer should have ridded her of all doubt. But today she'd discovered it was more complicated than that. Mike was more complicated than that. Of course, she had to admit that he personally hadn't given her any reason to doubt him; it was Rob's fear that she would end up hurt again that made her cautious. And sadly so had remembering how she and Alan had done so much together, shared so many good times. She'd once believed that such sharing was all a relationship needed.

So how could she trust her response to Mike? Only two weeks into this new adventure, and she was falling in love with him. Or maybe she was only falling into lust and couldn't tell the difference.

Four years of struggling with her physical well-being had left her rather barren in other areas. She felt that her emotional maturity had regressed to about age seventeen. Teenagers tended to think with their hormones, and maybe that was all that was happening to her.

Except, deep down, she didn't believe that. Mike looked at her with more in his eyes than desire. When they laughed together, it felt like a meeting of the minds. And he wasn't put off by her occasional weakness. Wasn't that a sure indication that he honestly, truly cared?

OLD FAITHFUL WAS disappointing. After waiting half an hour in a chilly wind, they joined the heaviest crowds since Portland to watch it erupt. Instead they saw steam. The hot water of the geyser condensed in the cold air as soon as it left the ground, creating billows of clouds.

"Do you wonder if they faked all those pictures you see in books of a pillar of water rising into a cloudless sky?" Rob complained.

"Maybe we'd have had more of a chance if the sky had been cloudless," Mike suggested philosophically.

Kelsey noticed he'd taken a stream of pictures in spite of having nothing to see.

"We could come back tomorrow," Rob suggested.

"I'd rather go on," Kelsey said.

They'd already visited the northwestern part of the park and seen the sights there. It had been overcast and drizzly the whole time, giving the devastation from the 1988 fire an eerie quality. Meadows of wildflowers, brilliant against the stark barrenness of skeletal lodgepole pines, promised the renewal of the park, but in the cold even the birds had sense enough to take shelter.

Kelsey was fascinated by the patterns of the fire. In the middle of huge burned areas were places that had been jumped—like most of the Old Faithful area. The inn still stood, but some of the cabins had been destroyed. The weather, however, killed much of her curiosity. After two days of cold, the chill seemed to penetrate clear to the marrow of her bones, and she could think of little besides getting warm again.

She'd worked at keeping this new discomfort to herself, but every once in a while she saw Mike watching her with concern in his eyes. It disconcerted her. She didn't want him to see below the surface. She didn't want to think he could perceive something she was able to keep from Rob.

Taking her park map from the clear vinyl pocket of her pack, she traced the road with her finger. "Let's ride around this loop and stop at the spots we haven't seen yet, then stay here at the Canyon campground tonight."

When Mike leaned over her shoulder, she handed him the map.

"Sounds good to me," he said. "What do you think, Rob?"

"It's cool. I can always buy a couple of postcards of the geyser and claim I saw it."

"Good plan. Postcards would probably have the sun shining." Kelsey turned her bike toward the exit and threw her leg over the crossbar. "Then tomorrow we can head into Wyoming."

Rob laughed and wheeled his bike next to hers. "We're already in Wyoming, sweetie."

"*Real* Wyoming. Where the cowboys are."

"Want to take a bet on how many cowboys we see?"

"A lot." She laughed over her shoulder as she tucked her foot into the toe clip. "They're on every license plate."

Since the ride around Yellowstone Lake was fairly flat, it should have been easy. It wasn't. The drizzle started again. Barely wet, Kelsey wouldn't say it was rain, but with a mild wind it seemed to soak through her rain gear and into her skin. When they got to the campground, she signaled a stop.

"Let's call it for today. We can see more tomorrow."

Immediately Rob was at her side. "You okay?"

"Just tired and cold."

"This place has showers. Why don't you take one, and I'll set up the tent?"

They found a spot, and Kelsey silently unloaded her bike and took dry clothes and a towel from her pack. Mike, unloading his own, watched her closely, and when she headed for the shower, he went with her, his towel tucked under his arm.

In an area completely untouched by the fire, the lodgepole pines towered straight as sentinels into the gray sky. Darkened by rain, they made the narrow road feel like a chasm. Low clouds gave the air an ethereal quality. Except for the cold, Kelsey would have enjoyed the effect. Instead she merely limped toward the showers.

"Why do you try to hide that you hurt?"

"I'm okay."

"Like hell."

She turned on him in frustration. It seemed as if she'd been fighting pain all her life, rather than just four years, and fighting for the physical independence she'd once taken for granted. Giving in, acknowledging, accepting—all were paths to defeat.

"Damn you, Mike. Leave me alone."

Grabbing her shoulders, he pulled her toward him. His eyes were as stormy as the sky, his mouth a tight straight line. "I can't. I care. I want to help."

Sorry she'd snapped at him, she smiled and shook her head. "There's nothing you can do. Please let me go so I can shower. I have to get warm."

Opening his jacket, he drew her inside close to his chest, unmindful of how wet her poncho must be making his jersey. His body heat felt like climbing under an electric blanket, prewarmed to exactly the right temperature.

"I can do this."

She leaned against him, absorbing his warmth and reveling in the comfort of his arms.

When she stopped shivering, he released her just enough to shift her to his side, and they headed together for the showers.

"I'll be here when you get through," he said.

"There's no need, really."

"There's every need."

The room was warm. At least, warm enough that she could undress without turning to ice. She put three quarters in the coin box and turned the water on full blast. For a while she just stood under it, letting the heat pour over her. Even so, it took several minutes to dispel the deep chill that made her bones feel like ice cakes breaking apart in a spring thaw.

She'd be glad when they left the mountains. This time of year she'd expected it to be chilly, not bone-jarring cold. Since she'd met the challenge of steep, steady grades, and conquered, that point didn't need to be proved further.

Leisurely she washed her hair and soaped her body. Touching her hip, she felt the scars and hesitated. For the first time she wondered how Mike would react to them.

Heaven knew, he talked about beauty often enough. She recoiled at the possibility of seeing horror in his eyes when he looked at her. She believed it wouldn't matter to him. She hoped it wouldn't. She wondered if she'd be brave enough to put it to the test—if they ever got to that point.

Of course, she knew the smartest approach would be to delay any potential relationship with Mike until after the trip. As she'd learned the hard way, it was too easy to equate the shared excitement of a fantasy situation with love.

A WEAK SUN FILTERED through the clouds, making a small but significant change in the temperature. Kelsey didn't seem to notice. She hardly spoke on the way back to their campsite, and Mike wished that the shower had cheered her spirits as much as it had helped physically. She was hardly limping at all. Additionally the shampoo she'd used made her hair smell of wildflowers.

But now there was no reason to pull her against him for comfort and warmth.

Rob had a weak flame fighting for life in the fire circle, with damp wood propped above it to dry. Just the thought of heat made Mike feel mellower toward Kelsey's brother. Actually, if Rob would quit acting like the entire queen's guard where Kelsey was concerned, he wouldn't be half-bad. He certainly knew his way around a fire, and tonight they all needed a good strong one.

"Feeling better?" Rob asked Kelsey.

Kelsey hunched down by the fire and held out her hands. "Terrific. What's for dinner?"

"Soup, hot chocolate, company. A couple of bicyclists. Their tent's only a few sites away."

As Mike rolled a rock closer to the fire for a seat within touching distance of Kelsey, he felt Rob's resentment. Too bad.

"Where are they headed?" he asked.

"Mount Rushmore, and then up into Canada," Rob answered without looking up.

"Where are they from?" For the first time all day Mike heard a note of excitement in Kelsey's voice.

"San Diego. Oh, here they are now." Rob stood up and motioned to the new arrivals. "Come and meet my sister."

Both the man and the woman were in their mid-twenties. They wore sweaters and windbreakers rather than custom rain gear. The woman had dark hair pulled back into a long braid and almost colorless blue eyes; the man was blond and bearded.

Rob introduced them as Bliss and Courtney Iverson. Kelsey welcomed them warmly, and Mike wondered which was which. Their names were too generic to tell. When Kelsey caught his eye, he saw laughter there, and he knew she had the same question.

"This is Mike Kincaid," she said, filling in where Rob left off. "He's riding with us. Grab a rock and sit down."

Mike immediately kicked his closer to Kelsey's.

"Get some soup first," Rob invited. "It'll be too cold to sit if we're not ingesting warmth at the same time."

The Iversons sat close together while they ate, shoulders and legs touching. Mike resisted the temptation to follow their example.

While they ate, the Sumners began to exchange stories with the Iversons of what they'd seen in Yellowstone, their impressions of the way the park was recovering and where they'd been before that. Mike unobtrusively placed his recorder on his thigh. Eventually the conversation turned to travel plans, and Kelsey turned eagerly toward the woman. "Rob says you're going to Canada."

Mike recognized the look of anticipation in her eyes. He'd caught it in his photographs of her, and seen it in action on the Salmon River. Did people hold the same fascination for her that she found in adventure? He doubted retold stories could provide her with the same adrenaline kick.

Yet here she was, more animated than she'd been all day, pulling a response from their guests.

"We're working our way as we go," the man said. "Courtney's uncle knows a guy in Alberta with a ranch who will give us jobs for a couple months."

Ah, then Courtney was the woman.

"When did you leave San Diego?" Mike asked.

The couple exchanged glances. "We've lost track of time." Bliss laughed. "Last October, whenever that was."

Kelsey leaned closer. "Where did you spend the winter?"

"Phoenix!" they both exclaimed at once.

"We left there about a month ago, I guess," Bliss said. Mike noticed that so far Courtney had made no attempt to actually join the conversation. "We want to take our time, because once we settle into a new place, we'll probably be there awhile."

"Spending a winter in Alberta doesn't sound too terrific to me." Rob set his metal bowl on the ground and grinned at Bliss. "You should go back to Phoenix."

Again, Bliss and Courtney exchanged glances. "We have to work over the summer, and then Courtney's going to have a baby in October."

Immediately images of disaster formed in Mike's mind. Bicycle touring itself had an acceptable risk level. Doing it while pregnant changed the odds dramatically. Concern and horror battled for supremacy in his mind as the reality of what they were doing took hold.

Kelsey didn't seem to share his anxiety. "You're four months along? You don't even show."

"And *bicycling?*" Mike couldn't keep his voice neutral.

"We don't go very fast," Courtney said defensively.

"But what if you fell?"

Laughing lightly, Kelsey touched his arm and spoke to the Iversons. "If you encourage him, he'll recite a huge list of all the reasons to play it safe. He's an insurance agent."

"Irrelevant." Mike turned seriously to Bliss. "Don't you feel a little anxious about letting your wife continue riding?" Without waiting for an answer, he switched his attention to Courtney. "Have you noticed any change in your balance? What if you fainted?"

Rob snorted his disdain but kept his opinion to himself. Courtney looked beseechingly at her husband.

"Sure," Bliss said. "We considered all those things. We checked with a doctor. Courtney's in good shape, and he said she could continue doing anything she was used to. Since we don't have a set schedule, we can ride for just an hour or for half a day, depending on how she feels. And we can take time off if she gets too tired."

The pressure of Kelsey's hand on his arm increased. "It's their business, Mike. I'm sure they thought about it carefully before they decided to keep going."

Since Mike wasn't sure how much careful thought Kelsey gave to her own decisions when it came to adventure, he wondered why she imagined other people did.

Courtney shivered and Bliss stood up quickly. "Look, we better go. Courtney feels the cold real easy. Thanks for inviting us over."

Mike heard the withdrawal in Bliss's voice. He knew it was because he'd come across so judgmental about their situation. He didn't particularly care. When people did things that foolhardy, they had to accept that those with more sense might not condone their choices.

Rob hunkered down by the fire and began stirring the coals into the damp ashes surrounding it. "What are your plans for tomorrow?" he asked.

With his arm around his wife's waist, Bliss lifted a shoulder. "Depends on the weather and how well Courtney sleeps."

Kelsey moved toward the edge of the campsite with the Iversons.

"If you want, we could ride together," she suggested. Some kind of unspoken message passed between Courtney and Kelsey. The knot of tension in Mike's stomach increased. For Kelsey, Courtney's pregnancy only added to the romance. He could see it in her eyes.

It didn't make sense. After having met disaster personally, it would be logical for her to become more cautious.

Instead she still seemed to possess that belief of personal invulnerability he witnessed constantly in risk takers.

Why? He knew she'd come on this trip to prove herself again. Obviously it was a totally physical thing, to prove her body could cope, not to determine if she had the courage to face danger again.

If he learned to understand the way her mind worked, the book for Seastone would be even better than he'd first visualized.

"I'd like to," Courtney agreed, for the first time making a decision without silently consulting Bliss.

"Then it's settled." Kelsey touched Courtney's arm before stepping away. "We'll see you in the morning."

Mike watched the exchange between the two women carefully. Courtney didn't seem like the type to appeal to Kelsey. She was too quiet, too indecisive. It had to be Courtney's pregnancy.

As soon as the Iversons were out of earshot, Rob dropped the stick he was using on the dying fire. "What did you do that for? You know they'll just slow us down."

"We're not exactly setting land-speed records." Kelsey's voice held no hint of anything beneath the surface. "They'll probably only be with us for a day or so."

Mike shoved his hands in his pockets and kicked dirt onto the dead fire in frustration. "Four months pregnant. Bliss has to be a stupid damn fool not to see the risk he's taking. Letting her take."

"Garbage," Rob sneered, his antagonism almost tangible. "You ride defensively, you don't take chances—everything's cool."

"You want chapter and verse on how some activities increase your potential for disaster? I can give them to you."

Kelsey quickly stepped between them. "Neither of you has a voice in what Courtney and Bliss decide to do. And we already know we have different ideas about which risks are acceptable and which ones aren't.''

Mike couldn't read her expression in the dark, but he heard the warning in her tone. He decided to let it drop. He wouldn't convince either of them. And Kelsey was right. It wasn't his concern.

She turned without another word and touched Rob's cheek. ''I'm going to bed. It's been a long day.''

''Sure.'' Pivoting away, Rob looped his arm around her shoulders and guided her toward the tent.

Mike watched them go, his impatience suddenly changing both tone and focus.

Standing alone in the cold, he wondered what the hell he was doing there. Neglecting his business and pursuing a woman. And a damn complicated woman at that. She was headstrong and foolhardy. But he'd never before met a woman who stirred his soul more than she excited his body.

It would be better if he could concentrate on putting the book together for Seastone, if he could pretend Kelsey were his sister. He laughed softly to himself. That was impossible, and Rob wouldn't like it any better than he liked the way things were now.

Far overhead the moon peeked through a hazy break in the clouds. The wind rustled the rain-wet pines, and in the distance a couple of squirrels quarreled.

Mike heard Kelsey's voice, soft and muted, then her laughter mingled with Rob's.

Ten weeks. Surely ten weeks were more than enough.

Chapter Nine

The morning dawned bright and clear for the first time in days, making Kelsey feel energized and confident. She was delighted when the Iversons arrived early and ready to ride.

"How about breakfast first?" she invited with a sweep of her hand. "The day's young, and a morning like this shouldn't be rushed. Besides, Mike brews the best."

"That's really why he's here," Rob said dryly. "To keep us in good coffee."

"Usually we snack on stuff in the morning that doesn't require a fire," Bliss said. "I'm not that good at making them."

Courtney laughed self-consciously. "And I'm worse."

It took Bliss a minute to get his bike to balance on its kickstand. It was an older ten-speed without extra climbing gears, the rust and dents on its frame testifying to years of hard use. Kelsey guessed that unloaded it probably weighed forty pounds and marveled that anyone would decide to take an extensive trip on such a clunk. Courtney's bike, she noticed, was of similar vintage and condition. Her opinion of the pair went up another notch. She admired anyone who decided to put their dreams into action in spite of less than ideal conditions.

Mike poured coffee for the Iversons first, then emptied the pot in Kelsey's mug before starting more. To her relief, this morning he didn't give any hint of his disapproval of them.

"How anxious are you to leave the park?" she asked. "There are a couple of sights we haven't seen yet."

"No problem." Bliss positioned two rocks close together so that Courtney's back rested against his chest. "Like we said, we're not in any hurry."

Half an hour later, when they were ready to leave, the camp looked as deserted and untouched as when they had arrived. The sun glinting through the trees had melted away the dew wherever it touched. When Bliss and Courtney began discussing their first stop with Rob, Mike wheeled his bike next to Kelsey's.

"Do you think there's any way to convince them to take a bus or something to wherever they're going?"

So here it was. She supposed she should have expected it. Last night he'd been too vehement to let it lie this morning, but she wasn't going to make it easy for him.

She looked at him sharply. "Why?"

His eyes flashed briefly with impatience. "It isn't safe for her to keep riding. Surely you can see that."

"It isn't my decision to make."

He plunged his free hand into his pocket, and his shadowy eyes focused at a point just beyond her shoulder. "You know I'm interested in people who do daring, foolhardy things." He swung his attention back to her. "People like you. I admire you for pitting yourself against the odds. But Courtney's pregnant. She's not the only one who could get hurt. She should be thinking of the baby."

Kelsey met his eyes steadily. She still didn't know where he drew the line between observing life and living it. His attitude about Courtney brought the edges into closer focus. "You could tell her that. But I think you should give her credit for thinking it all through for herself. You heard Bliss. They consulted a doctor. They go slow. I'm sure they wouldn't ride under hazardous conditions. I doubt anything you could say would change their minds."

"You admire her, don't you? For you, that element of added risk gives their trip some kind of special appeal." He made it sound like an insult.

"Please, credit me with a little common sense. I think danger for its own sake is stupid. But adults should be allowed to make their own choices. In this instance, I would do exactly the same thing."

"What if she gets in an accident and loses the baby?"

"What if you get in an accident and die? If you believed that could happen, you wouldn't be here."

Although Courtney and Bliss were still talking to Rob, both had straddled their bikes. Rob was refastening a bungie cord around his sleeping bag and the tent. Mike watched him for a moment, then dropped his attention back to Kelsey. "I know nothing I say will change your mind. But you're wrong. In a situation like this, there's too much risk."

Rob finished and flashed a grin at the Iversons. When he turned to Kelsey and Mike, a fleeting cloud shadowed his eyes. Since Mike's expression was grim with frustration, Kelsey didn't blame him.

"You guys coming?" he called.

She smiled to deflect his concern. "Sure."

It didn't work. His glare sharpened, then he shrugged and threw his leg over his bike. Flinging his arm forward in a theatrical gesture, Rob pointed down the road. "Wagons, ho!"

Courtney's soft laughter lifted onto the breeze and dissipated. Bliss waited for his wife to start, then followed her onto the road. Rob, Kelsey knew, would wait for her.

Well, she couldn't appease both men at the same time. She wasn't sure she wanted to. As far as she could see, Rob had no reason for resenting Mike, and Mike had no right to criticize the Iversons.

Mounting, she wondered if his concern for Courtney wasn't an example of the empathy that forged his fascination with risk takers. In every example of his work that she'd seen, he made the viewer feel a part of the subject, a part of whatever activity he photographed. Knowing the man behind the camera, she saw the contradiction between his opinion about risk and his fascination with those who pursued it. It made him complex.

Was that why he intrigued her so much? If so, she should throw reluctance to the winds and grab whatever he offered. Wasn't that what she'd decided? To find someone firmly rooted to the ground? Now she wasn't so sure. Mike didn't seem able to accept even the most minimal of risks. If they were back in Portland, living their normal lives, they probably wouldn't look twice at each other.

But they weren't in Portland, and wouldn't be again for over two months. Glancing over her shoulder, she saw him watching her as he rode.

THEY STOPPED at several scenic spots before leaving the park, and of them all, Kelsey liked Inspiration Point the best. Overlooking the Grand Canyon of the Yellowstone, breathtaking vistas stretched as far as the eye could see in three directions. The fire hadn't reached this part of the park, so she could almost pretend the world was still perfect.

The height of the cliffs brought back feelings of power, excitement and vigor, emotions she hadn't felt since her accident. Looking down, she remembered how it was to be airborne, to soar on currents high above the earth, hearing only the sound of the wind.

Mike fixed a long lens on his camera, but stayed well back from the edge. Kelsey was glad. She had to come to terms with wanting something she knew wasn't good for her. At least, something that wouldn't be good for her in the long run. Unless she was willing to accept saying goodbye to Mike once they reached Maine, she should keep Rob and his protective animosity firmly between them.

Rob walked with Bliss and Courtney as they wandered hand in hand along the trail, pausing at each sign that explained the view. For a while Kelsey stood by herself at the rail. She let her eyes drift to the mountains across the gorge. Far to the north a thunderhead towered into the sky. In the sun it looked white and peaceful, a shifting sunlit monument built from water and ice.

She looked down into the canyon, its sheer cliffs ending in the rushing river hundreds of feet below. Only the steel-and-rock railing held people back from disaster. It was easy to draw a parallel with her own situation. Unfortunately in real life it was hard to recognize a precipice, and there were no protective barriers. Only feelings and fears.

When Kelsey turned, she found Mike watching her. He sat about twenty feet away, his forearms propped on his knees and his camera, cradled expertly, negligently, in both hands. Impulsively she skipped over to him, caught his hand and tried to pull him toward the railing.

"Come and see the view! It's too wonderful to miss. The colors and the distances. It's not the same as flying, but it's probably as close as you could come and still stay on the ground."

With a reluctant grin he shook his head. "It's closer than I like, thanks."

She challenged him with laughter in her voice. "Chicken."

"Damn right."

"Come on, there's a nice, sturdy railing for you to hold on to."

He shook his head firmly. "Give me a break, Kelsey. The last time I followed you, we ended up in the river."

"This time there's a fence."

His eyes were blue and light with laughter, but he stood his ground. "Heights and I don't get along well. Of course, I don't expect you to understand, since you've never been afraid of anything."

She stopped. Did she really seem that confident, or were his words only part of the game? Of course, fears came in many shapes and forms. Her own anxieties were strong enough that she could hardly belittle his.

"I do understand, although I don't know how you feel. If you'd like to leave here, we can."

With a wave of his hand he dismissed the idea. "Go enjoy it. I'll stay back here and watch you."

"Why are you really here, Mike," she asked suddenly, "if you don't like the best parts? It's as if you have some ulterior motive."

Mike arched a brow and met her eyes directly, but he didn't smile. "I do."

There it was again, that wild flare of longing. Their opposing approaches to life seemed suddenly irrelevant. This was man and woman, reaching for each other in the most primitive way. She swung her head away, holding back the need to touch him.

He slid his hand around her neck and sifted his fingers through her hair. "I'm going to make love with you, Kelsey. Soon."

"Don't, Mike. Please. Let's just go on as we are for a while."

"How long is a while? A day? A week?" The play of his fingers on her skin sent flames of desire coursing through her veins. If they'd been alone, in spite of all logic to the contrary, she'd have turned to him.

And then she'd have had to face the consequences, whether or not she was prepared to.

He dropped his hand and she felt bereft. "We're walking a fine line, Kelsey. You want us to be friends. So do I. I want us to be lovers. So do you."

What would it take for her to conquer her fears? "Yes."

"When the time is right, it will be easy."

She searched his eyes and found promise. She wished she could accept it without qualms. Thoughtfully she returned to the rail without him.

Mike was different from any man she'd ever known. Rob, of course, had always matched her stroke for stroke in any adventure. Except for work, Blaine never stayed in one place long enough to take a deep breath. And Alan. If anything, Alan had kept a step ahead, sometimes pushing her even farther than she wanted to go. At least Mike wasn't like that.

Kelsey knew Mike confronted life aggressively. She'd seen it in his office and the way he dressed, in the way he'd come back to rejoin them and the way he assaulted her defenses. But he had different objectives; he placed his emphasis in areas unfamiliar to her.

When she turned back to him, he had his camera pointed at her. She made a face and heard the whir of his shutter. Laughing, she struck a Marilyn Monroe-type pose, one hand behind her head and her hips thrust forward. In her touring shorts and jersey, that one would be particularly ridiculous. She stuck her tongue out at him.

"Have you finished risking your neck at the edge of the cliff?"

With another quick glance at the view, she nodded. "I wish you'd come take some pictures of it for me."

"Not a chance."

As they returned to their bikes, she looked up at him. His eyes were still clear and blue. Deep.

"Have heights always bothered you?"

"Ever since I can remember. Have they always fasci-nated you?"

She grinned. "Ever since I can remember. Shall we catch up with Rob and the others?"

"Do we have to?"

A simple enough question, said lightly. She decided to ignore the ramifications. Letting her laughter drift behind her, she turned up the path in the direction Rob had gone.

Hearing Mike behind her, she felt a little like the teasing girls in stories who want their men to chase them and expect to get caught.

FOUR DAYS AFTER LEAVING Yellowstone, they reached the summit of the Powder River Pass in the Bighorn Mountains. Rob got there first, then Kelsey, then Mike. Bliss and Courtney were somewhere behind, separated by the steepness of the grade.

The ride across the Bighorn Basin had been uneventful, and the climb up the west side of the mountains difficult. In fact, it had taken two days to make the summit, which a sign said was 9,666 feet. A cold wind blew down from mountains still towering high above them. Mike pulled his windbreaker on.

Rob's eyes lit up when he looked at the road going down. "This one's going to be a record breaker."

Mike shuddered, but kept his reaction to himself. The way Kelsey and Rob took descents made the hair on the back of his neck prickle. He knew they were sure and competent, but the pace gave him a sick feeling in the pit of his stomach.

"What's our best speed so far?" Kelsey asked.

"Forty-two. We hit that coming down out of Yellowstone." Rob had a bike computer on his handlebars that provided all kinds of fascinating data. Kelsey, to Mike's surprise, didn't own one.

"Wanna race?" Her eyes gleamed as she tightened the strap on her helmet.

Just below the crest of the summit, a sign warned trucks of the steepness of the grade, then the road below them curved sharply out of sight.

"It looks dangerous," Mike said.

Kelsey only laughed. "I know you. You're the guy who doesn't like speed." She touched his arm, her smile as alive as it'd been that day on the river. Perhaps danger was one of the essential elements needed in her diet. "Relax. It'll be great. Just stay in the center of the lane to avoid debris on the right and prevent cars from passing on the left."

"Maybe I'll wait for the others."

"Whatever you want."

What he wanted was to make sure that she got to the bottom of this mountain safely.

On the other side of her, Rob wheeled forward. "Come on. Let's go."

Kelsey sent Mike a sparkling smile before joining her brother. It was stupid and he'd hate it, but Mike decided to follow them.

Leaning over on the drops with his hands gripping the brakes, he pushed off in Kelsey's wake. Within seconds he was overtraveling his pedals and fighting to keep his center of gravity stable. He applied his brakes on the first bend, and she shot ahead of him. Determined not to let her get out of sight, he loosened his grip. Probably only because he weighed more and could coast faster, he gained on her.

Picking up momentum all the way and working with the weight of his packs, he managed to keep Kelsey and Rob in sight. Pressure built in his forearms and wrists; his neck and shoulders tensed. He marveled that anyone could enjoy this. The wind whipped his face and whistled through his helmet as they flew around the curves in a wild, terrifying thrust of speed. Kelsey let go a whoop of excitement, and the wind carried it back to him.

They raced around a hairpin turn, and Mike spotted a truck in the lane ahead. He tightened his hands, making the brakes sing against the rims. For a breathless minute the weight of his packs seemed to carry him along. He gripped tighter, his heart in his throat, and held the bike steady until the brakes grabbed.

Ahead of him, Rob swung toward the middle of the road to pass the truck. Suddenly a car came around the curve in the opposite direction.

Mike heard Kelsey scream Rob's name. Rob clung to the center yellow line, the truck on his right, its brake lights flashing, the car coming fast on his left. There was no room for error on either side.

Oh, God, Kelsey. No!

She held back, practically riding the truck's bumper. Mike couldn't help her and he couldn't stop. His own pace demanded his total attention. He leaned as hard as he dared into his brakes, trying to watch Kelsey and the road and the truck all at the same time.

She was okay.

He loved her.

He never wanted to experience such terror again.

Within seconds Rob disappeared ahead of them. The truck continued on, and to Mike's relief, Kelsey held her brakes the rest of the way down. His hands cramped, and his shoulders ached. Adrenaline and emotion pumped crazily through his veins. He couldn't erase the images of disaster from his mind.

At the bottom they found Rob pulled off the road, standing beside his bike and calmly drinking from his water bottle.

"What a ride!" he yelled when Mike and Kelsey came up to him. Exultation filled his eyes.

"You're insane," Kelsey said without a trace of recrimination in her voice.

"Forty-seven miles an hour! I couldn't believe it when I passed that truck. You should have seen the look on the driver's face!"

"You should have seen the look on mine. I thought you were a goner."

Inside Mike fear surged into anger. His world turned red, hard and dangerous. He let his bike drop to the ground and advanced on Rob. "You fool! You could have been killed. I'd like to rip you apart." He grabbed the front of Rob's jersey, wanting to force the other man's smile down his throat. Never in his life had he felt such raw, elemental fury. "What if you'd been hurt? *What if she had?*"

"Mike!" Kelsey jerked on his arm with both hands. "Stop."

"That was the stupidest thing I've ever witnessed," he continued. "Hasn't she been through enough already?"

Rob tore free of Mike's hold and bent forward aggressively, his legs spread apart. "What the hell business is it of yours?"

Instead of answering, Mike swung at Rob. Rob ducked, then drove his fist into Mike's chin.

Mike staggered and Kelsey darted between them.

"Stop! Both of you!"

Rob elbowed past her. "Clear out, Kelsey, this is between me and him."

"No! Rob, oh, no!" She threw herself against Mike's chest, pushing him back. As if from a distance, he heard her sob. "Damn you. Damn you both."

With Kelsey pressed against him, Mike's vision began to clear. His chin hurt like hell, and two paces away Rob still clenched his fists for combat.

But the main thrust of his anger was gone. Looking down at Kelsey, he saw that the color had drained from her face.

Her skin was damp with sweat and her lips were white. Her beautiful eyes were dark and wet with tears. In them he read fear, the kind of fear that had nothing to do with physical risk.

But she was whole and unharmed. He pulled her against him, as if needing a tactile reassurance.

"God, if anything happened to you."

Her helmet bumped into his, but he didn't care. He brushed his lips across her cheek and down toward her mouth.

She pushed against him, hard, but instinctively he tightened his hold.

"You're mad! It's not Rob's fault, and he's not responsible for me. I make my own choices. Besides, Rob...Rob came closer to getting hit than I did." By the time she finished, her voice was only a harsh whisper.

Suddenly Mike felt sick. Never in his entire life had he wanted to hurt someone else. Never had he used force to solve a problem, and the only thing he'd accomplished was to cause Kelsey more distress. Guilt engulfed him and he stepped away.

"You're right. I'm sorry."

Rob stepped forward, his expression a mixture of reserved hostility. "Next time, watch whose business you go sticking your nose in."

"There won't be a next time." Between the ride down the mountain and his attack on Rob, Mike had learned a great deal about himself, and most of it he didn't like.

IN SILENCE THEY WAITED for Bliss and Courtney. Kelsey sat off by herself, her back against a tree, her thoughts in turmoil.

Damn Mike! No one got hurt. Why had he made such a big deal out of it? Why, when they were fighting, had she run to him instead of Rob?

A tear trickled down her cheek, and she wiped it away impatiently. Maybe she should find a way to make him go home. He upset her equilibrium, he confused her, he made her want things. They were an awfully long way from Maine.

Hearing footsteps behind her, she looked up expecting Rob. Instead it was Mike.

He held out his hand to her. "Come for a walk with me."

"I'd rather not." In fact, she could think of a dozen things she'd prefer to do.

"We need to talk."

"There's nothing to say."

"Isn't there? I need to apologize, if nothing else."

"Mike—"

"Come on, Kelsey." Without waiting for agreement, he took her hand and pulled her to her feet. Moving into the trees, they climbed away from the road. Soon the noise of the occasional traffic faded into the background.

When he stopped and turned toward her, his eyes were dark with emotion. "I'm not feeling very proud of myself at the moment."

"Perhaps it would be better if we didn't discuss it."

He shook his head emphatically. "No. I need to clear the air on this. I don't usually go around striking out at someone who makes me angry."

Involuntarily she touched his chin where it was beginning to darken into a bruise. "I'd say you got the worst of it."

Almost instantly his hand covered hers, holding it against his face. "Maybe next time I'll think before I attack."

She saw more than regret in his expression. Guilt was there, and so was fear, neither of which she fully understood and both of which annoyed her. The facts were clear. Mike had made an ugly scene, Rob hit him, Rob was still mad. But he'd get over it. Where they went from here was also clear. By tomorrow it would probably all be forgotten.

She pulled her hand free of his. "Apology accepted. Shall we go back now?"

Before she could walk away, he caught her hand. "You don't understand, do you? You're only looking at what I did, without considering what you did."

Letting go of her, he paced away. "To you, that ride was a game. A chance to court death and win. To me it was like watching the destruction of everything that's good." His eyes turned still darker as he talked, and suddenly he slammed his palm against the nearest tree trunk. "You know what I saw? Just as if it were actually happening, I saw you hit that truck and fly off your bike onto the road. When you kept riding, it took me a second to catch my bearings. And Rob! Urging you on, then bragging about it."

"Mike, life is risky."

"After what you've been through, how could you put yourself in such jeopardy again?"

"Why do you think I'm taking this trip? To test my strength and endurance, certainly, but also to prove I can still take risks. I refuse to spend the rest of my life afraid."

Placing both hands on her arms, he looked down at her. "I refuse to spend the rest of my life without you."

Joy rose inside her like a bird in flight, only to fall like sudden death to the ground. No matter how much she was attracted to Mike, no matter how much she wanted to believe there might be a future, today had proven how wrong it would be. Maybe she would never again want a relationship with someone as obsessed with turning life into a game as Alan had been, but Mike stood on the opposite end of the scale. Kelsey found that equally unrealistic.

"Rob will be wondering where I am." As a protest, it didn't work.

Mike slipped his hand into her hair and brushed it back away from her face. His touch was so gentle, so tender, it brought tears to her eyes. What would it be like to love him, just once, and know the happiness he could give her? If she could only believe they'd have anything to build a future on after this trip was over.

"Once upon a time, a very wise woman gave me a stirring lecture on risk. I believed everything she said, and I thought she did, too." His lips touched her forehead, and she could smell wind and sun and perspiration on his shirt. "What are you afraid of, Kelsey?"

Uncertain, she turned away, and to her relief he didn't try to stop her.

When she got back to the road, the Iversons were with Rob.

"Hey, Kel. Come look at Courtney's chain, will you?"

"What is it?"

Courtney smiled apologetically and pointed to the chain stay. "I don't know. It just started dragging. It clinks on this bar here when I stop pedaling."

"Unload your gear, and I'll check it out."

"Can you?" Courtney asked incredulously.

Kelsey laughed and turned to get her tools from the wedge pack under her seat. "I can try."

It was something to do, something to concentrate on. Kelsey forced herself to focus on Courtney's derailleur. Rob held the back wheel off the ground while she turned the pedal. Unfortunately, even under adverse conditions, the job didn't require her full attention. Her mind kept wandering to Mike.

He and Bliss were standing off to one side, watching and talking quietly. Shorter and thinner than Mike, with nondescript features, Bliss didn't draw much attention to himself by his presence. But Kelsey had watched him with Courtney. Theirs was a good kind of low-key relationship, and obviously successful. No two people could travel and work together the way the Iversons did without totally loving each other.

Kelsey stood up, brushing the dirt off the seat of her shorts. "There you go. I think I got it, but just to be sure, I'll follow you for a while. Work through the gears a few times even though the road looks pretty level, okay?"

"Gee, this is so neat of you." Courtney began reloading her gear, and Bliss came to help her. "It's great that you knew what to do and had the tools and everything. I'm really lucky that we were riding with you when this happened. Otherwise, I don't know what I'd have done."

It was the most she'd ever heard Courtney say at one time. With a shrug Kelsey put her tools away. "You could have ridden with a problem that small for a long time. I'm just glad I could help."

When they were on the road again, Rob held back with Kelsey. Mike stayed with Bliss, obviously continuing their conversation.

"Look," Rob said almost immediately. "I've been thinking about what happened, and as much as I hate to admit it, maybe Mike was right. Either one of us could have gotten hurt."

"That was a fluke, and you know it. We've done lots of runs like that before."

"You'd flown a hundred times before you crashed, too."

"People get killed in cars even when they're wearing their seat belts." The argument was getting old. Kelsey had restated the same things too often lately. And now she was saying them to Rob, the one person she shouldn't have to convince.

"It's not worth the risk. Let's just take it easy from now on. Okay?"

She shrugged. "Sure." It seemed strange that she should be the one most unconcerned about danger. By rights, her accident probably should have made her overly cautious. She certainly didn't feel invulnerable anymore. It was just that the trip tended to reaffirm that she couldn't lock herself away from life. There were too many adventures out there still inviting her to pursue them. So why couldn't she treat her attraction to Mike the same way?

Chapter Ten

When they left the Bighorns, they left the Rockies. The Great Basin stretched out before them, flat and grassy almost as far as the eye could see. In Buffalo, a little town in the middle of Wyoming, they realized they had two choices: make a loop up into the northeastern corner of the state or follow the interstate. According to the map, going by interstate was thirty miles shorter, but there wasn't even a dot to indicate a town. They decided to take the state road.

After twenty miles Kelsey began reminding herself that at least they weren't being passed by eighteen-wheelers. Twenty more, and she was sure she'd seen enough barren plains to last a lifetime.

Even in spite of the relative flatness of the land, the group began to spread out. When Rob got so far ahead that she couldn't see him, she glanced back to see how far behind the others were. She couldn't see anyone else, either. She shifted into an easier gear to spin for a while, hoping Mike would soon catch up. After five minutes she considered backtracking, then decided that might imply things she wasn't ready for. Instead she pulled off the road to stretch and get a drink.

She rolled her bike into what little shade an ancient clump of sagebrush would provide and took her binoculars out while she waited.

Nearly twenty minutes later, when Mike finally came into view, relief drained through her body and she discovered she'd begun to worry. She didn't stop to wonder why she wasn't equally worried about the Iversons.

When he got close enough that she could see his face, she waved. He immediately pushed into a sprint. When he came abreast of her, he leapt off his bike before it came to a complete stop.

"Are you okay?" he asked breathlessly, hurrying to her side.

"Of course. Why wouldn't I be?"

With a sheepish grin he shook his head. "No reason, I guess."

"I was just waiting for you."

"Oh, were you?"

"And bird-watching," she added quickly.

She caught a glint of something in his eyes, and then he was sitting beside her. "All right. And what have you found that's interesting enough to sit here in the sun?"

Kelsey handed Mike the field glasses and pointed to a flock of birds, circling and swooping as they feasted on insects.

"Swallows mostly, but the larger ones are swifts."

"They all look the same to me."

"The swifts have white throats."

"White throats?" He adjusted the focus and leaned forward to rest his elbows on his knees.

Scooting closer, she pointed and described until he saw the difference. Eventually he handed the binoculars back to her.

"Fascinating." He'd fixed an expression of awe on his face, but it was the hint of sarcasm in his voice that gave him away.

With a light laugh she stood up and brushed off the seat of her shorts. "You asked."

His laughter mingled with hers. "You're right, I did." Standing, he touched her cheek. "You don't miss much, do you?"

Where he was concerned, no, she didn't miss much. She just wasn't sure her interpretation was always correct. Right now, for instance, he was looking at her with such intensity she could believe he wanted her, maybe even cared for her. Or was he still just intrigued that someone who liked speed also had the patience for bird-watching?

"I think we'd better go," she said, putting her binoculars away. "Rob will be wondering what happened to us."

"And we certainly wouldn't want him to add two and two together and get five, would we?"

"No," she said firmly. "We wouldn't."

About the time Kelsey was thinking a lunch stop would be nice, they caught up with Rob. He sat with his legs hanging over the edge of a culvert that allowed a thin, muddy creek to run under the road. Courtney and Bliss didn't show up for nearly an hour, and by then it was time to hurry on.

The afternoon was just more long, empty stretches of road, except the sky began to cloud over. Kelsey considered that a blessing. Water stops were farther apart than she liked, and they would probably drink less if the sun weren't beating directly down on them.

About three the wind began to blow. Hard. It came from the southwest, hitting them almost head-on. It was like riding against a twenty-mile-an-hour resistance shield, and the gusts blasted them with sand. After half an hour of fighting it, Kelsey stopped and got out her map. Rob had again pulled so far ahead she couldn't see him, which meant she wouldn't be able to discuss alternatives with him. Still, she wanted to know what she was up against. To keep the map from blowing back on itself, she turned away from the wind.

Mike, who had stayed with her most of the day, pulled alongside her.

"Any idea where we are?" he asked.

"From the mile markers and the map, I'd guess we're still twenty miles out of Gillette."

Without getting off his bike, he rested his hand at the base of her neck to look over her shoulder. "With nothing between here and there."

His glove was damp with perspiration, but his fingers were dry and she could feel each one of them as they gently massaged her skin. It felt good, heavenly, easing away some of the tension of riding against the wind. Without thinking, she leaned back so that her shoulder rested on his chest. The pressure on her neck increased, sending soothing waves of relief down her spine and across her shoulder blades.

"The wind will slow us down, but we don't have a whole lot of alternatives." She glanced at her watch. "We should still get there before sunset."

"How far behind us do you suppose the Iversons are?"

"Who knows? They're slow under good conditions." She straightened to slip the map back into its pocket. "I guess we'd better go on."

He half turned her toward him. "Or we could take advantage of being together and alone."

Oh, yes, they could do that. A gust whipped sand against her cheek. The sparse grasses bent almost flat. "Here? Now?" In spite of herself, she laughed.

Bending closer, he brushed his lips across the back of her neck. "Sometime soon."

"Mike, I'm not sure—"

"What are you afraid of, Kelsey?"

She injected a note of lightness into her voice. "Only that I'd lose my shirt to the wind if I took it off."

That made him chuckle. "I wouldn't care."

"No?" Another gust, stronger this time, pelted them. "You'd lose yours, too."

"I could live with that."

Because of the direction of the wind, she couldn't turn to look at him without getting dirt in her eyes. "I think we'd better go."

"Kelsey—"

She wanted him so badly she could taste it. And if it were a physical challenge, she'd rise to it without hesitation. Why, when it came to her emotions, was she afraid of an uncertain future? "The weather's only going to get worse."

"You're right." Without another word, he pulled away and pushed off. Swearing silently, Kelsey followed. She knew it might be days, even weeks, before they were alone again. Maybe with Mike one chance was all you got. She didn't know him well enough to second-guess him.

He stayed in front, breaking the wind. With each mile the sky became darker, more foreboding. The storm continued to build, requiring the ultimate effort to make each turn of the pedals.

Suddenly thunder cracked almost directly overhead, and lightning slashed through the sky. With no more warning than that, rain washed down on them in torrents.

Mike pulled back beside her. "Let's stop. We can put up my tent for cover."

Fighting wind and rain, it seemed to take forever to slide the poles through the channels and stake the tent. By the time they got their gear safely inside, they were both soaked. The storm brought an early dusk, making everything dim and shadowy.

Kneeling there, dripping wet, Kelsey looked at Mike. Blinking the water out of his eyes, he pulled off his shoes and socks and tossed them distastefully into the corner of the tent. His hair lay wet and flattened on his forehead, his jersey clung to his chest, clearly defining every line of muscle, and the slope of his shoulders indicated fatigue. She could sympathize; she felt exhausted. Struggling with wet nylon in the wind, the rain so dense she could hardly see, had drained most of her energy away.

Mike looked at her and smiled. "You look like a drowned cat," he said.

Since that was exactly how she felt, she started to laugh. She sat flat on the floor of the narrow tent and let a humor born of fatigue roll out of her.

To her delight, Mike started to chuckle, too. His laughter mingled with hers, and it seemed as if they'd crossed a line of demarcation. Suddenly she was in uncharted territory, and none of the rules she knew continued to apply.

When his hand curved around her neck, drawing her against his chest, she went without hesitation. On contact, water squished out of both their jerseys, which made her laugh still harder. She leaned against his shoulder and wriggled her toes, and water seeped from her shoes, mixing with the mud they'd tracked in.

"Your tent will never be the same," she said.

"Not because of the rain," he said, "but because you're in it." He bent closer and pressed his mouth to hers.

Electricity flared between them, more potent than the lightning flashing in the distance. It ignited the carefully banked embers of her repressed desire, and she could no longer hold the flames at bay.

Eagerly she wound her arms around his neck and accepted the promise of his lips.

He skimmed his mouth over her cheeks and down her neck, then up to her ear. Leaving a trail of heat, he tasted and caressed, his lips molten against her skin.

As her flesh came alive, she shivered in response.

Still holding her, he drew slightly away. "We've got to get you warm."

"I'm not cold."

"No?" His chuckle, rich and warm and inviting, washed over her like a tropical sun. "Just wet?"

Before she could protest, or even think about it, he pulled her jersey over her head, then took off his own. Without a word his mouth found the pulse point in her neck as he took her into his arms again. His chest felt damp and chilly against her breasts, but heat coursed between them. An ache, too powerful to ignore, expanded inside her. Responding, she wrapped her arms around his neck and pulled him closer still.

From her scalp to her toes, her body tingled; she felt alive, whole, wonderful. His kisses fell on her bare shoulder, her neck, the curve of her breasts, and a deep, soft chuckle rose in her throat.

Mike rolled her onto her back and looked into her eyes. "I love to see you happy."

"Oh, Mike. Mike." She plunged her fingers into his wet hair and pulled his face down until his lips met hers. Hungrily she tasted, explored, let her tongue seek the pleasures of his mouth.

His hands roved all over her upper body. Wherever he touched, he awoke nerves that had forgotten how to feel. Her shoulders, her sides, her breasts, her stomach. She arched toward him, letting feeling alone guide her. His mouth slid lower, leaving a trail of fire from her throat to her breast. He took her nipple in his mouth, and pleasure burst free within her.

Her hands traced his body. Absorbing joy with her fingers, like a sponge filling with liquid, she learned the slope of his shoulders, the width of his back, the solid strength of his chest, the narrowness of his hips.

Anxiously her fingers unfastened his shorts, seeking every hidden part of him. A faint moan rumbled from his chest, vibrating through her sensitive nerve endings.

Within seconds they were both completely undressed and he was above her, his mouth seeking hers yet again.

Longings surfaced, newly born feelings guided, demands meshed. Soaring, she opened herself to him, and he took her to heights she'd never before experienced. She wrapped her legs around him, letting the waves of sensation wash over her, lift her, carry her beyond the threshold of reason.

Then slowly, so slowly it seemed as if she were awakening from a dream, Kelsey floated back to reality. She heard the wind whipping at the tent, forcing the rain against the fabric. Inside, it was as dark as night. Thunder rumbled, and she realized she'd been oblivious to the storm roaring around them. The uneven rocky earth bit into her flesh. She began to feel Mike's weight.

When she stirred, he lifted himself on his elbows and looked down at her. Tenderly he brushed her hair away from her face and traced her cheekbone, then her lips. "My beautiful love."

At his words, uncertainty of the future edged back into her heart. For a few brief moments she and Mike had shared a piece of heaven. What if it turned out to be a lie?

Like Scarlett, she would worry about that tomorrow. Tonight she would savor this gift of happiness.

LOVING KELSEY HAD BEEN incredible. She took, totally, yet gave more. The very first time he'd seen her, he'd recognized passion. She attacked life with too much enthusiasm to be limpid. And still, what she'd given him defied imagination. Mike smoothed his hand from breast to waist.

"Not much of a bed, is it?"

"I have no complaints." Her voice was low, sensual and so inviting he felt desire stir again.

"Let's unroll our sleeping bags."

Before she could answer, he levered off her and reached for the closest one. His. By the time he had it open, she'd unzipped her own. She was only a shadow in the darkness, but the way she moved reminded him of earlier times, chance encounters when he'd known only her name, when he'd watched her, moving like a bird in flight or a cat landing on its feet. She was grace and beauty. She was his.

When she spread her bag out flat, he lay down beside her, pulling his over them. As though they'd spent a hundred nights together before, she turned into his arms, and the seeking, needful urgency started again.

This time he wanted to savor her, to let spirit and body merge slowly and completely. But she slid her hand down his chest and circled him with her fingers. The fire roared to life, fully grown and demanding, too strong to fight.

Kelsey loved with her mouth and hands, and with the movements of her body. Mike responded, meeting challenge with challenge, until at last they lay together, sated.

Lightning flashed, too far away to brighten the inside of the tent, then thunder rolled distantly. There were no words strong enough, and none were spoken.

Mike didn't want to sleep. What he felt was too new, too unlooked for to miss any moment of it.

Never before had he experienced anything as wonderful as loving her. She'd let herself go completely, flowing with the emotions, responding to his touch.

In the morning he woke before she did. Pleased, he waited, wanting to learn how she greeted a new day.

She surfaced slowly. First a sensual stirring, a slight shifting of her body, as though making sure every part of it still worked. Then stretching, like a cat. Finally she opened her eyes.

"Good morning," she said.

"The best."

She kissed him, then sat up, keeping the sleeping bag tucked across her breasts. To his surprise and delight, she leaned over and kissed him again. "I like sleeping with you."

Hunger surged through him. Maybe, in twenty years or so, he would grow indifferent to her. For now he wanted to know her again.

Instead he touched her lips with his fingers, traced them, then trailed his fingers down her neck. The coming of the day brought complications he hadn't considered in the dark.

"Kelsey, we didn't do anything to protect you from getting pregnant."

Her expression clouded briefly, then she smiled brightly. "I won't get pregnant."

"That's good." Relief rushed him like a wave. Images of his father jeering at him, criticizing him in front of his friends, swinging his belt in anger. The last thing he wanted was to have that kind of power over another human being. "You have an IUD?"

She twisted away to reach for her panniers, exposing the bare line of her back. It was white, in stark contrast to the tan of her arms and neck. It was sleek and long and lovely. He smoothed his forefinger from her shoulder blade down her spine to the curve of her buttock.

When she stiffened, he dropped his hand.

"Oh, much better than an IUD. I have a damaged body." She tossed the words at him like a joke, but underneath he heard the pain. He wanted to comfort her, reassure her. Her blunt, flippant attitude held him back. One night of passion didn't give him the right to touch a subject so obviously sensitive to her. Yet. In the meantime he'd play it her way.

"Then we have nothing to worry about," he said lightly.

"Not a thing." With her back to him, she pulled a tank top over her head.

"I'm glad." But even as he spoke, he caught a vision of Kelsey carrying his baby. She'd be so beautiful. Impatiently he pushed the sentiment aside. For a dozen reasons the only logical emotion in this situation was relief. He had no experience with long-term relationships, so it was best to take this one a step at a time. Bicycling and pregnancy didn't mix. He'd make a lousy father.

She shrugged into her shorts, and the sleeping bag fell to the ground.

This was not the way he'd imagined their first morning together. No slow rediscovery, no soft words, only a tension he couldn't disperse.

Too much like a stranger, she unzipped the tent and wriggled out into the bright morning.

KELSEY DRANK IN the clear, fresh day. The mountains in the distance seemed like pale silhouettes etched on the horizon. Absolutely cloudless, the sky straight overhead looked indigo, fading to robin's-egg blue near the earth. The sun made the shadows of low, windblown brush stretch long across the ground. Dew still clung to the clumps of short grass.

After such an exquisite night of love with Mike, she should be feeling on top of the world. But she would never, never forget the relief in his voice when she'd told him she wouldn't get pregnant.

So what? He obviously didn't want children, and she couldn't have them. What could be more perfect? Why did she feel so damn depressed?

A meadowlark sang. She spotted it sitting on the jutting dead branch of an ancient sage. Automatically, following the patterns of a lifetime, her spirits began to rise. She waited, and her patience was soon rewarded.

Of all the tiny pleasures nature provided, this one never failed to make her happy. The bird sang again, and she was able to follow its multinote trill. The world *was* perfect. She just needed to let herself tune in and be a part of it. Indulging in depression, especially over things she couldn't change, took too much energy. She drank deeply of the sweet, clean air and let unpleasant emotions slide away.

Behind her she heard Mike leave the tent and turned to him expectantly.

"Listen."

"What?"

"Shh. There! Did you hear it? That's a meadowlark."

His hand settled on her shoulder. To her surprise, he whistled the exact same pattern of notes.

"Mike!" She looked up at him in surprise. "I had no idea. Do it again."

He did, and the bird sang in response.

"I love that."

His fingers tightened slightly, then he dropped his hand. "I'm glad I do something you like."

Lifting her face, she met his eyes. They were gray and somber. "I'm sorry. I have a problem. I didn't need to take it out on you, and I'm not going to dwell on it today."

Gently he cupped her face with his palm. "You could trust me to understand."

She shifted her eyes to the empty road, stretching farther then the eye could see. Trust. Funny how many different levels of existence required it. She trusted the laws of nature, gravity, motion, combustion. She trusted her equipment, her bike, her pack, as long as she checked them regularly. She trusted her family. And she did trust Mike. She'd trust him with her life. She'd trust him with her love. But trusting him to understand the loss she felt?

She hardly understood herself. Four years ago, learning she'd probably never have children had seemed insignificant when compared to being alive. Now she was learning that it still mattered. Especially if a baby could have been Mike's.

It didn't make sense. She should be happy he didn't want something she couldn't give.

She brushed her hand across her abdomen, then pivoted away to crawl back inside the tent.

MIKE HESITATED, wondering if he should follow her. The uncertainty in her eyes had been unmistakable. And he hadn't missed the way she'd touched her stomach.

He closed his eyes against the memories of the night before. Without even trying, he could feel her body under his hands, the lean firmness of her limbs, the soft ripeness of her breasts. She'd been the woman of his dreams; now she was the woman of his life. What would it take to convince her that whatever troubled her would be better faced together?

The meadowlark sang again, and softly he repeated the call. He understood why Kelsey liked it. Even though nothing had actually changed, it lifted away some of the gloom.

Instead he heard the whir of a bike. Turning, he saw Rob riding back toward him.

As soon as he was within hailing distance, Rob called out, "Is Kelsey with you?" He rode up close to the tent.

"Luckily, since you had the tent. How did you fare?"

"I didn't see it coming soon enough to avoid getting wet. How about you?"

Surprised at Rob's neutral tone, Mike responded in kind. He guessed the challenge would come later, after Rob assured himself of his sister's safety. "Nope. Soaked to the skin before we got the tent up."

"It was kind of stupid to get separated by so far."

Kelsey crawled out of the tent and grabbed Rob's arms. "Are you all right?"

"Fine. Starving. You have all the food."

She took a step back and looked him over. Mike felt the old familiar jealousy rise again.

With a light laugh Kelsey shook her head. "Such as it is. I think we have instant oatmeal and oranges left—but not enough water to cook with. We were supposed to make it to Gillette yesterday, remember?''

"Give me an orange before I die from hunger."

Laughing again, she pulled her panniers out of the tent.

Observing them, Mike tried to put his feelings into perspective. Disappointment still ranked at the top. Then came frustration, and finally a sense of being excluded.

Trying to ignore Kelsey and Rob, he ducked into the tent to pack up his gear.

Behind him he heard Rob's voice, in a whisper that carried clearly. "I tried to get back to you. Did he try anything?"

Kelsey didn't answer immediately. Mike could almost see the shadows cross her face as she weighed her words. "I was glad he was close enough to share his shelter," she said at last.

"If he touched you—"

"It'd be nobody's business but my own."

"Look, Kelsey, I've seen the way he looks at you. Some guys don't wait for permission."

Listening, Mike couldn't stop his muscles from tensing. For the second time he wanted to swing out at Rob Sumner.

"Since what you fear the most didn't happen, why don't you just stop playing protector? Mike and I spent the night together in his tent because of the storm. Today I'm fine. I wonder how Courtney and Bliss managed."

Mike's spirits rose. So there were things she didn't share with her brother. Good.

"You don't sound all that fine. Look, if you need to talk—"

"There's nothing more to say, Rob."

"Okay, okay. We have two oranges left? That's all?"

"We can share, and it won't take more than an hour or so to get to Gillette, with no wind."

Mike finished rolling up his pad. The floor of the tent was filthy, and out here in the middle of nowhere, there was no way to clean it. He hauled his panniers and sleeping bag out into the open.

Kelsey brought him the larger part of a peeled orange. "Here." When she handed it to him, their eyes met. Hers were the color of the earth, browns and greens woven together like sage and sand. And distressed over her conflict with Rob. Every instinct urged him to take some physical action to reassure her.

Instead he jammed his free hand deep into his pocket. "Thanks. So what's the plan?"

"We wait for the Iversons, I guess," she said. "Or else we ride back to find them."

"Let's wait," Rob said. "They'll come soon enough." He wandered off a couple of yards and broke a piece of dead branch off a sagebrush. Taking out his pocketknife, he sat close enough to watch and listen.

Mike bit into a section of the orange. It was warm and sweet, and not much of a breakfast. He'd have preferred to ride on, but they couldn't very well leave before the Iversons showed up.

Impatient with the delay, he finished the orange, then started taking down the tent. Kelsey came to help him. Without saying a word, she knew exactly what to do, making it a cooperative effort.

Her hair shimmered like dark gold in the morning sun, shiny and inviting. Her movements were smooth and efficient. But somehow her face seemed more angular, the planes more abrupt. The tension she held inside showed in the set of her mouth.

Impulsively he whistled the meadowlark's song. She looked up immediately, her eyes suddenly brighter.

"That's magic," she said.

"Only if it works."

She smiled. "I guess it does." In a spontaneous gesture, she laid her hand over his. "I'm sorry. I didn't mean to be moody."

Turning his hand over, he closed his fingers around hers. "Let's forget it, okay?"

Lightly she returned the pressure of his fingers, then withdrew her hand. "Sure." She gathered up the scattered poles and folded them into their pouch.

She was a confusing woman. Beautiful, intriguing, exciting, frustrating. But last night he'd made her his own, and no one could take that away from him. Not even her.

Chapter Eleven

Waiting for Bliss and Courtney turned into a patience marathon. While Rob whittled away the time, Kelsey and Mike resorted to playing tick tack toe in the dirt with sticks. The sun crept higher and hotter, and they were miles from any shade.

"It's not that I mind the time, but I think I've got this piece of country pretty well imprinted in my mind," Kelsey said.

Mike shaded his eyes and pointedly scanned the vistas. "Hey, come on. This has got to be one of the premier tourist spots in Wyoming."

"That's why we've seen so much traffic the last two days." She brushed away the old game and scratched another crosshatch pattern.

"You want company?" he asked incredulously. "The way your hair looks this morning?"

That made her laugh. It had dried in a mess and, although she'd brushed it, she hadn't wanted to waste any of their limited water on trying to calm it. Her only consolation was that his looked almost as bad, and so did Rob's.

"Why should I care? I don't have to look at it."

"I'm not looking at it, either." He marked an X in the center square. She put in her O. This would be another blocked game.

"There's got to be something better to do."

Immediately he threw aside his stick and took her hand. "Walk with me."

She let him pull her to her feet. Turning away from the road, he led her through the rough, sparse grass. Peripherally she saw Rob glare after them. She chose to ignore him.

"When I first came west," Mike said, "I couldn't get over how big the sky looked. I guess because you can almost always see from horizon to horizon. And the sky's bluer, especially here where the air's so dry."

She matched her pace to his. "I've never been to the Midwest."

"South America, Europe, the Pacific, but never the Midwest. It's an interesting life you've led."

"That's one of the reasons I wanted to make this trip. To see as much of the United States as I could, as intimately as I could."

"You probably picked the best way for that."

Her hand, enclosed in his, felt warm and comfortable and secure. "Tell me about your family," she said. Suddenly she stopped and looked up into his wonderful gray eyes. "I just realized I don't know anything about your past, except that you grew up in Duluth and went fishing with friends."

With a casual shrug he started walking again. "Not much to tell. My dad's a longshoreman. He works the docks on Lake Superior. My mother's a supervisor on the assembly line of an electronics company. I have two sisters, both younger. Susan's married and lives in Ohio. She has four kids already. Linda's divorced. She and her little boy live a couple of miles from my folks."

"It sounds like a nice family. I bet you have a lot of fun when you get together."

He laughed softly, but without humor. "We never get together."

She stopped again and again searched his eyes. "Mike. Never? Not even at Christmas?" She didn't understand, couldn't comprehend, but his voice held no emotion, no longing. Her family were the most important people in her life. It was a good thing the night she'd spent with him would have no unwelcome repercussions.

His fingers brushed her face. "Not everyone has a happy family, love. We get along much better from a distance."

"Is that why you came west? How old were you?"

"Seventeen. I left the day after I graduated from high school."

"Have you ever been back?"

"Once. When Susan had her first baby. That was nine years ago. I was only twenty-four and had just signed my first big corporate account. It was going to bring me about five thousand a year, so I was flying pretty high. Of course, the baby was the most important thing, or should have been. But it was only a girl. All my dad wanted to talk about was the Super Bowl. Unfortunately I still didn't give a damn about football."

Words, stripped to the bone, but beneath them she heard everything he didn't say. "It doesn't sound like a very congenial reunion."

With another light laugh, this one free of strain, he rested his arm across her shoulders and began to walk again. "It wasn't. And it took me a while to put it in perspective. I was a success. My work was satisfying and so were my hobbies. My value system differed from my dad's, but that didn't invalidate his. He's okay."

"But you haven't been back."

"Not since then. Maybe someday. I keep in touch with my mom."

Knowing how hurt her parents would be if she ever walked out of their lives without a word, Kelsey tried to picture Sunday dinners, one place not set. She could imagine his mother thinking every once in a while about the son who wasn't there, and his father missing the give and take of his only boy.

Before she could formulate any of the questions budding in her mind, Rob called them back.

Turning, they saw the Iversons just dismounting their bikes.

Mike glanced at his watch. "And it's only nine forty-five. Nothing like early to rise."

Kelsey bumped him with her hip. "Be consistent, Mike. You don't think Courtney should be riding, but since she is, you want her to go fast?"

"She probably spent half an hour trying to decide what to wear."

"I think she's got a lot of inner strength, even if she seems indecisive."

Mike snorted. "Maybe I should be grateful they gave me this extra time to be with you."

"Yes, you should be."

Mike stuck close to Kelsey all the way into Gillette. Today, of course, there was no threat of storm, with the sky bright and cloudless. But the fabric of their new relationship, woven so painstakingly, seemed too fragile to leave to chance. It made him feel that if he lost sight of her, he'd lose her completely.

THEY INVITED the Iversons to come to the radio station where Kelsey and Rob would spend half an hour on the air. Since that wasn't scheduled until early afternoon, Bliss and Courtney went off to find the city park and rest for a while. Kelsey watched Mike's face as they rode away, and she saw both concern and impatience. Slowly she was learning he had no use for decisions based on emotion. He preferred logic and rationality. It made his fascination with risk takers all the more intriguing. It made her wonder about the future. Back in the real world, he would have no use for her spur-of-the-moment approach.

Since the trip offered little privacy anyway, she decided to be content with what she had and not wish for more. If last night turned out to be a one-time experience, at least it had been the best.

At the post office Kelsey collected the mail: a pale green envelope, she smiled as she sorted past it; a note from Cindy—Blaine never wrote letters; a blue airmail letter with Greek stamps; an envelope with an Ohio postmark. Her pulse quickened. Mike had gotten something from home. Good. It had been forwarded from Portland and had hit each of their past three mail stops, so it had been en route for well over a week. She hoped the news wouldn't out of date. Last there was an envelope embossed with the logo of Seastone Books in San Francisco and addressed to Mike.

Her eyes widened. She knew he was talented, but she hadn't thought past the magazine features she'd seen. Impressed, she hurried back outside to distribute the mail.

Tucking the Seastone letter indifferently into the back pocket of his jersey, Mike opened the one from home first. Kelsey tried to keep her curiosity to herself while she opened the envelope from her parents, and Rob tore open the one from Angela.

Brimming with news about finishing their work in Greece, Kelsey's mother filled three pages before mentioning the move to Barbados. Kelsey checked the postmark, then counted on her fingers to decide what the date was.

She touched Rob's arm. "Mom and Dad left Greece last Saturday. She sent this letter from the airport. They want to meet us in New York after we finish."

"Sounds terrific," he said without enthusiasm. "Anything else?"

"Not much. What does Angela say?"

With a slight frown he shook his head. "You know what makes relationships suck? Expectations."

She waited for more, but he turned on his heel and stalked away, leaving her to stare after him.

"Bad news?" Mike asked.

"I doubt it was good, but he didn't say. What did you hear from home?"

He handed her a card. A birthday card signed, "Love, Susan."

Surprised, she looked up at him. "When?"

"The seventeenth."

"You were with us then! Why didn't you say anything?"

"It wasn't important."

"Not important? Birthdays are the most important days of the whole year. Better than Christmas, or Halloween."

"Halloween?" Lifting an eyebrow, he took the card and put it back into the envelope. When he looked up again, his eyes were shimmering with laughter. "Halloween."

"A great holiday. One of my favorites."

"I can imagine."

"Don't knock it till you try it."

"I'll bet you still dress up."

"Sure. Don't you?"

Sliding his arm around her waist, he turned her toward their bikes. "No, Kelsey, I don't."

"I wonder why I find that easy to believe. What else did your sister say?"

He shrugged. "Nothing."

"Nothing?"

"I told you, we're not a close family."

"Obviously. She didn't even know where you were. Are you going to write back?"

At their bikes he faced her. "What if I don't?"

Why did she hurt, for him and for his sister? Because she knew what they didn't have? It was none of her business. "That's your choice."

"But you'd be disappointed with me."

She smiled sadly. "I hope I wouldn't judge you. But Susan opened a door. You don't have to be the one to close it again."

"Okay. I'll send her a postcard. But I promise you, we don't miss what we've never had. Now, we need to get to that radio station, or you'll be late."

Not until later did Kelsey remember the letter from Seastone. Mike hadn't mentioned it at all. She wondered what it said.

THE LETTER FROM SEASTONE burned like a brand in his pocket. Even when he wasn't thinking about it, Mike knew it was there. He'd managed to read it while Kelsey was on the radio, and it left him with a bad taste in his mouth.

Darlene Yim was pressing for a deadline. In an incriminating tone, she'd noted the lack of publicity since Boise. She implied he should be contriving more, rather than merely recording the trip.

Mike didn't know exactly when they'd reach Maine. He did know that after he got home, it would take him at least a month to get his photos all developed, to sort and review them, and perhaps two more months to organize the outline and write the text. If he worked on the book to the exclusion of all else.

He knew his first priority at home would be his agency. It might be six months before he finished the book for Seastone, and Darlene sounded as if she wanted it the day after their return.

Worst of all, the letter put the night he'd just spent with Kelsey in a different perspective. *He* knew loving her had nothing to do with writing about her. Would she?

Or would she feel used?

Of course she'd feel used. She'd think he'd come first for the book and that he'd pretended to love her to get her to accept it. At every turn he'd encouraged her to promote the publicity rather than run away from it. In spite of the chemistry that flared between them, in spite of how he really felt, logic pointed to his duplicity.

Reluctantly he decided he had only one choice: to keep a safe distance for a while. Making love with her again would only complicate an already difficult situation. Until he could build a real relationship with her, he'd have to keep sex out of it.

That would be damn hard. Just thinking about her and the night he'd spent with her, his body started to harden. Of course, the way Rob continued to watch over her, there probably wouldn't be much opportunity anyway.

THREE DAYS LATER, after seeing Mt. Rushmore, they parted company with the Iversons. Even though pacing kept them separated most of the time, Kelsey was sorry to see her new friends go. Courtney wasn't much of a conversationalist, but Kelsey still felt an affinity to her.

"Write, okay? Let me know about the baby. You have our home address."

Courtney glanced at Bliss and smiled shyly. "You've been so kind to us. I'll never forget you."

"Gee, I hope not. I thrive on being remembered." Impulsively Kelsey kissed the other woman's cheek. "Just take care of yourself."

By the time all the goodbyes were said and they headed off in the opposite direction, Kelsey had a lump in her throat. The Iversons had qualities she admired and a relationship she envied.

What did it take to make a marriage like theirs? Or one like her parents had? Love and commitment, certainly. But shared goals and similar likes and dislikes, too.

Mike rode ahead of her, and she watched him thoughtfully. Did Courtney's blood sing when Bliss touched her? All day the questions persisted, as steadily as her feet turned the pedals.

And when they stopped to set up camp, Kelsey still had no answers. At supper, sitting across the fire from Mike in a campground at the south end of Wind Cave National Park, she knew he'd become an intricate part of the fabric of her life.

Except for the past three days, he'd been treating her more like a sister than a lover. Which, since Rob was slowly relaxing around Mike in response, was probably for the best. It didn't stop her from wanting, but since the future was so uncertain, she preferred to take things slowly.

It was easier to think of other advantages to having him along. She appreciated his advice. His argument about the publicity had helped her come to terms with it. She now realized that it was only a matter of degree. Neither one of them had anticipated this side effect when Mike joined the trip and began to write about it, but it was too late to turn back.

After her appearance on the radio, they'd looked up the local newspaper. By the time they left Gillette, another fifteen hundred dollars had been pledged to the Children's Medical Center.

Good weather favored them all the way across South Dakota; they raised nearly thirteen thousand dollars in pledges in Sioux Falls, and had dinner at the home of one of the members of the city council.

Mike's attitude began to confuse her. As days lengthened into a week and he gave no indication that he still wanted her, her insecurity grew like a black cloud churned by some distant wind to hang over her and block her sun.

Of course, Rob stayed close, too close for any intimacy. But Mike hadn't let that stop him during the first part of the trip. Before they'd made love.

Whether she liked it or not, she had to face the possibility that he had been repulsed by her body. Even in the dark he would have felt the scars. It was a repugnant thought, but one she could understand. Alan, after all, had also had trouble with her imperfections. But she didn't really believe that of Mike. Or maybe she just didn't want to believe it.

Sometimes at night, when Rob's steady breathing told her he was asleep, she'd replay those hours of passion when only feelings had mattered, when she'd slipped into a dimension separate from reality and tasted the full fruits of what love could be.

Then morning would come, and reason would return. She and Mike had established a comfortable routine with each other. She decided her best course was to accept things the way they were. Then there was no question of what the future would bring.

THEY SPENT a day at a place on the river called Devil's Gulch, where Jesse James had a hideout, then rode on into Minnesota. And it seemed as if the minute they crossed the state line, it began to rain. It rained for two days straight. They rode in the rain, they saw what sights they could in the rain, they stayed at a motel to dry out from the rain, and for the rest of her life, Kelsey figured that whenever she thought of Minnesota she would think of rain. She marveled that Mike hadn't grown up with webbed feet.

Then, suddenly, the sun came out. It wasn't the bright, dry sun of Wyoming, because it had to seep through the humidity generated by a thousand lakes, but it definitely wasn't rain. The roads, though, were still wet enough for the wheels to splatter mud on their legs and gear.

As they approached a town about fifty miles west of Minneapolis, Rob called over his shoulder to Kelsey, "Okay, we've been slumming long enough. Race me to the city limits."

Kelsey pulled abreast of him and slipped onto the drops to lessen the wind resistance. "I'll lose. What kind of masochist do you think I am?"

"Come on. It's just for fun, and we haven't had an all-out push in weeks."

Flashing him a grin, she stood on the pedals for a quick thrust. "Give me a head start!" she yelled.

Once she'd established the rhythm of the ride, she glanced in her rearview mirror. Rob was a wheel length behind, so she geared higher and stood up again, pushing harder as he gained on her. Her heart pounded in her chest, and the sweat gathered on her forehead, but the thrill of the pursuit overshadowed the physical discomforts.

Then she realized he was riding in her draft. He was letting her break wind for him, wearing her down until the end, when he'd pull ahead and sprint to the finish. But it was too late now to change strategy.

She swerved to miss a chuckhole in the road and felt her wheels plane through a puddle. It was insanity, racing along on a rain-wet road, but something in the air, a freshness that washed over her like sun-spun gold, drove her on.

Then from behind, a cry ripped the fragile threads of excitement. In her mirror she saw Rob's wheels fly out from under his bike as it plowed through the water. In less than a second he was down, sliding across the asphalt on his shoulder and hip, his feet caught firmly in the pedals.

Kelsey grabbed her brakes, slipping one foot free to balance herself, and skidded completely around. Rob was on the ground, twisted awkwardly under his bike, imprisoned by his toe straps.

"Rob!"

Pain lined his face as he tried to right himself, and she let her bike drop away unheeded as she hurried to help him. Mike got there first.

"Is anything broken?" she asked urgently.

"Maybe," Mike told her. He took Rob's weight, and she loosened the straps.

Perspiration beaded Rob's forehead, but as soon as his feet were free, he struggled to sit up.

A motorist pulled off the road to help. "Is he all right?"

"We don't know yet," Mike said. "Rob?"

"I'm not dead," he replied grimly.

The man at Kelsey's side chuckled dryly. "Good sense of humor."

"For what it's worth," she retorted.

They got Rob farther off the road, and Kelsey knelt to explore the extent of his injuries. When she smoothed her hand gently down his calf, he winced.

Old remembered agonies racked her body in sympathy, but she forced them back, deep under the surface. "This is going to require some attention," she told him.

"I'll go call an ambulance if you like." For the first time Kelsey really looked at their knight of the road. He was middle-aged, with graying hair, and wore a business suit without the jacket. Just before he left to call for help, she saw concern in his close-set eyes.

"Hey, you guys," Rob protested. "I don't need to go to the hospital. It's probably just a sprain."

"You want to try walking on it?" Mike suggested.

Rob's mouth grew taut at the idea, and he shook his head ruefully.

"Try to relax," Kelsey said. The color had completely drained from his face, and he was beginning to shake with the shock. She scooted around to let him lean against her and to share some of her body heat while Mike left to move the bikes away from the road. "I don't know how long it will take for help to come. How does your arm feel? It's all scraped up, too."

"Right now it's numb."

Kelsey frowned. Rob's road burns looked as bad as any she'd ever seen. With no way to clean even the surface dirt and gravel off his injuries, she felt totally helpless.

To her surprise, the man who had assisted them before returned within minutes. "I thought you might need some help with the bikes," he offered.

Then she heard the wail of a siren.

As it turned out, they decided Kelsey could ride in the ambulance with Rob.

"I'll be there as soon as I can," Mike told them, squeezing Kelsey's hand briefly.

"Just take care of my bike," Rob said.

"Your bike's fine, but I'm afraid your right pannier has a big rip in it."

"Oh, hell. You sure it was my right pannier? Damn. That was my favorite one."

Mike chuckled, but Kelsey only climbed silently into the ambulance. She sat across the narrow space from Rob and held tightly to his hand. The paramedics closed the door, and the vehicle began to move. Because she was watching closely, she could tell that Rob was trying to hide his pain.

Guilt fell over her like a shroud. To race had been stupid, but she'd taken up his challenge. If only she'd refused, they'd have continued at a reasonable pace and Rob wouldn't be hurt.

Chapter Twelve

Rob was still in the treatment room, and Kelsey had almost regressed to biting her nails by the time Mike arrived. He immediately took her in his arms, and much of the weight of her fear seemed to shift onto his capable shoulders. With Mike beside her she felt as if she could handle whatever happened next.

"How is he?"

She shook her head against his chest. "I don't know yet. Oh, Mike, it's all my fault."

His hand smoothed across her cheek and cradled her head closer. "Of course it's not."

"I shouldn't have agreed to race."

"If we could turn back the clock, he shouldn't have suggested it."

"I didn't have to accept."

"Maybe he'd have gone ahead anyway."

"Mike—" She stepped back and he loosened his arms, but he didn't let her go. Tipping her head to look up at him, she tried to convey with her eyes the remorse she felt. "Rob's in there hurt and I don't know how bad, and I'm scared."

"He's going to be all right, Kelsey."

Because she wanted to believe him, she took a deep breath to force away all the worst-case possibilities that kept creeping into her mind.

"It's probably nothing more than a broken leg," she said.

"I'm sure of it." He guided her to a row of chairs with his arm still around her shoulders and sat beside her.

"But he was pretty badly scraped up. Maybe there are internal injuries. Maybe that's why it's taking so long."

"Not likely."

"But we were going so fast!"

"Kelsey." He cupped her chin and tipped her face toward his. "Stop worrying. He'll be fine."

The calm assurance of his voice helped. Some. "What if he *is* seriously hurt?"

He shook his head, but she could see he wasn't totally unconcerned. "He was sitting up and talking to us before the paramedics arrived. He wasn't unconscious or coughing up blood."

His firm logic helped even more. This wasn't the first bicycling accident she'd ever seen, nor the worst. Rob had been wearing his helmet, and he'd been fully lucid after his fall. Mike was right; she was overreacting. But if Rob was badly hurt...

As if reading her mind, Mike caught her hand and brought her fingers to his lips. "Rob will be fine, Kelsey."

"I know." At least, she hoped.

"Thanks to the man who stopped to help us, I found a motel fairly close to the hospital. It'll be a lot easier on Rob if we don't try to camp tonight."

The thought made Kelsey smile. "*That* would have been impossible."

"Hey, Kel. Look at this!" And there was Rob, in a wheelchair, his leg propped up in a cast that stretched from thigh to toes. Kelsey knew his grin was forced.

"Oh, Rob," she wailed, rushing to his side. "I'm so sorry. We're only halfway, and you looked forward to this for so long. Oh, I'm sorry."

He gripped her arm, not too hard but firmly enough to get her attention. "You said that already, Kel. And I don't know what you're sorry about. It wasn't your fault I wiped out."

"I should have had the sense to realize how dangerous it was."

Rob looked past her at Mike. "Has she been carrying on like this the whole time?"

"All the time I've been here," Mike said.

"Hell. I suppose it was your fault the road was wet, too? And that there was a chuckhole?"

Kelsey sighed. Whatever they thought, she knew the lion's share of the responsibility was hers, but there was obviously no point in continuing to say so. She'd get no confirmation, nor absolution, from either of them.

"All right, you win. Let's get out of this place, okay? I'm not overly fond of hospitals."

They took a taxi to the motel, carefully trying not to jar Rob's leg. Thick bandages covered the abrasions on his arm, and that injury made navigating on crutches more difficult. At every tiny moan or groan he made, Kelsey winced in empathy. Her own body remembered too well the immediacy of pain. She could imagine exactly how he felt, and she wanted to cry for him.

It took a while to get Rob settled into bed, then Mike slipped out to leave her alone with her brother. Between the effort and the pain pills, Kelsey could see he was exhausted by the time she pulled a blanket up to his chin.

"Are you going to be okay? Do you need anything else?"

"I'm fine, Kel. Don't hover."

She managed a laugh. "I'm just giving you a little of your own back."

"You were a real invalid. I'm a phony."

"What rot. Agony is agony."

"Look," he said, shifting his weight slightly. "I know you're worried, and I know you'll stay awake all night worrying, and nothing I can say will change that. But I'm fine. Now, will you just leave me alone for a while? I'll take a nice nap, then you can come back and feed me supper."

He made her feel foolish, unnecessary and less anxious all at once. She nodded and dropped a kiss on his cheek.

"If you have to be macho in your misery, far be it from me to interfere. I'll go for a walk or something."

Both their bikes were parked against the far inside wall of the room. Kelsey got her running shoes out of her panniers and sat on the second bed to change. "Do you want to watch TV?"

"No, Kel."

"You understand I won't be near enough to hear if you call, so if you need anything, you better speak up now."

"I don't need anything," he said firmly, but she heard the laughter trying to break free. "Is this really how I treat you?"

"Worse."

"Okay, okay, I get the point. Really, I'm fine."

"I'll be back in a while."

"Make it a couple of hours."

Taking the key and turning off the light behind her, she left him alone while she went to discuss with Mike what arrangements they'd have to make to go home.

WHEN HE HEARD the knock on his door, Mike stretched the phone cord as far as it would reach to answer it, and he still had to hold the receiver an arm's length away from his ear.

It was Kelsey. A sudden burst of love surged through him as he motioned her in while trying to catch the words coming from the other end of the line.

Would he ever get used to the rush of excitement he felt whenever he saw her? Suppressing it—again—he indicated with a wave she should sit on the bed, then he grabbed the pen to scribble down the information coming over the phone.

"One-thirty. Great. Thank you."

Hanging up, he tore the sheet off the pad and handed it to Kelsey. "There's a flight to Portland tomorrow afternoon. It requires a plane change in Denver."

She took the paper, looked at it, then folded it, carefully aligning the corners. "Thanks."

His heart went out to her. Although he'd resented Rob frequently in the past few weeks, he'd gained an appreciation for how intensely Kelsey felt about her brother. This couldn't be easy for her.

"How is he?"

"Fine. He's resting now, and he should sleep all night. The painkillers will probably knock him out."

With one step he eliminated the distance between them and folded her in his arms. She relaxed against him naturally, automatically. Was he a fool? Would she believe him now if he told her he loved her? Would he be able to keep his hands off her if they were alone?

Unfortunately her thoughts were full of her brother. Holding her close, Mike massaged her back and neck lightly. "How are you holding up?"

"Oh, I'm fine. I hate to see Rob hurting. And then not being able to finish this trip."

As soon as she spoke, a wheel began to turn inside Mike's head. He realized they'd all assumed Rob's accident meant they would go home. Why? Of course, the trip had originally been Kelsey's and Rob's together. But just below her distress about Rob's injury, he could hear her disappointment.

"Why do you have to quit?"

She leaned back to meet his eyes. Hers were shadowed, uncertain.

"Rob needs me."

"This isn't the same as when you were hurt. Rob'll be walking on his cast within a day or two."

"It would feel like desertion."

The more he thought about it, the more strongly he believed she should go on. With him. She needed to finish for the sake of her own self-confidence and for the commitments she'd made to promote the rest of her trip. But more than all the rest, he knew as surely as if the answer had come through some spirit guide, she needed to break her dependency on Rob.

He wondered what it would take to convince her.

Glancing at his watch, he decided to let the idea take root before trying to cultivate it. "Why don't we go get something to eat? It's been hours since breakfast, and neither of us got any lunch."

"Rob didn't, either."

"We'll bring back a hamburger just in case he's not asleep." He tipped her chin gently upward. "What do you say? The world will look a whole lot brighter if you're not feeling faint from lack of food."

She smiled up at him, and his arms ached to hold her. For now, however, she mostly needed a little comfort, some humor, a meal.

"I'm so hungry I could eat an extra-large, superdeluxe combination pizza by myself."

"That I've got to see."

With his hand at her waist, he guided her to the door. Visions of what the next few weeks would be like filled his mind. Riding side by side, sharing a tent, learning to know each other better, teaching her to trust him.

Oh, yes. It was exactly what he wanted, and what they needed.

WALKING BACK to the motel with half an unfinished pizza for Rob, Kelsey realized how much comfort she derived from Mike. His touch, his strength, his ability to think clearly when her emotions got in the way. She wished she had something to give in return.

Instead she was going to ask for more. For the past two hours her mind had repeatedly returned to Mike's suggestion. What if they went on together? She tried to separate her deep need to finish the trip from her feelings about spending the next five weeks with him and found the two were inexorably combined. At first, while planning the trip, she'd been scared and uncertain. It looked too big. But between her own determination and Rob's encouragement, they'd made it this far. Now she wanted to finish for the sake of completion. Three thousand miles on a bicycle. From sea to shining sea. After four long years of agony and recuperation.

And she wanted to do it with Mike. If five weeks was all she'd ever have with him, then she'd take it happily.

Of course, the whole idea made her feel guilty. Rob was her brother. They'd rescued each other from scrapes since early childhood. Rob had gotten her back on her feet. Rob was her best friend in the whole world. Right now Rob needed her. His accident gave her a chance to repay him for the past four years.

Except what would the sacrifice gain, and what would it cost?

Mike was right when he said Rob would be walking on his leg in less than a week. It would be a limited mobility, and he'd need some help, but he wouldn't be bedridden. A couple of calls to Portland, and someone would come to the rescue.

Just thinking about it wound Kelsey in knots. How could she even consider it?

Sneaking a glance at Mike, she knew. The road ahead looked rocky with problems. The situation was too unrealistic to believe in an easy readjustment to real life. They still had so much to learn about each other. But for right now she wanted to be with him.

She tucked her hand under his arm. "Mike?"

Slowing his pace, he looked down at her.

"Back in your room, when you suggested I go on, were you volunteering to go with me?"

"I wouldn't let you go alone."

"Why?"

"Because I love you, Kelsey."

She searched his eyes. He'd never said it before; he hadn't acted like it since Wyoming.

"Then why have you been so indifferent lately?"

"You're like an addiction. One taste isn't enough. Rob would not have looked on kindly if you'd started sleeping in my tent."

With a soft laugh she shook her head. "No. Is that the only reason?"

"What other reason do you think there could be?"

That one night was enough for him? That she was afraid he didn't want to look at her damaged body? Faced with saying such words out loud, she realized they all seemed foolish. "None."

Cupping her face with both hands, he kissed her forehead, then captured her mouth. She drank of him, needing to quench the two-weeks' drought. Holding the pizza box out of the way, he pulled her close until her body molded against his. Every inch of her came alive. He renewed her. He filled places she didn't know were empty.

"You're considering it," he murmured.

"I've decided. If I can find someone to meet his plane."

"How about the woman of the green envelopes?"

With her head pressed against his shoulder and his lips whispering against her hair, she felt his chuckle rather than heard it.

"She may not want to."

"Of course she will. Isn't his being gone the whole source of the conflict?"

Kelsey drew back slightly. "How did you know? He hasn't said anything."

With their arms around each other's waist, Mike turned again toward the motel. "I read minds."

"I'll remember that. I think I'll try to call her before I say anything to Rob."

"Yes."

"Will you come with me?"

"He's not going to like it."

"Why else do you think I need your support?"

To Kelsey's surprise, Rob sat propped up in bed watching television. All too aware of what turning it on must have cost him, she accosted her brother.

"You got out of bed! You're supposed to be resting."

He shrugged indifferently. "I got bored. Good, you brought me food."

"Which you don't deserve." But even as she spoke, Mike handed the white box to Rob. "I offered to stay and help you, to wait on you hand and foot, to fulfill your every need. And what do you do? Send me away, then turn on the TV all by yourself."

"Don't be a nag, Kel." With relish he lifted a huge slice of pizza to his mouth.

Mike pulled the one chair the room offered off to the side, out of Rob's direct line of vision. Kelsey sat on the edge of the bed. From her pocket she took the piece of paper on which Mike had written his notations.

"There's a flight home tomorrow. How does that sound?"

Rob levered himself back against the headboard. "Fine. Look, I'm sorry things had to end this way. I'll make it up to you sometime, I promise."

Chewing on the inside of her cheek, she took his hand between both of hers. "What would you say if I told you I wanted to go on?"

His grip tightened around her fingers. "Go on? Alone?"

"With Mike."

With effort Rob twisted around to glare at Mike, then swung back to Kelsey.

"No."

"Why? You know he can ride."

Rob lowered his voice. "He's not good for you, Kel. He'll hurt you."

"You've said that before, but Mike hasn't given me any reason to agree. I told you before, I'm ready to take a chance."

"Kelsey—"

"Please, Rob. You know I wouldn't ask if I thought you really needed me. I called Angela to meet your plane tomorrow."

"You *what?*"

"She said she'd be happy to."

"So she can break my other leg."

"Angela? With what? Her briefcase? Maybe I'll come home with you just to watch."

A smile tugged at the corner of his mouth. "Don't make me laugh, Kel. It makes my shoulder hurt."

"Poor boy."

He sobered and turned her hand over in his. "Are you sure you want to go on?"

"Do you remember before we started, when you said if Mike wrote about me it would give me a reason not to quit?"

"Yeah." The word came reluctantly. She knew he'd regretted that argument many times.

"Well, you were right. All those commitments I've made have become important to me. I need to finish what I've started."

He twisted back to Mike, and she knew what it cost him. They needed to let him rest.

"You'll take care of her?"

Mike left his chair and came to stand beside Kelsey. "You know I will."

"If anything happens, I'll come after you."

"If anything happens, you won't need to."

Rob dropped back against the pillows in silent acceptance of her decision.

With a smile she dropped a light kiss on his forehead. "Go to sleep. We can work out the details in the morning."

GETTING ROB OFF the next day proved challenging. They had to pack his bike and equipment, arrange for transportation to the airport, make sure he would have adequate assistance in changing planes, call Angela Newberry again and let the television station in Minneapolis know they couldn't get there until afternoon.

To Kelsey's relief, the station said they'd like to have her on just after the evening news.

It was harder than she'd expected to watch Rob's plane take off. He'd been both nursemaid and constant companion since her accident, and it felt like losing a part of herself.

"I think it's a good thing we're not riding today," Mike said.

She smiled ruefully up at him. "Why? Do I look that frazzled?"

Like a caress his eyes drifted across her face. They stood facing each other, barely a foot apart, and his hands were plunged deep into the cargo pockets of his shorts. Perhaps it was because she felt so lost without Rob, but she wanted Mike to touch her. She wanted him to hold her close and reassure her that she wasn't alone.

"I'm the wrong person to ask," he said solemnly. "To me you're always beautiful."

"Oh, Mike."

He cupped her face with both hands. "It's okay to miss him, but going on was the right decision to make."

"Promise me that. Promise me he'll be okay."

"He'll be fine. And so will you. You have my word."

"We have five weeks to go." She drew a deep breath and smiled tremulously. "Let's make them the best."

His own smile came lazy and sensuous. "You have my word on that, too."

MIKE COULD FEEL Kelsey's tension the minute they got in the cab to go to the television station. As if determined not to let apprehension get the best of her, she'd been telling him about the time she and some friends climbed Mt. Rainier when she was in college.

He thought about the Rainier book he planned to write and wished he'd known her then, been able to photograph her climb. He took his recorder out and flipped it on. She was so accustomed to it now, she went on with her story without noticing.

Her group had gotten caught in an unseasonal snow-storm, were stranded for two days in a blizzard, kept themselves alive because they were prepared for the unexpected and shared body heat.

As he listened, Mike was appalled that she took the whole thing so lightly. Before, when all he'd known of her was what he caught on film, the reckless confidence in her manner had intrigued him. He'd been seduced by the fire in her eyes.

Now it frightened him. In vivid detail he remembered every second of the spill in the Snake River, the wild ride down the mountain in Wyoming. Loving her made it difficult to deal with such risks objectively. Watching Rob fall had been bad enough. If it had been Kelsey...

The cab slowed to a stop, and Kelsey stopped her narrative in midsentence. Looking at her sharply, Mike knew she would never totally accustom herself to the publicity. She put on a good show, frequently reinforcing the reasons why she'd decided to go on. But she would have preferred anonymity.

Inside they were greeted first by a receptionist, then the producer of the spot, then the interviewer, who was a woman in her mid-forties.

"I'm Jennifer Delaney," the woman said. "We're excited to have you with us." She shook Kelsey's hand, then turned to Mike. "You must be her brother."

"No, I'm Michael Kincaid. I wrote the first articles about the trip, the ones that started the whole thing."

"My brother had an accident yesterday and had to go home," Kelsey said.

"Oh, my. I'm sorry to hear that. Was he hurt badly?"

"He'll be fine."

Because he knew her so well, Mike saw the flicker of pain that crossed Kelsey's eyes. It occurred to him that in leaving, Rob had tied Kelsey to him more firmly than ever. The familiar flare of jealousy rose again. How could he compete with someone two thousand miles away?

By loving her. Suddenly the conflict with Seastone seemed insignificant. He had her, he needed her, he wanted her. He wouldn't be able to spend even one platonic night with her. And this time he'd want it to be in the light, maybe even in the sun. Heat would pour over them and grow inside them. He'd undress her slowly, savoring every minute and watching hunger fill her eyes.

". . . on camera with us?"

With a jolt Mike realized Jennifer was talking to him. "No, I don't think so," he said quickly. "This is Kelsey's trip. I'm just along for the ride."

Kelsey grabbed his hand. "You have to, Mike," she whispered urgently. "I can't do it alone."

"Of course you can. I've watched you. You're always terrific."

"Rob's always been with me."

And essentially he'd promised to take Rob's place, to be for her what Rob had always been. "Okay, then. Tell me what to do."

The interview went well. Since it was short, Jennifer took only a few calls from viewers, but even before the show ended, pledges started to pour in. At least Kelsey had finally adjusted to the money, and Mike saw excitement light her eyes as the total increased.

When the lights dimmed and the camera moved away, Kelsey reached for Mike's hand. "Thanks."

"I didn't do much."

"It was enough."

Jennifer shook both their hands. "The local hospital's excited by what you're doing. If you want to call in the morning, we'll tell you how much you raised. It's too bad you're not going to be here long enough for us to create a full-fledged telethon, but for a cause like this every little bit helps."

Mike watched Kelsey respond as graciously as a society matron who had done things like this all her life, and his admiration increased. He knew she'd hated every minute of the interview and was uncomfortable with the attention. But she did feel strongly about the possibility of helping even one child become more functional.

When they were finally able to break away, she touched his chest and he wrapped his arm around her waist. Outside, the sun was still hot and the humidity heavy. Kelsey looked as if she could use a long bath and dinner in bed.

Instead she drew a deep breath and turned to him with determination in her eyes. "Let's get our bikes and leave now. I've had enough of this place."

"Minneapolis is a great city. We could go for a real change of pace and have a night on the town."

"Is that what you want?" she asked.

What he wanted was to take her somewhere private and make love to her until morning. "I want for you to be happy."

She looked past him at the heavy traffic, the flowing stream of pedestrians, the buildings shutting out the sky. "Let's leave."

THEY RODE north to a quiet, isolated campground on the Mississippi River. The location delighted Kelsey because it was practically in the Upper Mississippi Wildlife Refuge, although it seemed strange to have Rob gone. His not being around would take some getting used to. Not just because she missed him, but for the simple, everyday things like setting up camp. The familiar routine didn't work without him.

She unloaded her panniers and sleeping bag from her rear rack. Something wasn't right. Something was missing. She sorted through her stuff, naming items on her fingers.

The tent. She didn't have the tent. There had to be some mistake. How could she have missed separating it out when she'd gotten Rob's stuff ready to send home with him?

Pivoting around, she saw Mike engrossed in his own preparations.

"Mike?"

From his crouched position, with his tent spread out on the ground in front of him, he looked up.

"I don't have a tent."

"No," he said calmly. "I thought it would work just as well for you to share mine. Then you wouldn't have to carry the additional weight."

Excitement coursed through her. He wanted her. He did!

"Do you have a problem with that?"

Fear engulfed her. It had been dark that night in Wyoming. They'd been driven by passion and the storm. How could he know what she really looked like? How would he react when he saw her scars?

"Of course not." But she knew she'd need a little time to accustom herself to the idea. She'd need to steel herself to accept his reaction to her body, whatever it was. "I'm sure it will be better not to hassle with the extra weight."

Grabbing her binoculars, she glanced at him. He was watching her expectantly, and she wasn't ready to answer his unasked questions.

"I'll be back in a few minutes," she told him.

The late-afternoon sun lit a brilliant swath of orange across the relentless waters of the river, and the occasional song of a bird lilted across the air.

Something about the isolation and beauty of the place tugged at the strings of Kelsey's memory, turning her thoughts to the life she'd led while growing up. With a singleness of purpose her parents had traveled all over the world, exploring new places and writing about them, never letting undue fears interfere. Kelsey and Rob had been raised in an atmosphere of exploration, one of seeking new challenges and overcoming all obstacles that might stand in the way.

Certainly difficulties had arisen, and sometimes plans had to be changed. Once, her parents had decided to leave Belfast sooner than planned; another time they'd been denied visas to a country in the Middle East. And always they'd insisted that current challenges be faced head-on. The

enior Sumners had taught their children that once they
made a decision, they were honor-bound by any commitments that decision involved.

She'd made a decision to go on with Mike. That didn't
necessarily mean she'd made a commitment to sleep with
him, but it did mean she'd accept the challenges that came
her way. And the first challenge was obviously going to be
whether she trusted him to love her the way she was.

Every cell in her body and every impulse of her mind
urged her to believe that he would. That he did.

"Going anywhere special?" At the sound of Mike's voice,
she spun around to face him.

"Just . . . just bird-watching."

"Then you don't mind if I come?" The words and his
tone could have been those of a casual acquaintance sug-
gesting an afternoon stroll together. Only the intensity in
those blue eyes indicated this was more.

This was Mike, asking again if she objected to sharing the
same tent.

"Of course not." She laughed and linked her arm through
his. "Just don't hog the binoculars."

They stayed by the river for about an hour. Returning to
the camp, Kelsey noticed a return of uncertainty. She wanted
this time with Mike as much as she'd ever wanted anything.
She wanted, she trusted, she believed, and yet from somewhere deep inside there remained a niggle of doubt.

As if sensing it, Mike looped his arm over her shoulder
and pulled her close. "Are you still worried about the
sleeping arrangements?" he asked.

"You might have included me in the decision-making
process."

Turning, he took both her hands in his and held them next
to his chest. "It's the most logical arrangement. You were

willing enough to share with Rob. Can't you consider me a substitute brother for a few weeks?''

''No.''

A knowing grin lifted the corners of his mouth. ''Good.''

''Oh, Mike.'' She could feel the rhythmic beat of his heart against the side of her hand, far more measured than the rapid pounding of her own. ''I'm not sure this is a good idea.''

''You don't want to sleep with me? I'll promise not to seduce you.''

She almost laughed out loud at that. Everything about him was seductive. ''You forget, I know how small that tent is. I don't see how we can share it.''

His hands tightened around hers. ''This is what we've both been waiting for. To be alone.''

''Yes.''

''Then accept it.''

When they got back to camp, she saw through the open vents that her sleeping bag was already spread out beside his. It gave her a warm sense that she belonged with Mike, seeing her gear side by side with his. Smiling to herself, she began gathering twigs and sticks for a fire. The evening was warm and pleasant, but she knew they'd want one in the morning for coffee.

His footfalls silent on the soft earth, Mike came behind her without warning. His arms circled her waist as he pulled her back against him. His breath whispered on her hair.

''Do you have a compulsive need to be busy?''

''No.''

''Is there anything specific you need to do in the next hour or so?''

''No.''

Turning her gently, he brushed his lips across her forehead, touched her cheek, found her mouth. "Then come with me."

He led her to the tent. The low, westering sun slanted across their sleeping bags. Once inside, she didn't resist when he pushed her slowly onto her back and bridged her with his body.

"I want to know you in the light," he said.

Chapter Thirteen

Mike kissed her. Before she could reason, her arms circled his neck, pulling him closer.

His mouth moved gently over hers, and when his tongue urged her lips apart, she welcomed the deepening contact. Emotion ran between them like warm mercury, heavy and liquid. Her fingers plunged into his hair, releasing the scents of sun and wind, then trailed across his cheek.

When he lifted his face away, his eyes searched hers. Not blue, not gray, they sparkled with intensity; they probed the depths of her soul. With his fingers spread so that she felt the touch of each one, his hand circled her throat. Sensation flowed outward, washing over her, robbing her of strength and reason. She wanted to drown in what she felt.

Almost without severing contact, Mike stripped off his jersey. "I need you to touch me," he said, coming back to her.

She needed to touch. His chest was broad and toned, with a light sprinkling of dark hair, and tan. Not as dark as his arms and neck, but a rich, wonderful color from occasionally riding without his shirt. Running her fingers from his shoulders to his waist, she let them sift through his hair and linger on his nipples. He was the most beautiful man she'd ever known.

She pressed her mouth to his neck, tasting the salt of his perspiration with her tongue, savoring the texture of his skin.

He unzipped her jersey and traced his fingers along the V, down to the exposed point between her breasts. "I need to touch you," he said.

Before she could object, she was bare above the waist. Instinctively she pressed her arm across the scar that had saved her lung. He took her hand and forced her arm above her head. Pinned, exposed, she watched his eyes. She felt his fingers trace the line left by the surgeon's knife.

"I didn't know you had a scar here. When we made love before, we didn't take the time to know each other's body," he said. "Now we have all the time in the world."

His hands flowed over her like silk, her breasts, her arms, her shoulders, her waist, the scar. It was if he were trying to memorize her with his touch. Eventually she realized the pounding of her heart came more from excitement than anxiety. The scar didn't stop Mike; he didn't mind. He wanted to touch her in spite of it.

"You are an incredibly beautiful woman. I guess finally being able to look at you has been worth the wait. Love me, Kelsey. Please make love with me."

WHEN KELSEY AWOKE the next morning, the sun had not yet brought the day to their tent, but the music of dawn swelled the air. Mike's hand cupped her breast, and his leg weighted hers. She could see the rise and fall of his chest, make out the shadow of his hair falling across his forehead. Softly, to avoid disturbing him, she let her hand float over his shoulder and arm and chest. Love filled her, fuller than she'd ever imagined, because of him, for him. When planning this trip with Rob and hoping to become whole, she hadn't dreamed of such completeness.

"I love you," he said.

Edging closer, she kissed him. "I didn't mean to wake you."

His hand began to move across her breast and down her side. "Don't apologize for something I enjoy so much. According to the calendar, it's been a mere two weeks and six days since I first made love with you. According to my heart, it's been an eternity. I don't want to miss a minute of being with you."

"Will it always be like this?"

"You should know better than anyone that life doesn't offer guarantees. But short of circumstances beyond our control, yes, it can always be like this."

Snuggling contentedly against him, she smiled in satisfaction. "Good, because I will never stop loving you."

Propping himself up on his elbow, he looked down at her. "A promise?"

"If you need one." In the growing light she could see that his eyes were blue, as deep as the sky, as warm as summer rain. His jaw was strong, his mouth sensuous, his expression one she wanted to etch in her memory. She touched the faint line of a scar on his chin. "How did you get this?"

"I fell off my bed when I was about ten years old and cut myself on a roller skate."

Kelsey laughed. She couldn't help it. "You fell out of bed when you were *ten?* What were you doing? Acrobatics?"

"Actually I was sleeping. A thunderstorm came up suddenly in the night. I woke up terrified and screaming. I got tangled in my blankets and fell when I tried to get up. My poor mother, there was blood all over the place."

"So did your parents rush you to the hospital?"

"Mom did. Years later I realized that Dad stayed home because he was embarrassed about having to explain it to anyone. If I'd been in a fight, he probably would have carried me into the emergency room on his shoulders."

Sympathy for the boy Mike had been pulled at her, rejected by his father and left without a role model. Yet from somewhere inside himself he'd found his own strengths and made the most of them.

With her arms around his neck, she pressed her lips against his chest. He folded her close, searching for her mouth, and when they melded together, it was as if all the lyrics to all the love songs blended into a melody written only for them.

THEY FOLLOWED the back roads through Wisconsin for several days, leisurely letting their moods guide them, making publicity stops in both Eau Claire and Wausau. There would be no more until they got down into lower Michigan. It meant they could simply be together.

Riding when they wanted to, they stopped to make love often. Kelsey felt as if she were on a honeymoon, as if the wonder of loving Mike and being loved in return would never wear off.

At a mail stop she finally got a letter from Rob. He mentioned Angela Newberry once, but only to say that she'd been at the airport when he arrived. Kelsey knew she wouldn't learn a thing more until she got home.

Mike got a couple of letters, too. One from Jerry, his partner, which he enjoyed. The other had the Seastone logo in the corner. While reading it, he became pensive, but before Kelsey could ask about it, he'd stuffed it in his pocket.

Obviously he wasn't glad to hear from Seastone. She watched him swing silently onto his bike and wondered why. Maybe this trip was taking too long, keeping him from work he wanted to do for them. Maybe they'd rejected some project he'd proposed.

Either way, she wished he'd share it with her. She tried not to feel hurt that he didn't. She had no claims on him, certainly none that gave her the right to intrude on his privacy.

But didn't love count for something? She'd hoped it would mean they could share each other's joys and sorrows, each other's problems.

Or maybe this wasn't real love. Maybe their relationship would end when they got home and resumed their normal lives. That possibility had been there from the beginning. It had been just beneath the surface in all Rob's arguments. She decided the joy she shared with Mike now was worth it. She decided not to let an unknown future plague the present.

The route through Wisconsin took them through some of the most beautiful country Kelsey had ever seen. Riding, she savored the smells and sounds, the winding curves of the road and the patterns of shade that fell across the road.

She didn't want to hurry. As if her body and her mind conspired to make sure she filled her senses completely, she found herself slowing her cadence. More and more frequently Mike edged ahead. Every half hour or so he'd end up waiting for her to catch up.

She offered no apologies. Instead she'd take a deep, exaggerated breath with her face tipped to the sky. "Savor, Mike. We may never come this way again."

"If anyone had suggested, when we were climbing through the Rockies, that before the trip was over I'd be outriding you, I'd have suggested tests for mental stability."

"Maybe it's the heat and humidity."

Laughing, he wiped the sweat from the back of his neck. "Or maybe you have no staying power. You're worn-out. Washed-up. Finished."

Maybe lethargy slowed her down, but it hadn't changed her. Accepting the challenge in his voice, she pushed off ahead of him, determined to stay ahead for maybe an hour, just to prove a point. Then, if she wanted to, she'd slow down again.

LATER THAT WEEK, while riding through the Nicolet National Forest in northeast Wisconsin, they met up with two other bike tourists. The four of them rode together for the rest of the afternoon. After the few days they'd spent with the Iversons, both Kelsey and Mike decided the two young men were excellent company. They all decided to camp together that night.

But it was only when they were pooling their food supplies for dinner that introductions were made.

"I'm Mike Kincaid and this is Kelsey Sumner," Mike said, offering his hand to the nearest of the two men.

"I'm Dave Milford. Glad to meet you." Dave was shorter than Mike, and his hair was a light brown color, which had probably been very blond when he was little. Kelsey guessed he was a couple of years younger than she.

"And I'm Leon Girard." Thin and dark, Leon wasn't more than twenty-one or two, and he had a constant, contagious smile. Kelsey warmed to him immediately.

"Where are you two from?" Dave asked.

"Oregon. On our way to Maine," Kelsey told him.

"Ah," Leon nodded. "Transcontinental. We're from Quebec." He spoke with a very slight accent.

"So you're French Canadian?" Mike asked.

"Oui." He grinned. "But not Dave, of course. He is Anglo."

"Wrong side of the channel," Dave agreed, giving Leon a friendly punch on the shoulder. "We're touring the Great Lakes, and we'll be damn glad to start heading east again. Of course, we've seen some nice country. No denying that."

"What difference does the direction make?" Mike asked.

"The wind," Kelsey told him. "The prevailing westerlies. It's why we're going from west to east instead of the other way around."

"Don't tell me I've been doing so well because the wind's been at my back? All this time I thought I was king of the road."

Kelsey tucked her arm through his and smiled up at him. "You are. And the wind has nothing to do with it."

"So," Leon said. "You are going across the peninsula of Michigan?"

"We plan to spend several days there," Kelsey told him. "Then we'll head back up toward Maine."

"Say, we know this terrific place to stay." Dave took a handful of maps out of his front pack and sorted through them. When he found the one he wanted, he spread it out on the ground for Kelsey and Mike to see. "In New York, between Fulton and Wolcott, you take this little road. It's not marked, so you have to watch for it. After about two miles, there's a farmhouse, and this old couple lives there. The Ridgeways. Probably early seventies. Real spry. Woman's a great cook. They love to have bicyclists drop in and spend the night. Won't charge you a thing—they just want to listen to where you've been."

"Isn't that out of our way?" Mike asked.

"Well, sort of," Kelsey agreed. "But what are itineraries for, if not to change?"

"You just ride up and say, 'Here we are, feed us'?"

"Yes. It's true," Leon said. "We heard about them from some other bikers. When we left, they told us to pass the word."

Kelsey could see Mike's reluctance, but it appealed to her immensely. She loved exploring back-road places and meeting the interesting people who lived there. She suspected that once they were alone, it would take very little to convince him they should seek out this elderly family. "Hey, these noodles are done. Anybody hungry?"

Over dinner they all exchanged stories of the places they'd been. Dave and Leon had been averaging a little over a hundred miles a day and expected to be back home in about a week. They laughed at Mike's expression of incredulity.

"No, it is not difficult," Leon said. "Perhaps the first day or two. But after that, what is a hundred? Only a couple of hours more than sixty. We have only two weeks—therefore, we must hurry."

Dave, lying back with his head propped on his still-rolled-up sleeping bag said, "You've really got it made. Taking three months and strolling along. What kind of work gives you that much freedom?"

"I'm an insurance agent and Kelsey owns a bicycle shop. We both have people back home holding down the fort."

"Why are you not married?" Leon asked bluntly, thoughtfully. "You seem so, I don't know, compatible."

Kelsey felt her cheeks warm. She felt married to Mike. In fact, she felt as if she'd been married to him all her life. But there were still secrets not shared and feelings not tested. Although Kelsey kept them at the back of her mind, she knew they were there.

"Not yet," Mike told them. Shooting a knowing look at Kelsey, he stood up. "And now, it's getting late. If you don't mind, I think we'll hit the sack."

Dave and Leon stood up, too, and Kelsey turned to them. "It's been a wonderful evening. I'm glad we met up with each other."

"The pleasure has been ours," Leon said.

Dave picked up his sleeping bag and began to unroll it. "We'll see you in the morning. What are your plans for breakfast?"

"Lately we've been riding awhile, then stopping somewhere," Kelsey said. "Do you want to join us?"

"We'd love to," Dave agreed.

The next day they continued to ride with Dave and Leon until their routes separated.

"If you're ever in Oregon, look us up," Kelsey invited. "Maybe we could ride the coast highway together."

Agreeing in the way people do who don't expect such a thing to happen, the two men rode off and Kelsey and Mike pointed their bikes eastward.

"You know what I like?" Mike rode beside her, and she loved the way his eyes smiled when he looked at her.

"What?"

"The easy way you invited them to look *us* up."

FLIPPING IDLY through the pages of Kelsey's bird book, Mike's attention kept wandering from the pictures to the woman beside him. Sitting next to him, half-hidden behind a stand of brush in the Ottawa National Forest of upper Michigan, she had her binoculars focused on a bird some twenty feet away. Her hair had grown longer since they'd been on the road, and it now reached her chin. Frequently she'd tuck it back behind her ears with a quick, impatient flick of her hand.

Now it had fallen forward again, but she was so engrossed in her study of the bird, she hadn't noticed it. He propped his forearms on his knees and glanced at the book again.

"I think it's a black-backed, three-toed woodpecker," he said softly, grinning to himself. It had certainly been educational watching her watch birds. He might never understand how she could take anything so seriously and so lightheartedly at the same time, but lately he'd been thinking of all the ways to do her justice in the book for Seastone.

Laughing, but still holding the field glasses firmly to her eyes, Kelsey dug her elbow into his side. "Why would you think that?"

"Because it's on the rare, uncommon or endangered list."

"That's why it's just sitting right out in plain sight on that limb, right?"

"It must have known we were coming."

"And that's why it's brown."

"Let me see!"

Kelsey handed him the glasses, watching him while he studied the bird in question.

"You're right. It's brown, kind of a russet color. What is it?"

"I think it's a hermit thrush." She turned to her spotter's guide. "Does it have 'small, dark, wedge-shaped spots' on its breast?"

"How do I get it to turn around so I can see its breast?"

"Listen to it. Maybe we can identify it by its song."

Moments later Mike handed the glasses back to her. "I don't think it's going to sing for us."

"Sure it will." She refocused on the bird. "If we wait long enough."

"How many of these babies have we identified today?"

"Hmm. Six or seven, I think."

He slipped his arm around her shoulder and pushed the glasses away from her eyes and into her lap. "Bird-watching is boring."

"Oh, what would you rather be doing?"

"I thought you'd never ask." He leaned over, capturing her lips, his hands holding her shoulders against the ground.

But the more demanding his mouth became, the more she tried to wriggle free. He saw that her eyes were full of laughter, so he refused to let her roll away. Every time she tried to escape the probing exploration of his tongue, he deepened the kiss.

Finally, though, she pushed him away long enough to take a breath.

"There's a root jabbing me in the back." Though her tone complained, her eyes were still alight.

Mike groaned, rolled to his feet and extended his hand. "No wonder you were acting as if my kisses were one of the stronger forms of torture."

Without pausing to brush off her backside, she moved into his arms and laced her hands behind his neck. "They are. When you kiss me, I'm compelled to tell you everything I know, to do anything you say."

Her words incited heady desires to hold her close, to kiss her into mindlessness, to protect her forever. *"Anything?"*

"Within reason."

He waved imperiously at the binoculars and field guide. "Gather your belongings."

Shooting him a laughing glance, she picked them up.

"Precede me to our camp."

She started walking backward, her eyes never leaving his. "And what do you have in mind, oh great and magnificent one?"

"A great destiny stretches before you, to spend the rest of the day—"

Stopping suddenly, she pressed outstretched hands against his chest. "On my back?" she demanded.

Not exactly what he had in mind, but close. Before he could protest, however, she went on.

"Oh, no, you don't. We're still on my time. You promised me a full morning of bird-watching."

"I was out of my mind."

"That's beside the point. A promise is a promise."

"And in return?" He slid his hands underneath her T-shirt and rubbed his thumbs just inside the bottom of her bra. Her breasts felt full and warm; he wanted to let them fill his hands. But Kelsey drew back slightly when he touched her nipples, as if they were tender.

"In return?" She lowered her voice and smiled seductively. "I'll show you how wild with desire I can become," she said. "I promise."

"I don't think I ever realized how sadistic you can be."

With a chuckle she freed herself from his hold, then took his hand and led him deeper into the forest. "Just think, if we do find a black-backed, three-toed woodpecker, you'll be able to tell all your friends about it."

"I'm sure they'll be appropriately astounded."

TWO DAYS LATER they set up camp at an isolated site where the peninsula jutted out into Lake Huron. Mike suggested a swim, but Kelsey brushed him off. The sun was warm, the day calm; she felt languorous and lazy.

"I'll watch, thanks, or take a nap."

"Watch? While I do? That's supposed to be my line."

"You're a doer," she protested.

"Don't change the subject. And don't make me beg." He slipped his hand into her hair and brushed his lips across hers. "Come swimming with me, Kelsey."

This wasn't begging; it was blackmail. Kelsey accepted his kiss and demanded more. Every time was like the first time, full of wonder and joy. When he drew her closer, she wound her arms around his back.

"Coming?"

With a laugh she pushed him away. "I guess you know your tactics are unfair."

"As long as they're persuasive."

The water was cold. Icy. But the sun was warm, and the slope into the lake very gradual. As Kelsey waded out into it with her hand in Mike's, the contrast felt delicious on her skin. Not since the accident had she experienced this particular combination of sensations.

Laughing, she abruptly dived into the water. She came up gasping. The cold made her breasts ache deep into her chest, but now that she was here, she wanted to enjoy.

"Try it."

Mike shook his head. "For some reason I've suddenly lost interest in actually *swimming*."

"Chicken."

"Damn right."

Except this time neither height nor speed was involved, so Kelsey knew he was teasing. Still laughing, she dived again, grabbed him by the knees and pulled him under.

The cold cut into her like a knife, and when Mike came up, he pounded the water to send it spraying over her. "Not kind, Kelsey."

She smiled against the ice invading her body. "You're the one who made me come."

"Obviously a lapse in judgment. Come on, now that we've made the commitment, let's swim." Grabbing her hand, he started toward deeper water.

The ache in her breasts began to feel like a vise, and not even the heat of the sun helped. "Let's go back, Mike, before we catch pneumonia."

"People don't catch pneumonia in the middle of the summer."

She held out her arm. "Look at me. I'm covered with goose bumps. Go swim. I'll watch from the bank, and if you get in trouble, I'll ride off for help."

He captured her mouth in a quick, hard, possessive kiss. "You'd better come after me."

The water lapped around her hips, and each gentle wave sent cold ricocheting through her body. She grinned to hide the ache that now pulled at the steel in her leg. "Here's the deal. You try to come out in one piece, and I promise to save you if you don't."

Before he could answer, she turned toward shore. The water slowed her pace, and by the time she reached the bank she was shaking. She stripped off her cold suit and clutched the towel to her breasts. They hurt worse than her thigh.

Why hadn't she suspected the lake would be so cold? How could Mike stand it?

As soon as she stopped trembling, she unrolled her sleeping bag and stretched out naked on her stomach to let the sun warm her.

Propping her chin on crossed arms, she watched Mike. His arms cut through the water with a smooth and even rhythm. Every few strokes the sun would glint on water running over his back.

Not at all to her surprise, he stayed out only a few more minutes. As he waded to shore, the water clinging to his body shimmered in the sun. He looked like a god rising from the sea. His skin bronzed, his shoulders wide, his hips narrow. He came slowly against the weight of the water, and she watched every second of his approach. The weeks of riding had firmed and defined his already healthy physique. There were strips of white where his bicycling shorts covered skin that his swim trunks didn't—places where the sun never touched. She knew that tan-all-over was supposed to be sexy. On Mike, nothing could look better than the way he was.

He trotted up the beach to where she lay and shook water out of his hair onto her back. The sudden cold made her jump.

"You're tempting fate, lady."

Unselfconsciously she rolled over and looked up at him. The sun was directly behind his head, so she couldn't see his features in the halo of light. "Oh?"

"You're tempting me."

"I don't care." She wanted him to love her, fully and completely.

When he came to her, she gave back to him, withholding nothing. She was in love with Mike Kincaid.

She'd been on the road with him for about two months; they'd been full-fledged lovers for a couple of weeks. And now her earlier fears seemed foolish. This was not a love that would end with this trip. Of course, the rhythm of their love would change when they got back to their normal routines, but what she felt for him would remain constant. She'd been worried about his level of adventurousness, as if that were the only thing that mattered.

Now she knew that the essential elements were harmony of spirit, trusting each other and that special communication that had nothing to do with words.

She also knew that although she wanted a full and wonderful life with Mike, if the world ended tomorrow, the love they shared today would be enough.

THAT CONFIDENCE in their relationship continued to build as the days passed and the miles added up. But almost as soon as they passed the sign welcoming them to Ohio, Kelsey started to sense a new pensiveness in Mike.

He supported her with his advice and his presence through two radio spots, a television appearance and a newspaper interview in Toledo. When they turned south to detour around Cleveland and Akron on their way to Pennsylvania, however, he seemed to turn in on himself.

The ride was beautiful. The land rich and fruitful, the farms well tended, the roads quiet. Kelsey loved it. She even loved the sultry heat. Mike didn't seem to notice.

After weeks of riding with him, she'd learned he didn't talk about himself without prodding, and even then he didn't say much. She suspected it was a result of having lived alone most of his adult life. She wondered if it was too much to wish he would share with her whatever troubled him.

They stopped for lunch and to check for mail in a little town southeast of Akron. Mike ordered and ate in silence, and Kelsey felt as if she were slipping into an undertow. A force beyond her control was influencing events, and because she didn't know its cause, she had no idea how to fight it.

When Mike pushed his plate away and leaned forward with his arms crossed on the table, she pulled her bottom lip between her teeth. He'd come to a decision; she could see the steel in his eyes.

"I have a favor to ask," he said.

Hardly aware of it, she held her breath.

"It means backtracking, and I know you wanted to avoid the bigger cities whenever possible, but I'd like to visit my sister Susan. She lives in a suburb north of Akron."

Like water flowing from a leaky bucket, the tension drained quickly away.

Automatically Kelsey touched his arm. "I'd love to meet her."

Enclosing her hand in his, Mike shook his head. "It won't be the way you expect. We're not close. But she has three kids I've never seen."

"It'll be terrific." She figured she knew better than he would what the reunion would be like. She'd had lots more experience with family relationships. "How far do you think it is from here?"

"About fifty miles." He said it so readily she realized he'd figured the distance before saying anything.

"Do you want to ride up today, or wait until tomorrow?"

"I think I'd better call first."

After paying for their lunch, they found a phone. Kelsey waited expectantly. In spite of Mike's caution, she couldn't help visualizing it from her own perspective. If Rob called suddenly after a long separation, she'd be wild with excitement.

Mike's voice gave nothing away. His words told her little more. When he hung up, his expression was just as serious, just as noncommittal. "She'd like us to come tonight. I told her we could probably be there for supper."

With a glance at her watch, Kelsey agreed. "It's barely twelve-thirty. That gives us plenty of time."

Chapter Fourteen

Susan welcomed Mike with a genuine smile and an extended hand, but they didn't embrace. She met Kelsey with a nod but not a touch. If she'd had a child in her arms, that would have accounted for it, but the baby was crying somewhere in the back of the house. Kelsey caught back the impulse to find the child and cuddle away its tears.

When she looked closely, she could see a remote family resemblance between Mike and his sister. Susan's hair wasn't as dark, and her eyes were a solid gray, but the set of the eyes and the shape of the nose were the same. She weighed thirty pounds too much compared to Mike's totally fit, wonderfully proportioned body.

A toddler with a thumb in her mouth had her free arm wrapped around Susan's leg.

"Come sit down. Would you like something to drink? You must be thirsty."

She led them through the kitchen to a connecting family room decorated in Early American. The baby lay crying in a playpen in the corner. Absently sticking a pacifier in his mouth, she called two more children in from the backyard.

"This is Tiffany," Susan said. "She was just a baby the last time you saw her. Then Kimberly, and Brittany. And that's Brandon."

Mike knelt on the floor and shook each of his nieces hands seriously, with a twinkle in his eye. They looked like they'd been poured from the same mold. Long dark hair, fine bones, fair skin. They were close enough in age that Kelsey didn't think she'd be able to tell them apart if they weren't standing next to each other like stair steps. When Mike sat down, the middle one tried to climb on his lap. Susan shooed them all outside with a firm reminder for Tiffany to watch the others.

With the children out of the way, Susan chatted while she poured ice and soda into tall glasses. "You look great, terrific," she told Mike. "It must be wonderful to be able to take a couple of months off and do whatever you want."

Beneath the words, Kelsey heard the wistfulness. Four kids in nine years. Two of them under three. Who wouldn't feel tied down? She tried to ignore the twinge of envy that pulled at a distant corner of her heart.

"It's been a good experience," Mike replied. "How have you been?"

The next few minutes were spent catching up. Talk of the trip, talk of kids. It seemed surface and unemotional to Kelsey. Then Susan said she had to finish supper.

Mike and Susan were strangers to each other. Kelsey told herself it was only natural, since they hadn't seen each other for so long. She felt sad for both of them.

Susan bustled around the kitchen, checking a roast, making gravy, loading the dishwasher as she worked. Mike offered to set the table. When the baby started crying again, Susan swore.

"Please, can I pick him up?" Kelsey asked, welcoming something to do.

"Sure, go ahead. He might be getting hungry, but he's always such a brat this time of day. I can't get anything done."

Kelsey didn't really know how to go about it. She'd never done any baby-sitting as a teenager; she had no nieces or nephews. Most of her friends who married soon drifted out of her life when they no longer had so much in common. Still, she didn't think it would be too difficult.

He was heavier than she thought, and more mature. He held his head well and molded himself to the shape of her body when she put him against her shoulder. His tiny arm wound around her neck. She stood by the window, rocking him gently with her eyes closed. It was easy to focus her attention on the sweet baby smell of him and the weight of his body.

The murmur of voices mixed with the rattle of dishes. Once Susan laughed, and Mike's deep chuckle echoed it.

"No! Kimberly, no!" Suddenly Susan's sharp yell broke the serenity. "Tiffany, you're supposed to watch her." Something metal dropped into the ceramic sink. The door slammed. A child cried.

Drawn, Kelsey turned. Beyond the window Susan had one of her daughters by the arm while she spanked her. The older child stood off to the side, her head bowed. The littlest one sat on the grass with her thumb in her mouth.

"What happened?"

Mike shrugged and shook his head. "I think one of them turned on the hose." His jaw was tight, his eyes hooded. For a second she imagined he was seeing beyond the scene in the backyard. Then he turned away suddenly. "By example, by example and by example."

"What?"

"Just something Albert Schweitzer said about the way children learn."

When Susan returned to the house, she smiled apologetically. "They just can't stay out of trouble, but I guess that's the way kids are. Here, do you want me to take him now?" She held out her arms for the baby. "If I hurry, I can probably get some food down him before Glen gets here. It's always a race."

Dinner might have been pleasant if Susan hadn't been so intent on ensuring her kids made a good impression. Constantly she interrupted the conversation to reprimand one or another of them for their manners or for saying something she didn't think they should. Every time she did, Glen threatened to send the offender away from the table.

Kelsey tried to remember the last time she'd shared a meal with young children. It had been in Ireland with a large Catholic family. The oldest of the eight kids had been fifteen, the youngest, three or four. The meal had been rowdy, fun, spiced with laughter and free from tension. In spite of all the confusion, that had seemed civilized. This felt like chaos.

The talk floated over the surface of experiences, what had happened in the past eight years, Glen's job, references to Linda and the older Kincaids. They didn't talk about memories. Not once during the meal did either Mike or Susan say, "Do you remember when we—" More than anything else, Kelsey noticed that they didn't seem to share any common bond from their childhood.

Over protests from both Mike and Kelsey, Susan insisted they spend the night, claiming she wanted more chance to visit. Because there had hardly been a calm minute since they'd arrived, it seemed a valid request, although Kelsey didn't know what they'd find to talk about.

During bath time, Glen took Mike into the family room to talk about investments, and Kelsey tried to help Susan. Unfortunately Susan's approach made Kelsey uncomfortable. Since she had no personal experience, she wasn't sure how she'd have handled things differently, but she didn't like bribes or threats, and Susan used both, reinforcing the words with frequent swats.

The baby started crying again before the girls were quite settled, so Kelsey picked him up. There was a rocking chair next to his crib, and she sank into it gratefully.

Slowly the noises in the house quieted. A last reprimand from Susan, a rumble of distant male laughter, a toilet flushing. The hall light went off, leaving only the glow of the night-light to illuminate the room. Susan peeked in.

"Is he asleep?"

"Not quite. I'll just rock him for a while if you like."

"I'd love it. Come on downstairs when you're done."

Privately Kelsey thought she'd rather sit in the dark than rejoin the other adults. As the baby grew heavy on her shoulder, she smoothed her hand over his head and down his back, and tears filled her eyes. Leaning back in the chair, she didn't even try to stop the feelings. She was twenty-seven years old. For the past four years she'd lived with the knowledge that she would never have a baby. Before that, she'd never thought about it. Families were a given, something that would happen in the future when she found the right man, when the adventures of her youth were behind her.

Months spent in the hospital had given her time to understand what she'd lost. Holding Susan's baby made it clearer still. Gently she put little Brandon back in his bed and followed the voices.

There was a light on in the kitchen, but the stairs were shadowed. She could hear a television playing softly. Kelsey went reluctantly, thinking she understood Mike better now. If this was what reunions with his family were like, no wonder he made no effort to make them happen more frequently.

Near the foot of the stairs, she heard Mike's voice, low and confidential.

"...I've wanted to tell her, but now I'm afraid it's too late."

"You said she didn't want the publicity in the first place." Hearing a note of caution in Susan's voice, Kelsey paused in the shadows.

In the living room Mike stood in front of an empty fireplace, facing Susan, who sat on an overstuffed couch. Kelsey could see only his profile.

"Not in the beginning. Now she just thinks about the amount of money coming in and all the kids it will help."

That was true. As far as Kelsey was concerned, it was the only thing that compensated for the continual telling and retelling of her story.

Susan leaned forward with her hands clasped together. "Just tell her, Mike. If she doesn't understand, she's not worth the worry."

"Tell her what?" He paced the length of the room, out of Kelsey's line of vision. "That when I decided to do the book for Seastone, it meant more to me than being up-front with her?"

"That was two months ago. The situation's not the same anymore."

Silence filled the empty places when Mike didn't answer right away. Kelsey wished she could see him. Maybe if she could read the way he held his head or the color of his eyes, she'd understand better what she was hearing.

Finally he spoke. "Now there's more at risk. I might lose her."

"Not if she loves you."

Kelsey didn't want to hear any more. She retreated up the stairs and sat on the top one to think. Mike was writing a book. About her. It was why he'd come.

She should have suspected he had ulterior motives. Men like Mike didn't do things on whim. They had reasons for everything. She should have listened to Rob.

But the part that hurt the worst was that he hadn't been able to tell her about it.

She'd put so much on the line for him. Her fears and trust. Her love. Wasn't love a two-way street? Didn't it require the same of both people? How could he have doubted he wouldn't understand?

Because she tensed up every time she had to make an appearance. Because he wanted to protect her. And yet he'd thrust her into the situation in the first place.

There wasn't time to work it out. She saw Susan pass the stairs on her way to the family room. She heard Glen's voice over the sound of the television. Mike appeared in the doorway.

"What are you doing sitting there in the dark?"

"Nothing. Giving you and your sister a chance to talk."

He held out his hand. "Come on down. I think everyone's about ready to turn in."

Full of questions that had no answers, she put her hand in his. It was as firm as ever, as full of confidence and security. As far as he could know, nothing had changed in the past few minutes. For her, everything had.

When they entered the kitchen, Susan bustled over to them. "I pulled out the sofa in the family room. It's a pretty comfortable bed."

So Susan expected them to sleep together. Kelsey wondered what else Mike had told his sister. Misery tightened like a clamp around her lungs.

She was overreacting. Did she love him less because of this? No. Love didn't die any more quickly than it grew. But she was more afraid of the future. This trip was all they had in common. Back in Portland he had a life she knew nothing about, and the book for Seastone was only part of it.

A switch clicked, and the kitchen fell into darkness. Kelsey and Mike were alone in a little island of light.

"What's the matter?" he asked.

"Why don't you tell me?" Without glancing at him, she stripped off her shorts and top. When she turned, he stood with his hands jammed in his pockets and his eyes unsure.

"You overheard us."

"You should have realized that was a possibility."

He didn't reply, which didn't surprise her. What could he say?

"What I don't understand is why you could confide in Susan and not in me. You're not at all close to her, you haven't talked to her in years, but she's the one you tell all your problems to."

"When we started, I didn't intend to tell you until the end."

"So I gathered. How did you expect to get my permission?"

"Oh, I have your permission. You gave it to me when you signed the release for me to use your picture in those first newspaper articles."

She sank onto the bed, stunned. "You mean you could publish the book without any further word from me."

"Yes." The dismay she felt must have shown on her face because he quickly dropped beside her and cupped her chin with his hand. "But I wouldn't. When Seastone first approached me, I turned them down. They said they'd send someone else. I hated the idea that anyone else would share these months with you."

"You still chose not to tell me."

"I wanted you to like having me along, not hate me."

She stood, unable to think when he touched her like that, looked at her like that. "I could never hate you, Mike."

"But you hate the idea of a book."

"I'm not wild about it." There wasn't room to think. She paced into the kitchen and back again, which wasn't far enough. There were shades of circumstances here that needed to be analyzed separately. "Why are you doing it at all? Why did Seastone approach you?"

"I'm doing it because I'd always wanted to do a Seastone book. They approached me because they liked my work."

"Is that still why you want to do it?"

He closed the distance between them and took her arms in his hands. "Now I think your story's worth telling—a book would increase support for your cause."

"You'd mention in it where to send donations?"

He slid his hands down until they found hers. He brought them to his chest and held them close. Faintly she could feel the beat of his heart. "Of course."

"And why else?"

"The next question is, why would I choose not to?"

She looked at him sharply. His eyes were solemn.

"I want to keep you safe," he continued, "to make sure you're never hurt again. If the book would cause you pain, I wouldn't do it."

Doubts vanished as if by magic. She wrapped her arms around his neck and pulled his face down to hers. "I'm through being hurt," she said. "I'm alive, I'm well. I can handle anything."

Mike pulled her against him, and together they dropped onto the bed.

THE NEXT MORNING Kelsey watched Susan beat Tiffany with a wooden spoon. She came out of the bathroom in time to see it, but not soon enough to learn the reason. She didn't want to know. Not once in her entire life had either of her parents touched her in anger. It seemed immoral for an adult to use size against a child. Like hunting. Like colonialism. Sickened, she managed to keep her feelings beneath the surface for the remainder of their visit, but just barely.

Riding away, Mike seemed in more of a hurry than at any time before.

"God, I'm sorry," he said when they stopped for a light. "I should have known it would be like that. I shouldn't have insisted we visit."

"How could you know?" Kelsey asked. "You've never been to her house before."

Meeting her eyes, his serious and gray, he shook his head. "My folks treated us like that. Sometimes worse—and I could have guessed Susan would beat her kids if she thought the situation called for it. That's the way it works. Parents beat their children, the children grow up and beat their kids. It's a cycle with no end."

"Not always. People can change."

"Don't be naive, love." Bitterness weighed heavily in his voice. "You grew up sheltered. I'd bet you never had a spanking in your life."

When she didn't answer, he went on. "That's what I thought. Well, welcome to the real world."

"You wouldn't be that way." Having known his gentleness, his concern, his patience, his love, she knew the pattern would break with him.

His lips curled, but not in a smile. "Of course I would. If it's not in my genes, it's in my script. But I don't intend to let it happen. I'll never take a belt to a child."

"Because you'll never have a child."

"I'm just not sadistic enough to want one."

A deep sadness wrapped around Kelsey's heart. In a way, she understood, especially after watching Susan mistreat her kids. But in her heart, she knew Mike *would* be different.

The light changed, probably not for the first time since they'd stopped, and Mike pushed off. She should be glad. At least he would never be disappointed by her inability to have children—if they managed to stay together once the future became the present.

THEIR ROUTE TOOK them through Pennsylvania and on into New York. The country was so beautiful Mike almost wished they had an extra month in which to explore it. The weather stayed hot and muggy, so they rode mostly in the early mornings and late afternoons, resting or exploring small villages during the heat of the day.

When Kelsey suggested they ride through the wine country, up the west side of the Finger Lakes toward Fulton, Mike knew she wanted to visit the Ridgeways. Periodically she'd referred to them since Dave and Leon had issued their secondhand invitation. He knew she was dying to meet them.

He wasn't so sure. In the first place he hesitated showing up on the doorstep of people he didn't know. Second he considered the practice risky and foolhardy and didn't want to condone it.

While eating a lunch of take-out hamburgers in the village square of a small town at the south end of one of the Finger Lakes, Kelsey finally brought up the subject of the visit.

"I can't see popping in, invading their privacy and asking for a place to sleep," he objected. "How would you like it if some stranger knocked on your door with a request like that?"

"I'd invite them in, of course." She laughed while picking listlessly at another French fry. "Look at this from their point of view. Suppose you were old and unable to go anywhere you wanted, anytime you wanted. Would you like to be stuck away somewhere with no one new to talk to?" In direct opposition to the enthusiasm of her words, she lay back on the grass and closed her eyes.

Sitting next to her, his legs crossed tailor fashion, Mike leaned toward her. "Are you saying you're not transferring your values to them without even knowing them?"

"Thinking they wouldn't like to see us is doing the same thing in reverse. Let's just ride up, introduce ourselves and tell them that Dave and Leon suggested we stop by and say hello. Then the ball will be in their court, and if they invite us in, fine—if not, we'll leave. How's that?" Her voice drifted lazily on the still air. The afternoon was hot, sultry, somnolent. He didn't blame her for being sleepy.

He tickled her nose with a blade of grass and chuckled when she swatted at his hand and missed. "It sounds marginally reasonable. But let's not arrive at mealtime, all right? That would be too much like forcing them to be hospitable."

She rolled toward him and opened one eye. "You're very persuasive. You suggest a compromise, but it manages to get you what you want. No wonder you sell so much insurance."

Laughing, Mike pushed her onto her back and pinned her to the grass. "I thought this was an instance of you getting your own way. You're the one who wants to visit them."

"Isn't that the essence of a good transaction? Both sides feel they're getting the best deal?" She closed her eyes again. "Wake me when it's time to go."

His hold on her shoulders softened. "Are you okay? You never sleep in the middle of the day."

"I think it's the weather."

"The weather's been like this for days."

She cracked one eye open and grinned. "I've felt like this for days. Maybe I don't get enough sleep at night."

That was one possibility. Very lightly he inched his fingers up her throat and sifted them into her hair. "Are you complaining?"

She shook her head and he let his hand drift across her cheek. "I think loving you has become a habit."

"Even though it makes you sleepy during the day."

"On the other hand," she sighed, "we could make love during the day and sleep at night."

"What an excellent idea." Mike inched his fingers under her jersey and brought his mouth close to her ear. His life had changed since meeting Kelsey, and not just in terms of the trip. He felt more relaxed generally, and much less concerned about keeping schedules. Over the past few weeks he'd learned that there had to be a balance between work and play. He'd realized that spending a weekend photographing others wasn't the same as experiencing for himself. He'd never want to climb cliffs or run rivers, but he could imagine taking off occasionally and separating himself completely from his list of goals.

Kelsey jerked his hand away and sat up, laughing. "Mike," she protested. "This is a public square."

"I got your attention, didn't I?"

AS MIKE SUGGESTED, they arrived at the Ridgeways about two in the afternoon. Mrs. Ridgeway answered the door, and just as Dave had described her, she was old—and spry. Her white hair was fixed in a knot at the back of her head. She wore bright red slacks and a baggy T-shirt that had New York New York repeating itself down the right side. On her feet were a pair of Reeboks.

"Come in, come in," she invited immediately, peering past them at their loaded bikes.

"We met some friends of yours," Kelsey told her after they'd introduced themselves. "Two guys from Canada named Dave Milford and Leon Girard. They wanted us to drop by and say hello."

"Of course. We remember them. Delightful boys. Come on down and I'll call Papa. It's so nice of you to stop by." She almost sprinted out of the room.

"Well?" Kelsey whispered to Mike with a grin.

"It's as if a biking helmet were some kind of secret pass word. What if we were serial killers or something? These ol people wouldn't have a chance, letting strangers in like thi without question."

Kelsey turned to him with a grin. "This is not the time t get into a discussion on risk management. She probabl wouldn't listen to you anyway."

Mrs. Ridgeway bustled back in. "Mike and Kelsey, thi is Papa—all the kids call him that. And I'm Effie. Neve been called anything else."

The old man stepped forward, and Mike accepted hi outstretched hand. Like his wife, he wore athletic shoes, bu the rest of his clothes were more conservative: jeans and golf-style knit shirt.

"If you met Dave and Leon, then you know we expec you to stay here tonight. Wouldn't think of sending you on without a home-cooked meal and a night in a good bec Come on, Mike, let me take you out and show you around We have a real nice place here."

Kelsey grinned and nudged Mike to follow Papa. Th prospect of this kind of hospitality and of meeting nev friends was the reason that had prompted her to come.

"We can't tell you how much we appreciate this," she tol Effie. "Do very many bike tourists stop by?"

Effie led her into a kitchen that was decorated in pale blu and white, with a distinctly modern collection of appl ances—including a coffee mill and a pasta maker—occu pying the countertop.

"Some summers we see more than others. This year been about average. Come here, I'll show you." Hundrec of snapshots had been thumb-tacked to the far wall. Som had one person centered in the middle of the picture; mo had two. Men, women, couples, young people, old peopl one or two adults with one or two children, and all of th ubjects had a bicycle. "There's Dave and Leon," Effie aid, pointing to their picture.

"Do you remember all the names?" Kelsey asked incredlously.

"Oh, I wish I could," Effie admitted with a reluctant augh. "I write names on the back, so I can match them to he Christmas cards and letters we get. We hear from almost all of our visitors at some time or another. Some of hem, of course, just seem to stick in my memory. These girls, for instance." She pointed to a picture of two young women who Kelsey guessed to be only eighteen or nineteen. "They came two years ago. They were from Georgia, as I ecall, and they planned to ride clear around the United States. Most people who come by are from New England. Some are from farther away." She turned to the refrigerator. "Would you like a glass of iced tea? I have some already made, and we can take a tray out to the menfolk."

"I'd love some. It's been hot today."

From the refrigerator Effie took a gallon jug and, after pouring it into huge glasses full of ice cubes, she led the way across the yard to the barn.

Inside were two vintage automobiles in shiny mint condition. Papa Ridgeway showed off his hobby, telling Kelsey in detail about the restoration work he'd done on them. When Mike winked at her, she realized it was being repeated for her benefit. But the barn was too hot, even with doors open on both ends and a slight breeze moving the heavy air. She found herself thinking wistfully of the cool forests of Michigan.

Papa droned on, describing how he originally got the cars, the difficulties he'd had in finding some parts, how he'd fabricated pieces he couldn't find anywhere else, and Kelsey tried to forget the heat. But as the minutes ticked slowly by, she found it harder and harder to concentrate.

She began to feel sick, as if a cauldron were churning in her stomach. An ache that started at the base of her neck edged around to her forehead and began to pound. By the time Effie announced to the men that it was time to fix dinner and that she was going to enlist Kelsey, Kelsey was hearing only one word in five of the conversation.

"Good idea," Papa agreed. "And Mike here can keep me company while I milk the cow."

He waved the women away, and Kelsey followed Effie back into the cool house, thankfully accepted another glass of iced tea, and slowly began to feel more normal. Still, it was a relief to immerse herself in the undemanding task of slicing vegetables while Effie efficiently put together a wild-rice-and-chicken curry. With an inner smile Kelsey observed that the meat-and-potatoes tradition didn't seem to hold true in this house.

While the rice cooked, Effie took Kelsey to a sun porch off the kitchen, which had been transformed into a well-equipped art studio. Three large canvases in various stages of completion were propped on easels. Not one of them conveyed much talent, but the vivid vitality of the work told Kelsey that Effie was the artist.

Pretty soon Mike and Papa came back to wash up. Dinner was particularly pleasant, lively and interesting. By the time they finished eating and settled in the living room with coffee, it seemed as if the afternoon had flown.

Bits and pieces of Mike and Kelsey's trek across the continent had come out during the course of the afternoon, but now the Ridgeways wanted to hear it all. So Mike and Kelsey told about the places they'd been, about the Iversons, about Rob and his accident and about Kelsey's cause.

Effie was particularly interested in that, so Kelsey found herself telling about the various public appearances she'd made.

"It's sort of mushroomed. I feel like a pseudo celebrity, ut I'm glad some good is coming out of it."

Mike took her hand and leaned forward. "Everybody xcept Kelsey seems to understand why she's a heroine. It n't just that she survived a traumatic accident, but that she ut herself back together, that she's willing to take risks gain and that in spite of how much effort she's had to put nto herself, she still thinks of others first."

Embarrassed, Kelsey sat quietly beside him, wishing he'd top. Maybe because he loved her, a certain amount of pride /as allowed. She just wished he'd keep it to himself. Of ourse, at this point, a little private boasting seemed inci-lental.

When an old clock in the hall chimed midnight, Papa ook Effie's hand and suggested it was time for bed. Kelsey elt a tiny bit guilty that the conversation had drifted so far nto the night, but neither of their hosts seemed particu-arly tired or worn-out by the lateness of the hour.

"We're not too fussy about what time we have break-ast," Effie told Kelsey and Mike. "So just come on down /henever you like."

Impulsively Kelsey bent and kissed her lightly on the heek. "Thank you for a wonderful day."

Chuckling, the older woman patted her hand. "We hould be the ones thanking you. You young people bring he world to us, and far more of it than we could ever hope o see if we were out there trying to do it on our own. See ou in the morning, dear."

A huge four-poster bed nearly consumed the room that Effie had invited Mike and Kelsey to use, and an oversize vardrobe used up most of the remaining floor space. Both pieces of furniture were ornately carved and beautifully polished to a warm, seductive glow. Running her hand over the smooth finish of the wardrobe, Kelsey said, "I'm glad we came here. It's too bad Rob had to miss it."

"Do you still miss him?" Coming behind her, Mike turned her into the circle of his arms and brushed his hand lightly across her cheek.

"Yes." She smiled up into his eyes, which were now a smoky shade of blue. "But not as much as I would if I didn't have you."

"As long as you don't think of me as a brother."

With a laugh she edged his jersey up his chest and ran her fingers along the familiar line of his ribs. He still smelled of fresh air, even after an evening indoors, and lightly of sweat. It was an intoxicating combination, one she'd almost grown addicted to in the past weeks. "I thought that's what you were going to be to me. A substitute for Rob."

Smoothly he pulled his shirt all the way off, giving her free access to all the wonderful places she wanted to touch.

"Only a part of the plot, my dear, to get you where I really want you." He pushed her down onto the bed, and she sank so deeply into the softness of the mattress she found it difficult to move. But she had only to wait while he turned off the light, and then he was beside her and nothing else mattered.

The pale starlight, which spilled across the windowsill, seemed to fill the room with magic. Mike was a silhouette, a shadow, moving with the silent rhythms of the night as he touched and explored and demanded. Matching his pace, Kelsey gave to him, her life, her love and her future. Together they soared beyond the limits of confining, earth-bound bodies. Gripped by a madness, a need for deeper, wider melding of their souls, they reached the peak, then drifted slowly, indolently, back to the known and peaceful heaven of each other's arms.

Chapter Fifteen

Kelsey awoke sometime in the middle hours of the night and dressed silently in her shorts and shirt for a quick trip across the hall to the bathroom. At least tonight she didn't have to seek her privacy behind a bush. Her increasingly frequent awakenings annoyed her, and she could only attribute them to the quantities of liquid she consumed to compensate for the heat of summer.

But then she felt too awake for sleep, and even while she considered waking Mike, the unbroken rhythm of his breathing held her back. He could certainly use the sleep she wouldn't get.

Quietly she made her way down the bare stairs, hoping to avoid any creaks she wouldn't have noticed the night before, when an extra noise or two simply blended into the voices and movements of four people. Perhaps something warm and soothing to drink would relax her enough to make the bed appealing. Like milk. Then she smiled to herself. It must be this house, or the unembarrassed hospitality of the Ridgeways, but the thought of warm milk brought back old forgotten fantasies from her childhood. Fantasies of farms and grandmothers and other childhood delights that hadn't belonged to her.

Taking a pot from the cupboard, she poured milk into it and turned the heat to low. While she waited, she wandered over to the picture wall and tried to imagine the stories behind the faces.

Where were they from? Why did they come? What were they looking for? Had any of them been as lucky as she, and found the answer to a dream?

"Warm milk, my dear?" Effie's voice flowed across the hush of the quiet kitchen as though it belonged to the night and Kelsey turned, not startled or surprised. "I thought only babies and old women liked warm milk."

"It just seemed like what I needed. I couldn't sleep."

"Well, I think it's ready." Effie took a ceramic mug from the cupboard and poured the warm milk into it.

"Thank you. I hope I didn't disturb you."

"Not at all. I've always been a bit partial to these hours when everyone else is asleep. Over the years it's when I've done my best thinking. And lately I find I like to come down and paint." While she talked, Effie filled the teapot, then selected a tea bag from one of several small, colorful tins.

"Well, normally I sleep very soundly, but it seems the last week or two I wake up a lot." Kelsey grinned. "Usually to go to the bathroom. And that can get to be quite a hassle while we're camping."

With a chuckle Effie nodded. "Oh, I can imagine. When I was a little girl, my family lived out in the country and we used an outhouse. Now, those were the good old days."

They began to reminisce, sitting across the table from each other and sipping their drinks in the quiet of the night. Kelsey listened avidly to Effie's tales of growing up in the early decades of the twentieth century, then talked of the distant places she herself had lived. As they turned the pages of their lives closer to the present, Effie told Kelsey of her children, who all lived in different states, and of her grandchildren.

"It's hard to have people you love so far away, isn't it?" Kelsey commiserated. "My parents are in Barbados right now, and they spent the last two years in Greece."

"Maybe they'll decide not to travel so much when you start having children. Babies grow too fast, and it's easy to lose years without even noticing."

"Well," Kelsey said dryly, "that's not much of a possibility."

"Oh?" Effie seemed surprised. Taking her cup to the stove, she poured more hot water over her tea bag. Then she turned and faced Kelsey. "My dear, I hope you won't think I'm prying when I say this, but I'd thought you were pregnant now."

"You did?"

"Your sleeplessness seemed to confirm it. You have that special glow about you that pregnancy brings to healthy women. And you prefer to sit whenever possible, like you were tired. And then there's the way Mike hovers over you, as if you were fragile and he wanted to protect you."

"Oh, well, Mike's just—" Kelsey broke off in midsentence as little bits and pieces of the past few weeks rushed through her mind. Joy and despair washed over her in successive waves. It was a possibility she'd never considered, never even let herself hope for. But a five-percent chance was still a chance.

"Oh, my God." It explained so many things. The tenderness in her breasts, her inability to keep up with Mike, the longing to take a nap in the middle of the day. Even her lack of periods—although, even before the accident she'd had a tendency to irregularity. Her mind leapt back to that fateful, wonderful, precious night in Wyoming, the night of the storm when they'd taken refuge in Mike's tent. It was the only possible time. There hadn't been enough time since Rob left to develop any symptoms.

A baby. Mike's baby. Right now growing inside of her, already a viable, wonderful presence in her life, in theirs. The idea, once Kelsey's imagination caught hold of it, took flight. Mike would...hate it. And he'd want her to stop riding.

As vividly as if it had been yesterday, she remembered his attitude about Courtney Iverson. He'd been angry that she'd continue to ride while pregnant—and she was a stranger. How would he react to this news. What would he say?

He'd want to turn back now, even though they were only days from finishing. And the situations weren't at all the same. Courtney was four months along, Kelsey barely two. Courtney had weeks of riding ahead of her, Kelsey only days.

Worse, she feared that when she told him, the love she'd found in his arms would die. He didn't want children of his own. Ever.

She looked imploringly at Effie. "I have a favor to ask of you, and it may seem strange, but it's very important to me. Please don't mention this to Mike, or to Papa while we're here."

"But my dear, the secret isn't yours to keep. It belongs to Mike, too, and you should share it with him."

"I can't."

"How much longer do you have to go? You won't be able to hide this for long."

"About ten days, I think. Not more than eleven." She reached for Effie's hand. "Surely I can manage that."

"Only if you get enough sleep," Effie said with a smile. "Your baby won't flourish if you don't take care of your body, you know. Perhaps it would be a good idea to see a doctor."

Kelsey shook her head, trying to think. What would a doctor say? Stop? Go on, but be careful? In either event, she knew what Mike's reaction would be, and she didn't want to stop. She didn't want the magic to end.

She was in top physical condition. She was well used to spending long hours each day on the bike. Obviously the past few weeks hadn't hurt her. Soon enough she'd be back in Oregon and she could see her own doctor, and then, when she knew positively, she would tell Mike.

There was even a chance that both she and Effie were jumping to conclusions. One distant part of her even hoped so. Except in her heart, Kelsey knew that she was indeed carrying Mike's baby.

BEFORE THEY LEFT the next day, Papa took their picture with his instant camera, and they were able to see it assume its place among the others.

Effie drew Kelsey aside and handed her a package of sandwiches and fruit. "And you mustn't forget to send me an announcement when that little one arrives," she whispered.

"You'll be one of the first to know," Kelsey agreed. "And if I ever come back this way, I'll stop by and show him to you."

"Well, you be very careful and not let anything happen." Effie patted her arm. "But I know you will. God bless you."

Waving, they rode down their driveway, and when they reached the road, Mike pulled in to ride side by side with Kelsey.

"What was that all about?" he asked.

Kelsey shook her head. "Girl talk."

"That's not a very subtle way to tell me to mind my own business."

"It wasn't meant to be subtle."

They took six days to cross New York instead of five. But the pace Kelsey set puzzled Mike in ways he couldn't quite identify. She practically dawdled along, making excuses to visit places that didn't seem to interest her. She seemed too preoccupied to sightsee. She got a letter from her parents, with the date of their arrival in New York City, but the excitement he'd come to expect didn't accompany the news.

Ever since leaving the Ridgeways, she'd been different.

Why?

Something was bothering her. Mike thought about using the same arguments on her that she'd used when confronting him about the book. Love and trust went hand in hand. They had no need for secrets between them. Was it because they were so close to the end of the trip? Did she expect things to change?

He studied her face constantly, and although she seemed tense, she didn't pull away from him. If anything, she was more loving, more demanding—as if she were trying to hold on to something.

What was she afraid of? That what they had wouldn't last after they got home? It was the only reasonable answer he could find. And since that was a question he'd asked himself frequently over the weeks, he understood her fear.

On the day they were to cross the Green Mountains of Vermont, Kelsey seemed more edgy than normal. Mike swallowed an impulse to force her to rest, to insist she level with him. But in only a few more days the stresses of this trip would be over. He decided it would be better to wait until then. Then he could prove to her that the future belonged to them.

The road was as steep and winding as any climb they'd encountered in the Rocky Mountains. About a third of the way up they stopped for a rest.

"I love the mountains," Kelsey proclaimed, sounding more like herself. She took off her helmet, shook her damp hair free and wiped the perspiration from her forehead with the back of her hand.

"Well, I didn't expect these to be such a grind," he replied easily, willing to pretend nothing was wrong.

"It's the difference in elevation from the valley floor that matters, not the distance from sea level."

"Oh, of course. That's intuitively obvious, isn't it? At least the air isn't as thin as it was in the Rockies. How much longer to the summit, do you think?"

"Two hours? Three, maybe?"

"And then we fly down the other side."

He said it as a joke, and to his surprise she laughed and held up her hand in protest. "*Oh*, no. I don't take risks like that anymore."

KELSEY DIDN'T THINK she'd ever reach the top of the climb. Her legs ached, her head ached and her stomach felt ready to rebel at any moment. The wind blowing off the slope whipped against her in ever-increasing gusts, chilling her sweat-bathed skin. With every turn of the pedals her body complained at the effort.

She couldn't keep up with Mike, no matter how much he held back for her. But she kept seeing signs of concern in his face, so she forced herself to grin at him and wave as though he were simply enjoying an easy stroll through the trees.

When would it end? Every bend in the road simply opened up another stretch of winding uphill. She didn't dare stop for fear she wouldn't be able to climb on the bike again.

She saw Mike riding back toward her, for perhaps the fifth time in twenty minutes. She hated feeling as if she were holding him back. Even more, she hated imagining what he must be thinking. Thank heaven, he'd never suspect the real reason for her difficulty.

Eventually, realizing she had to rest, she coasted to a stop and took a deep, ragged breath to compose herself. When Mike coasted back down the mountain to pull up beside her, she smiled at him.

"You okay?" He stopped, facing her, his thigh brushing against hers, and his eyes far too probing.

"I'm fine, just not in any hurry. How much farther do you think it is?"

He waved his hand back the way he'd come, and she could tell he was concerned. "One more rise, but you'd better stop sight-seeing and get serious. It looks like rain."

She glanced around and saw that he was right. Ominous clouds rolled across the sky, threatening to block the sun. Her drooping spirits sagged even more. She felt so tired, so unsure. The mountain demanded more of her than she had to give. But on this quiet, remote stretch of road, there were no alternatives. "We'd better go, then."

Mike lifted her chin with a touch so gentle it made her want to lay her head against his chest and let his arms enfold her. "You look beat," he said solemnly.

"Thanks a lot!" Somehow she managed to inject a spark of humor into her voice, and his encouraging smile rewarded her.

"But you still look good to me."

"Wanna take a break?" she teased. By merely being there, he reassured her; knowing he cared eased her fatigue. Since leaving the Ridgeways, she'd tried to concentrate on his support because there was so little time left for them to be together.

He chuckled and brushed his lips across hers in a fleeting caress before turning back to his bike. "Nope. I want to beat this storm. Come on, I'll race you to the top."

She nodded her assent, but knew there was no contest. Just keeping her feet turning the pedals would tax her strength.

Mike was waiting for her when she finally gained the summit. She could tell from his stance that he expected them to begin the descent immediately, and she couldn't blame him. The first spatters of rain began to hit her face, driven by a cold and biting wind. With luck they'd be able to out-run it now that they were going down.

But her heart thudded heavily in her chest, too hard and too fast. She felt dizzy and nauseated. Sick. She kept her bike steady until she came even with Mike. Her feet touched solid ground, but she felt no answering reassurance in her legs. Mike sprang to her side before she could swing her leg over the crossbar, and the last thing she noticed was the strength of his arms catching her as everything went black.

MIKE LIFTED Kelsey into his arms, more frightened for her safety than he'd ever been in the past. Already the rain slashed down so fast it was useless to think about trying to set up the tent alone, and Kelsey needed shelter now. He carried her to the leeward side of a stand of trees and placed her gently on the ground before going back to his bike for something with which to cover them.

Kelsey was stirring when he returned. Shaking out his rain poncho, he snuggled close to her and threw it over both their heads.

"Are you all right?"

She shook her head against his shoulder. "I think I'm going to be sick." She rolled away from him, and he held her while she retched. Afterward he wiped her face with his rain-dampened handkerchief and then brought her back into the shelter of the poncho.

"I'm sorry," she said, and the way she lay against him told him more poignantly than words how worn and exhausted she was.

Flicks of anger curled through his concern for her. Why, if she knew she wasn't well, had she pushed on? "We didn't need to climb this mountain today. We could have taken a break."

"I was fine until that last push."

A vague note of defensiveness bracketed her words, and Mike knew she held something back, something she didn't trust him to know. So here they were, caught in a rainstorm, miles away from any possible help. Dammit. It was just like her to ignore good sense when it stood in the way of something she wanted.

"You haven't been fine for days," he said bluntly.

She stiffened slightly in his arms. "Why do you say that?"

"Your approach has changed. Even on straightaways you hardly manage ten miles an hour. You go through the motions of being a tourist, but you don't see anything."

"Oh, it's just that we're so close," she said lightly. "I can't think about anything except making it to the end."

"Bull." Taken by themselves, the words made sense, but something still didn't ring true. "It's more than that, Kelsey. I think it's past time for you to tell me what's bothering you."

She turned and pressed her face against his neck. "It's nothing, Mike. Just hold me." Her breath felt warm on his skin, and the dampness heightened the woodsy smell of her hair. Even as frustrated as he was, he couldn't deny her. He wrapped his arms more firmly around her, bringing her closer. He loved her, he wanted her, but a painful knot had tightened in his chest. Why didn't she trust him? Under his hand her heart beat unevenly, and although she molded herself close to him, she felt stiff and unpliable.

"You don't get sick over nothing. And a little hill like this wouldn't do you in. Come on, Kelsey, level with me."

She shivered, and he twisted to give her a margin of added protection with his body.

When she spoke, her words were lost against his shirt. He lifted her chin and was surprised to find tears running down her cheeks.

"What it is, Kelsey? I didn't hear you."

"I'm pregnant, Mike," she said again.

Chapter Sixteen

The hovering wisps of worry and frustration that had been nipping at Mike congealed suddenly and drove straight to his gut in a single surge of anger. He jerked her around to face him. "Pregnant? And you kept riding? You didn't hesitate to climb this mountain. My God, Kelsey, why didn't you tell me?"

Kelsey glared at him through her tears. "Because I *knew* this was how you'd react."

With cold knots of fear tightening his muscles, his fingers bit into her arms, and he could feel her flesh give beneath them. How could she have been so foolish? Dozens of things could have gone wrong. She'd totally ignored the possibility of disaster. "How long have you known?" he demanded.

"Since the night we spent with the Ridgeways."

"Don't you give a damn about the baby?"

She recoiled as if he'd hit her, but the sense of betrayal consumed him, driving him on. "Or did you hope you could lose it? A baby would change your life-style, wouldn't it. Were you wishing for a miscarriage?"

"No!" She wrenched free of his hold and scrambled to her feet.

Before he could stop her, she dashed down the slight slope to her bike. He leapt to his feet, but the ground was wet and slippery, causing him to lose his footing. He scrambled up, rain hazing his vision, and saw Kelsey heft her bike back onto the road and swing her leg over the seat.

Sliding after her, every inch of his body seemed to scream his fear for her.

"Kelsey!" His cry instantly dissipated in the rain. *"Kelsey!"*

Already she'd disappeared, lost in the mist and the turns of the road. He grabbed his bike, not caring that his poncho and helmet were still lying back on the hill. Nothing mattered anymore except catching up with Kelsey and keeping her safe.

But his mind couldn't ignore the questions pressing in on him. How had she kept the news from him? Why? Didn't she know how much it would mean to him to have her carrying their child?

No, she couldn't know. He'd insisted he didn't want kids. And until hearing the news, he hadn't.

Pain washed through him. Kelsey, a baby. A family. He realized suddenly that was exactly what he wanted—had always wanted. Within inches of having it within his reach, he'd thrown it away. What if he never got another chance?

KELSEY COULDN'T STOP crying. Between the driving rain and her tears, she could see little but the lines marking the road. A car passed from behind, going too fast and sending a spray of water over her, but she didn't care. Nothing mattered anymore.

Her bike seemed to skim along the surface of the road, carrying her at a pace all its own. She pulled the brakes, but they found little purchase on the wet rims.

She should stop. She should find some shelter and wait out the storm. She glanced down at her map, but there was too much water puddled on the top of her carrier. How far was it to the nearest town? A few miles? A dozen? She was cold. Colder than during her climb on Rainier. Colder than swimming in Lake Huron. The wind blowing through her wet clothes made even her bones feel frigid and useless. Where was her poncho? Tucked into her pack, or back with Mike? And her helmet? She didn't dare take her hands off the handlebars, but she shook her head and realized it was bare. What else had she left behind when she'd fled Mike's fury?

Now here she was, riding downhill through a biting storm with nothing to protect her from the rain or the road. Maybe everything Mike had said was true.

Another car raced past, and Kelsey gripped the handlebars even more tightly against the heavy gust of wind that followed in its wake. Her tires spun along as if coasting on glass, and a vision of Rob losing control in a puddle of water forced itself into her memory. God, would this mountain never end? She tightened her brakes again, but found little response.

When she seemed to slow, as if the slope had eased, she let her eyes leave the road and glanced around. Finally! A house here, one down the road. She'd enter a town soon.

Peru, Vermont. Population 312, the sign said. No chance of a motel. But at least the storm was easing. Kelsey stopped long enough to check her packs for her poncho, and released a sigh when she found it. Thank heaven the one she'd left with Mike had been his.

It seemed like hours before she finally saw a sign directing her to an inn. Two miles farther she saw the house, a beautifully restored Victorian with a delicately lettered welcome sign.

Never in Kelsey's life had a welcome been so needed. The woman who greeted her took her directly upstairs and even ran water in the claw-footed tub for her, assuring her that someone would take care of her bike.

Gratefully she slipped into the hot, chin-deep water, reveling in the momentary painful reaction of her chilled body. But as her body warmed, so did her mind, making room for delayed reactions and disjointed thoughts.

Snatches of her argument with Mike on the mountain replayed through her brain, none of them connected, all of them raw. He'd been angry, of course. Had she expected him not to be?

But if she'd told him sooner, she'd have lost the past few days. With it all over, every second she'd been able to lodge in her memory had become precious.

A fresh wave of pain and longing besieged her. She tightened her fingers against her flesh, as if physically searching for answers that didn't exist. They pressed into her stomach, and relief suddenly, urgently, replaced the despair. She hadn't lost everything. Through some miracle, some quirk of fate, she'd made that mad ride down the mountain safely. Growing inside of her was the baby they told her she couldn't have. Mike's baby.

Just the thought of it made the cold retreat. Nothing could replace Mike, but she would never be alone.

She ran more hot water into the tub and tried to think. She was stronger and surer now than when she'd packed her bike in May. In dozens of ways the accomplishment was bigger than she'd foreseen.

If she could only concentrate on that. She'd be able to make a home for this baby. A good home. One like her parents had made for her and Rob. Of course, it would be a one-parent home, but she had more than enough love. She had all the love she wouldn't be able to give to Mike.

Of course, she wouldn't finish the trip. There was no point now, with her life in a shambles. Her parents would be in New York day after tomorrow, which would give her plenty of time to get her bike shipped home. Then maybe she'd rent a car and drive down to meet them.

This time when the water cooled, Kelsey got out. Her body was more relaxed now, and she felt slightly more positive about the future than an hour before.

On the table beside her bed, a tray with tea and fresh scones waited for her. The fresh-bread smell filled the room, and Kelsey realized that she'd eaten only a banana since breakfast. She smiled ruefully. She hadn't felt much like eating for days, but this looked too good to resist. Then she'd have a nap. After all, she did have someone else to think of now.

She spread homemade raspberry jam on the scone and poured a cup of tea, then climbed between the sheets and cuddled the down comforter closer around her body. It wasn't like snuggling close to Mike, but she might as well start getting used to sleeping alone. She'd be doing it for a long, long time.

When Kelsey awoke, thin bars of sun filtered through the blinds, streaking the bed with light. Was it morning or late afternoon? She didn't know and she had no idea which direction her room faced. It didn't matter. She felt rested and at least partially restored.

Downstairs the enticing aroma of bacon and fresh muffins made all thoughts of everything except breakfast disappear. It must be morning, she decided. The dining room was decorated in ivory and pale blue, and, though the long table was set for a meal, the room itself was empty.

Kelsey waited in the doorway for a moment, letting the smells increase her appetite. She wondered if guests were supposed to help themselves.

She heard a step behind her and turned to find the woman who had greeted her the evening before. Today Kelsey noticed the smile wrinkles that bracketed her hostess's mouth and the humor that filled her eyes. A fresh dose of thank

ulness rose in Kelsey's throat. She couldn't have found a
more welcome port in the storm.

"Good morning," Kelsey said.

The woman smiled. "How are you this morning?"

"Much better. Warm, rested, hungry." With a smile Kelsey extend her hand. "I'm afraid I didn't catch your name yesterday."

"Janina Howard. Breakfast is ready."

"I've been standing here anticipating it. Should I just help myself? Or should I wait for the other guests?"

Janina grinned. "You're the first one up. Perhaps because you went to bed so early?"

"Probably," Kelsey agreed with a laugh. "First, though, I need to make a few phone calls. Can you tell me where the nearest airport is?"

Janina lead Kelsey into an alcove off the entry and handed her the phone book. She placed the first call and began to note the information on a slip of paper. Suddenly a hand closed over hers, and she looked up into Mike's eyes.

"Hang up, Kelsey," he said.

She could only stare at him, her heart in her throat, her pulse rattling through her veins. "What?"

"We need to talk."

Her mind refused to respond; it was too full of trying to find answers in his eyes. They were gray and solemn, and his mouth was drawn into a straight, unsmiling line. He took the phone from her and said something to the man at the other end before hanging up.

"Mike—"

"What was that all about?"

Her legs turned liquid, and she leaned back against the table for support. Words stuck in her throat. Did they have anything more to say to each other? She didn't think she could bear to hear him say out loud that it was too late.

"I'm quitting," she said tightly.

He touched her cheek, brushing away the moisture an settling his hand gently on the back of her neck. His finger slid into her hair, and she thought his touch had neve reached more deeply into her soul.

"I'm sorry," he said.

"No. Please don't, Mike." She stepped away. It was to hard to have him look at her like that, knowing it wa probably for the last time. "How did you find me?"

"There weren't too many places to look. I guess I got i about an hour after you, after asking at every house passed. By then I was so frantic I almost wanted to find yo lying beside the road just so I'd know where you were Janina told me you were okay, and that you'd gone to bec I decided you needed the rest more than you needed to se me."

"Why are you here? You made yourself quite clear yes terday."

"I said some harsh things."

"Maybe I deserved them."

"I was wrong." Mike's hand closed around her arm turning her toward him. His nearness brought every nerve ending in her body alive. "About everything."

Confused, she stood silently. Could she begin to hope?

"I want the baby. I want you. I never meant to hurt you."

"What's different now?" She had to be sure. There wa too much at stake to let her emotions guide her. If th wasn't real, if he was setting her up for a fall, she doubte she'd be able to pick up the pieces.

Taking her by the arms, he ran his hands down to her e bows then up again to her shoulders. His grip was firm, fu of tension. His hand slid to her throat. "I love you."

The room felt hot and close. She couldn't breath. "B: bies are forever. They don't go away if you get tired of ther or think you can't handle it anymore."

"I'm not saying I'm not scared, or that I think it will be easy. But watching you ride away yesterday was the worst moment of my life. Hunting for you, I knew if I found you in one piece, I couldn't let you go again. And I guess it took that to make me realize how much I want a family. I want what you and Rob have. I just never believed it was possible."

She cupped his face with her palms. If there was ever a time for reassurance, this was it. "You're not your father. You're not a carbon copy of Susan."

"I wish you'd told me when you first knew."

"I didn't want you to worry."

His arms came around her, letting his strength enfold her. "I'll always worry," he said. "I love you."

"Mike." She whispered his name. Then she said it again, as a prayer to the future.

"Yesterday was a nightmare I hope never to repeat."

"No," she assured him. "I'll never leave you again. Never."

He nuzzled her neck and ran his hands across her hips and up her back. "You were leaving today. I heard you on the phone."

"I decided to meet my parents in New York."

"Quitting never solved anything."

She leaned back in surprise. It was the last thing she'd expected him to say. "But you were angry when Courtney kept going. You said Bliss was a stupid fool to allow it."

Mike grinned. His eyes were not quite blue, not quite gray, and happier than she'd ever seen them. "Do you really want to stop short of achieving your goal?"

She chuckled wryly. "Of course not."

"We could be in Portland in less than a week."

"Portland, Maine." She could almost taste the salt in the air and hear the cries of sea gulls on the wing. But if he'd suggested they quit, she'd have gone in a flash. The only

ending that held any meaning anymore was a happily-ever
after one with him. Nothing else mattered but Mike and her
together, forever. His lips touched hers, so softly the pres
sure felt more like a promise than a kiss.

"I want to go on," he said.

She laughed, unable to hide the excitement that sprang
within her. "Oh, Mike. Are you sure?"

"On one condition. We'll do it my way. I'll say when to
ride and when to stop. You'll rest when I suggest it, you'll
eat what I provide. No more long hauls up mountains, no
more snacks on the run. No more disappearing acts."

"Getting dictatorial in your old age?"

"More like in my approaching fatherhood," he said.

"You'll be one hell of a dad."

He chuckled and looked consideringly at the ceiling. "I
think you'll be a pretty flaky mother."

"Mike!"

"Think about it. Poor kid will never know when his
mother will decide to go climb a mountain or sail off into the
sunset."

Because he was teasing, Kelsey couldn't help taking ad
vantage of the moment. "Oh, I don't know. Think how
lucky he'll be to have you always providing such a well
developed sense of caution."

"He'll need it to balance your unbridled sense of adven
ture."

She grinned. "Haven't you ever seen those little back
packs for babies? You can tie a sleeping bag on under
neath, and voilà, two for the road."

Mike pulled her against him and captured her mouth.
"Make that *three* for the road."

This October, Harlequin offers you a second
two-in-one collection of romances

A SPECIAL
SOMETHING

THE FOREVER
INSTINCT

by the award-winning author,

Barbara Delinsky

Now, two of Barbara Delinsky's most loved books are
available together in this special edition that new and
longtime fans will want to add to their bookshelves.

Let Barbara Delinsky double your reading pleasure with
her memorable love stories, A SPECIAL SOMETHING and
THE FOREVER INSTINCT.

Available wherever Harlequin books are sold. TWO-D

HARLEQUIN
Romance®

**This September, travel to England
with Harlequin Romance
FIRST CLASS title #3149,
ROSES HAVE THORNS
by Betty Neels**

was Radolf Nauta's fault that Sarah lost her job at the hospi-
al and was forced to look elsewhere for a living. So she wasn't
articulary pleased to meet him again in a totally different envi-
onment. Not that he seemed disposed to be gracious to her:
rrogant, opinionated and entirely too sure of himself, Radolf
vas just the sort of man Sarah disliked most. And yet, the
nore she saw of him, the more she found herself wondering
vhat he really thought about her—which was stupid, because
e was the last man on earth she could ever love....

---

you missed June title #3128, THE JEWELS OF HELEN (Turkey), July title #3136, FALSE
IPRESSIONS (Italy) or August title #3143, SUMMER'S PRIDE (Spain) and would like to or-
er them, send your name, address, zip or postal code, along with a check or money order
r $2.75 plus 75¢ postage and handling ($1.00 in Canada) for each book ordered, payable
Harlequin Reader Service to:

In the U.S.

3010 Walden Ave.
P.O. Box 1325
Buffalo, NY 14269-1325

In Canada

P.O. Box 609
Fort Erie, Ontario
L2A 5X3

lease specify book title(s) with your order.
anadian residents add applicable federal and provincial taxes.

JT-B9R

Harlequin Superromance®

Available in Superromance this month
#462—STARLIT PROMISE

STARLIT PROMISE is a deeply moving story of a woman coming to terms with her grief and gradually opening her heart to life and love.

Author Petra Holland sets the scene beautifully, never allowing her heroine to become mired in self-pity. It is a story that will touch your heart and leave you celebrating the strength of the human spirit.

Available wherever Harlequin books are sold.

STARLIT-A